Both Sides Of The Fence 3:

Loose Ends

Both Sides Of The Fence 3:

Loose Ends

M.T. Pope

www.urbanbooks.net

Urban Books, LLC
78 East Industry Court
Deer Park, NY 11729

ISBN 13: 978-1-60162-319-5
ISBN 10: 1-60162-319-4

First Trade Paperback Printing October 2011
Printed in the United States of America

10 9 8 7 6 5 4 3 2

*This is a work of fiction. Any references or similarities
to actual events, real people, living, or dead, or to real
locales are intended to give the novel a sense of reality. Any similarity in other names, characters, places,
and incidents is entirely coincidental.*

Distributed by Kensington Publishing Corp.
Submit Wholesale Orders to:
Kensington Publishing Corp.
C/O Penguin Group (USA) Inc.
Attention: Order Processing
405 Murray Hill Parkway
East Rutherford, NJ 07073-2316
Phone: 1-800-526-0275
Fax: 1-800-227-9604

Dedication

I dedicate this book to the black family and the black community. It's time to start communicating as a family and stop letting our children suffer from our loose ends. Peace!

Mildred Hooper
02/19/1945–12/10/2010

Rachel Shelton
01/21/1987–02/16/2011

One thing about the truth is, you don't have to believe it for it to be true.

—M.T. Pope

Most people usually won't believe what they can't see past their own two eyes.

— *X-Men 2: X-Men United*

We don't see things as they are, we see things as we are.

—Anaïs Nin

Acknowledgments

This is book number three for me. I owe it all to God for blessing me with a wonderful gift that he chose to spring forth at the appointed time. Thank you, God, for finishing another book for me. You poured out the words once again onto empty pages and made it flow so easily. You know, Lord, I agonized over if this whole writing thing was for me and if you were approving of it. You answered by filling up the pages once again. I thank you for the grace and mercy that allowed me to get this far in life. I am . . . because you are and I live . . . because you died and I will die because you showed me how to live.

To my mom, Lawanda Pope, a little woman with big strength. You make me smile every time I see you. You are the best mom in the world. I love you. My brothers and sisters: Shirley, William, Darnell, Darlene, Gaynell, Latricia, Nathon, and Yvette. I love you guys.

To my pastor, Melvin T. Lee and first lady Tanya Lee, for coming out and showing love at my first book signing and everything else I do in this life. I promise Dad that the Christian fiction is coming . . . LOL. To all my Because He Lives church family members: I love you with only the love that God shines through me. WE ARE! . . . BECAUSE HE LIVES!

To Tracey Bowden and Arnisha Hooper, my two best friends in the world. I can't even begin to say how much you mean to me. I don't say it enough and I don't show it

Acknowledgments

enough, but I can't pay for friends like you two. You put up with my mess and my mouth and I am grateful. For all the book signings you drove me to, all the books you sold for me, and all the bookmarkers you passed out, I appreciate it so much. There are just some things in life that you just know. I know that only God could have put together and you two were chosen just for me. I am honored to have you as my friends.

Carl Weber, once again, you had faith in what God has put in me to pour out of me. Thank you for this opportunity, and all that you do.

To all the Urban Knowledge Bookstore workers that pushed my book, it is appreciated. Will, Tracey, Renee, Daisy, Ruthanne, Tonya, Latonya, and any newcomers, thank you. May God bless you in all your endeavors.

To the Urban Books home office family: Carl, Karen, Natalie, George (Gee), Brenda, Shawn, Walter, Albert . . . you guys make this easier for me.

To Nichelle Washington, Darlene Washington, Ruthanne Ryan, Latricia Baker, Martina Doss, Karen Williams, Cearia Rice, Shawna Brim. Thank you for reading the first draft of this book.

To Kenneth Goffney: Again, I am totally blown away by God and how he used you to bless me. You came out of nowhere and lent a helping hand, when I needed it the most. I thank God for you and the time you've put into this project. Thank you, friend.

To all the book clubs that hosted me, thank you for the love and support as well. Especially my hometown book clubs: The Bmore Readers with W.I.S.D.O.M. Kudos to Tasha and Pat. ShayRod Book club, my first book club meeting. Y'all are the bomb. Dwayne Vernon and Novel-Lites.

Davida Baldwin, Oddballdesigns(www.oddballldsgns.com), thank you for another slamming cover.

Acknowledgments

To my editor, Maxine Thompson, I don't know how I forgot to put you in my acknowledgments before, but here it is now. Thank you for guiding my writing hand with your insightful eye to make my work flow better.

Thank you, Martha Weber for the excellent synopsis for the book.

I want to give a special thanks to couple of people who really supported me from a distance:

Martina Doss, for giving me my first official review and selling my books down there in Atlanta. Also, thank you for calling me and letting me know how my books moved you. You have to finish your book now . . . LOL.

Leona Romich, my Facebook friend, thank you for being honest and supportive and passing my book on to the appropriate people. You were such a great person from the first time we chatted. Thanks to Toka Waters as well.

My literary friend, J'son M. Lee (*Just Tryin' to be Loved*). Man, you are the best. We clicked from day one and we have so much in common. Thank you for answering the phone every time I call. I'm waiting on that second book, sir. Chop chop . . . LOL.

To Ashley & Jaquavis, you guys are the best at what you do and you always are humble when I see you or talk to you. Thank you for the encouragement and the support. Congrats on the new addition.

My author friends that supported me: Karen Williams, Anna J., Dwayne S. Joseph, Ashley Antoinette, Miss KP, Jaquavis Coleman, Wahida Clark, Michel Moore, Kiki Swinson, J.M. Benjamin, Anya Ellis, Amaleeka Mccall, Tina Brooks McKinney, Tra Verdejo, Kashamba Williams, Danette Majette, Tiffany Wright, Deborah Cardona(Sexy), La Jill Hunt, Kwan, Zoe Woods, Nannette Buchannan, Treasure E. Blue, Marlene, Dwayne Vernon, Mike Warren, Azarel, J'son M. Lee, Dell Banks(Shady), and so many others.

Acknowledgments

To the people that encouraged me along the way: Kenneth Goffney, your words are so inspiring. I am glad to call you friend. Marcel Emerson, boy, you are the coolest. Keep pumping out them hot books.

Deterrius Woods, an extraordinary Facebook buddy. Don't be afraid to finish your book. You have some great stories to tell, so get to work.

Kyeon, you have so much talent that it is ridiculous. So get started and get yourself out there.

My Wal-Mart family: Shernae, Tamara, Renee, Gary, Ms. Val, Danuiella, Keisha, Wayne, Sharon. Thank you, guys, for your love and support. I miss you guys . . . LOL. But, not the work . . . LOL.

My Baltimore customers that I can count on: Ms, Cheetah, Ms. Janet, Ms. Connie, Charlene(Gemini), Ebonee, Keyonne, Shavonni (Vonnie). Ms. Jennifer, Ms. Michelle Lawson. Mrs. Debbie.

If I left you out, put your name here:_____, because you are important to me too. Smile

I can be reached at:
www.myspace.com/mtpope
www.facebook.com/mtpope
www.twitter.com/mtpope
or e-mail: chosen_97@hotmail.com

Thank you for the love.

Remember . . . pass the word, not the book!

A Letter to the Reader

Well, here we go again. More drama. More crazy characters. More of the Black family. A part three was never in the plans for me, never. I wrote it because so many people wanted to know what happened after reading part two. I know what you are saying, Why? I said the same thing. . . . LOL, but I moved with it and here it is. The story wasn't finished like I thought it was and people still said I hadn't tied up all the loose ends (hence the title . . . LOL) Yes, James/Jerry Parks is dead and gone and he's not coming back. I know you loved/hated him, but again, I never planned on writing a part three. So I moved on. But it wasn't that easy to let go. When I wrote the first line, I knew it was on and popping . . . LOL. The road to finishing it was a rough one indeed. I quit several times in my mind and physically. It was just that serious. I can't speak for every writer, but I wanted this book to be entertaining and educational on a life and living basis. I wrote and rewrote so much that I was driving me crazy. I was never satisfied with what I wrote. I wanted this to be an experience. I didn't write it to get on a list , win an award or a five-star rating. My reward was to finish it and I did. I hope you get it. But, I'll live if you don't . . . LOL.

Anyway, as you may or may not know, some of James's traits were passed down to his offspring and that is where I started. We all know that the apple doesn't fall far from the tree in most families. In this final chapter, I will try my best to tie up all the loose ends. I introduce new characters with old wounds and hopefully by the end of the book you will see how one's loose ends can damage more than just one family for generations to come. So once again, take a trip with me as I bring everything full circle.

Just like the other two, I will be pushing the envelope and stretch you past your believability factor. So put *far-fetched* and *never* away while reading this book or any book for that matter, because things do happen outside of your little world. I may offend you and even gross you out, but hang in there with me. There is a point to all three books and by the end you will see.

M.T. Pope. . . . Enjoy!

Hello, reader, the next couple of pages is a recap of the previous two books. If you feel like you remember them, then skip it. If not, help yourself.

Shawn Black takes you back . . .

What's up y'all . . . give me a couple of minutes of your time before you jump right back into the drama of the Black family and the people caught up in the web of secrets and lies.

First, you were introduced to James Parks, the scorned bisexual from California, who set out to Baltimore on a path of wrath and destruction. He was hurt by a past lover and decided that he would take it out on every down-low brother he met in Baltimore, which included me.

Then, you were introduced to me and my wife and Mona Black, a middle-class lawyer and housewife. We

A Letter to the Reader

lived comfortably in Randallstown, Maryland with our six-year-old twins, Ashley and Alex. I was molested by my father and secretly pursued men. Mona, who thinks I was fooling around with another woman, is oblivious to my sexual attraction toward men, but I would soon find out that she has secrets of her own.

When James and I have a chance meeting, I unknowingly become one of his next victims. A few drinks are all James needs to set up me for the taking. After several mishaps and a mysterious condom wrapper, Mona gives me the boot and I'm out on the street. Waiting in the wings, James scores a touchdown when I opted to move in with him for a couple of weeks. As I moved in, James had to now juggle a sexual and monetary relationship with a drug dealer named Kenny, who is strung out on James and his white boss.

Later on in the story I walk into James's apartment and find my father being sexually dominated by James, and I fly off the handle. I punch and beat my father and then I proceed to sexually violate my father for all the pain he caused me and my mom. James watched on in twisted horror/pleasure as this takes place in front of him.

Next, a letter is then sent to my wife, Mona, by James, posing as me, telling her to move on with her life. She does not take it well and proceeds to confront me and my new "women" at my place of work. A fight ensues between Mona and Sherry, my new paralegal, and Mona ends up in jail. I convince Sherry to drop the charges and now Mona is a free woman. I then convince Mona to let me take a lie detector test, with her present, and prove to her that I was not cheating on her with another woman. I pass the test and Mona graciously takes me back.

A Letter to the Reader

James doesn't take the news that his new piggy bank is being taken back, so he sets out on a mission of damage control. He makes a house call to my residence and that is when the plot really gets thicker.

James arrives at the house, wanting to set me up by posing as a hurt husband who suspects his wife of cheating on him with me. But that plan goes out the window when the front door opens and Mona's well- hidden secret stands in her doorway. Unbeknownst to me, early in our marriage, Mona flew to California, alone, to bury a beloved uncle. Overcome with grief, along with a starving sexual addiction, Mona met James in a bar, got drunk, and they had a tawdry one- night stand, where no names were exchanged. During sex, the condom unknowingly breaks; Mona flies back to Baltimore and has sex with me within the same twenty-four-hour period. Weeks later she finds out she is pregnant with twins and she buries the secret, hoping to carry it to her grave.

James forces his way into the house and once again Mona gives in to her sexual appetite and his sexual advances and they have another sex romp right in our living room. Unbeknownst to Mona, I watched it all go down as I entered the house to surprise my wife with a short sexual quickie. I, in turn, left out quickly and quietly, confused about what I just saw, but I could not say anything, for the fear of my secret being exposed as well. I made it back to my office and receive a call from James telling me that he saw me while having sex with my wife through a picture frame and if I want my secret to stay safe with him I would have to do everything he asks of me. James makes another call and threatens Mona with exposure if she doesn't fork over a large sum of money. She reluctantly agrees.

A Letter to the Reader

Now James juggles me, Mona, Kenny, his boss, and my father in his web of destruction. He then demands Mona to pay him a biweekly hush fee to fuel his bank account and his lavish lifestyle.

Mona and I are too caught up into our own individual problems, so much so that the line between the truth and lies is now blurry. The last straw comes when James decides to throw a party in my honor. I entered the party optimistic, yet slightly on the defense. I was enjoying the party until the party turned on me. I was drugged and awakened tied up to a balcony railing and sodomized by a host of men, then taken back inside and violated by the last of the men, including my father.

I returned home and acted as if nothing was wrong, while Mona tried to stand strong against James. Her walls tumbled down when he forces her to be sexually assaulted in an alley by a homeless man for just five dollars.

Toward the end, I win a very important case and I am offered a position as a partner at the law firm I work for. James meets me outside and hops in my car to see how I was doing. A call comes through; I answer and place the call on speakerphone. It is my mother calling to invite me and Mona to my parents' anniversary cookout. James invites himself against my wishes.

A couple of days later on the ride to the cookout, I noticed Mona was acting a little weird. I question her and she tells me that she thinks she is pregnant. I am elated about the news, but Mona is far from enthusiastic about the situation. We enter the cookout with brave fronts on, both knowing that James may or may not show up to turn us or the party out. James does show up, but with a surprise guest. He has my paralegal with him. Sherry just happens to be James's cousin. We all socialize until I excuse myself to use the bathroom and James follows suit shortly after. In the bathroom, James offers me a deal: One last fuck and ten grand to leave me and my family alone. I accept the deal and walk back to the cookout a happy man.

Several minutes go by when everyone expects my father at the cookout. A loud disruption in the house ends with my father being escorted outside by a gun-wielding Kenny, James's drug-dealing lover. He holds everybody at gunpoint while he tells James that he was having him followed and that he knew all of his business. He tells how I had sex with my father, how James was sexing both Mona and me. The shock could be seen on the faces of the guests. But it wasn't over just yet. Sherry steps out the crowd to tell Mona that she indeed slept with me, but after the lie detector test. My mother then goes off and tells me that it was her fault and that I was the way I was and she knew all that time that I was being molested. She said she just wanted to keep her family together. Before Kenny could kill anyone, his baby's momma Keisha and the police come in and breaks up the party even further. It turns out Kenny was being followed too.

In the end, Kenny gets arrested and sentenced to twenty to twenty-five years in jail for drugs that Keisha had planted in his trunk. Keisha walks away with close to a hundred grand from Kenny and James's getaway and shacks up with Kenny's lesbian sister, Antoinette. Mona and I find out that James is the father of all three of my children. My mom evicts my father, leaving him to fend for himself, and James gets arrested for embezzlement and is sentenced to ten years in a federal prison. At the end of the book you are left with James reading a letter from a secret lover, telling him about his three offspring. He swears revenge and plots the destruction of his ex-boss, Keisha, Mona, and me, upon his exit from prison.

Wheffff! If that wasn't enough ten years go by and the drama continued to plague my family.

To start, more drama pops off when I give into my homosexual demons and get sexually accosted in the bathroom of a bar that I was not supposed to be in. Being drunk didn't help either. This only stimulates my already raging sexually deviancy. I barely make it home and it takes me a while to get in the house. This was only the beginning of a new adventure for me and my family.

Next, I learn that James is out of prison. I was not happy with that at all. I was in therapy for last past couple of years, trying to get past my past, so I did what my psychologist suggested and visited my father to get some closure, just to find out that James is shacking up with him. I fly off the handle and beat my father again. I make some threats and James makes some too. I proceed to leave the building only to be pulled up, before leaving, by some crooked cops that sexually assault me in the back of their squad car in an alley after they escort me out. These were some of the same guys that assaulted me at the party James had for me way back when.

Mona, is doing the best she can trying to keep the house in order and her own demons are pushing at the closet door, threatening to come out. I try my best to comfort her and be there for her but, with James now out my focus is on how to keep my feeling for him at bay and from her.

James doesn't seem to have learned a thing when he spent those ten years in prison. He pops up at my office and threatens me with my secrets and makes all sorts of demands that I know I can't do. If you don't know by now, I still haven't confessed to my children that I am not their biological father. I gave into his demands, so he could go on about his business, but I had no plans of doing what he asked of me.

My twins are sixteen years older now and they have lives of their own and their own problems as well. But we don't learn of them until it is almost too late. I will get to that later. Now let me tell you the rest of the story.

I go on with life trying my best to cope, just to be hit with a call that my father has been murdered. I wasn't devastated as much as I should be by the news, but my mom was. I confront James about out it, but he denies all dealings with it. I make a trip down to the detective's office to be interviewed and I conveniently drop James's name as a person of interest. Funeral plans were made, but I briefly attend the service because of me and my father's sordid history. I go home to find my ill daughter Ashley being attended to by her mentor Tony. Ashley and I have a father-daughter moment and she comforts me about the death of my dad. A couple of weeks go by and I have to attend the reading of my father's will. James shows up and shows off as usual, causing more drama than the law allows. Come to find out my father leaves me all of his bills and James walked away with a hundred thousand dollars. I was so livid that I hopped across the table and tried my best to strangle James to death, only to be dragged out by security.

A couple more days go by and I get a call from James to meet him at the restaurant that we visited when we first hung out. I was extremely reluctant, but he said it would be worth my while, so I went. What I found out at this restaurant was that I had a son by my old secretary and who happened to be James' cousin. He again manipulated some money out of me to help him "keep his mouth shut" . . . LOL. It's funny now but not when it happened to me.

Li'l Shawn was now a fixture in my life and I immediately felt a bond with him, so much so that I started to feel bad that I was giving him the attention that I use to give my other children at home. James had all but disappeared, except for the occasional call or pop up at my home.

After that Mona and I were both a little off, but that didn't stop us from having sex. That is, until she called out James's name during sex and I slept in my office the whole night.

A little more time passed and I was notified by the detective working on my father's murder case that James was cleared as a possible suspect. I was not happy with that, but I moved on.

More and more I was spending time with Li'l Shawn and less with my family. I was in love with the thought of having a son that was naturally mine, but I was feeling really guilty about the fact that I was sneaking around doing it.

Well, some more time went by and I was getting even more and more attached to Li'l Shawn and I was prodding Mona into adoption with the reasoning that our then youngest daughter, Diana, would need someone to play with since Ashley and Alex were too mature and she would need a live-in playmate. It was the only rationalizing I could use to get Li'l Shawn in the house without suspicion from Mona. That wasn't even necessary because on one evening when I was taking him back home I discovered his mom, James, and an unknown dude dead in the back of the apartment while he stood outside the door waiting for me.

A Letter to the Reader

I rushed out the house to tell my son that his mom wasn't home and called the police to let them know what I had found while he sat in the car. I instinctively took him to the next best place I could think of—my mom's house. She was not happy when I showed up to her doorstep with a new grandchild. I begged and pleaded for my mom to keep him and she did, after I insulted her and she hit me because of it. I thanked my mom and scurried off toward home like the punk I was. I breathed a sigh of relief now that James was dead, but I still had the burden to tell my new son his mom was dead and getting him in the house for good. I knew for sure my mom was not going to raise another child and I wouldn't let her, even though it did cross my mind. Slowly my anxiety level was peaking and it was nearing an explosion.

Again, I entered my house acting as if everything was okay, to find that my house not in order either. My wife was on edge and Ashley was having boy problems, it seemed.

Fast-forward to our second wedding and that is when all hell breaks loose. In the middle of the service, my new son pops up and shows his displeasure for me marrying Mona and not his mom. The entire population of the ceremony's mouths was on the floor. I plead with my eyes to my wife that she should not walk out on me and she didn't, but she did have me spill my guts in the limousine ride to the banquet hall. I also found out that I was going to be a father again for the fifth time.

Just when we thought we were in the clear as a family, up pops another surprise: My daughter's lover busts up into the reception drunk and screaming Ashley's name. After a short conversation with Tony (Antoinette), she exits and is never seen again.

A Letter to the Reader

We finally sit down as a family and Mona and I spilled our guts about James being Alex and Ashley's biological father and my homosexual desires. Their reactions were nonjudgmental and we moved on. Mona gives them all letters from James telling them that he really did love them, but could not care for them the way that me and Mona could have. He also left them some money to start them off in college. I also let Li'l Shawn know about his mom's death. He was surprisingly even-tempered about and gave me some reassurance as well. I was pleased that Sherry raised him the way she did.

Well, after all of that was finished I took a trip to the cemetery to visit my father's grave and let him know how I felt about our relationship or non-relationship so to speak. I cried and forgave him and gave it up to God.

Yep, that's the story up to now. It was rough, but we made it. I thought the drama was over but it wasn't. My children moved away and started to get into some trouble themselves and as you will see I didn't tie up all the loose ends like I thought I did. In this next chapter you will find out how my family and James's family were changed by one man's actions long before we met.

Get ready for another ride!

Prologue

Ashley

I was at the door turning the knob, when I heard what sounded like a gun click next to my ear. I turned to see it pointed right in between my eyes. "Bitch, where you think you going?" I saw him raise his hand and the pain of the butt of the gun hitting me in the head let me know this may not end too well. Then the room went black.

I woke up tied to a chair with a duct-taped mouth. My head was spinning and it was hard for me to focus. Once my vision started to become focused, I noticed that we were in a room alone.

"How does her pussy taste?" he asked me, inches away from my face. I blinked back tears, because I didn't know what he was going to do to me. I was tied up and light-headed. He hit me again with the gun across my face.

Wham!!!

"Mmm!" I moaned in pain but he was unrelenting. He hit me again. The room started to spin again. It was spinning so bad that I thought I "saw a putty-cat." I was just that dizzy.

"I can't believe she was playing me with you." He spit out a glob of spit onto my face. I felt it run down my cheek and hit me on my thigh.

Nobody knows I'm here and this crazy nut is about to take my head off. I don't know where his wife was. I was hoping that he had not killed her in a fit of rage. It wasn't looking good as he keeps on going back and forth to the window. It was like he was expecting someone else to come.

"So all you do is straight pussy?" he asked me. I nodded yes.

"So you never tasted a real dick before?" I shook my head no.

"Well, today is your lucky day." He laughed. I started to cry harder now because I didn't want to be raped. I watched as he unbuckled his pants and pulled out his penis.

"Mmm . . . mmm," I moaned in fear while shaking my head side to side. He had a big dick for the size of a guy he was.

"You like that?" He slapped me in the face a couple of times with it. I could tell it was getting harder with every slap on the face.

"You like it?" He yelled at me and slapped me harder with his penis. I nodded yes to appease him. "Well, you about to taste it."

He ripped the tape off of my mouth with force that caused me to cry out. "Ahh."

"Bitch, shut up!" He put the gun to my temple.

I hushed instantly.

"Open your mouth." I hesitated and shook my head from side to side. My heart was pounding and my mind was racing.

He hit me with the gun again. "Bitch, I said open it."

I obliged this time and opened my mouth. Salty, sweatiness is what I tasted as he pumped my face slowly. I was fighting for oxygen, because the girth of his dick filled my mouth. Even though I didn't do dick per se, I wondered why his wife would be dipping out on all of this. An average woman didn't just pass up on a dick like this. But, then *it* happened. He came. He was a one-minute brotha. Now I knew why she stepped out on him.

"Ahh . . . mmm" He began to shake violently and pulled out until the tip of his penis was on my lips. Then I felt the warmness of his seed hit the roof of my mouth.

"Bitch, you betta swallow that shit." He held my mouth closed to ensure that I did. I swallowed to assure him that the deed was done.

"Taste good?" he asked with his face inches from mine.

I silently nodded yes. He didn't know I had stored his seed underneath my tongue. I was not swallowing shit. Before he could blink I had spit his own seed right back at him in his face.

"You swallow that shit!" I boldly said. I knew I was going to die, so why not go out with a bang.

"You, bitch!" He slowly wiped his face with his shirt. "You gonna die for that shit." He stood up and aimed the gun.

In those few seconds as I watched him aim the gun at my head, my whole life flashed before me.

Chapter 1

Ashley
The Opportunist
April 1st 6:11 P.M.

"Look, Ms. Andrews." I walked to her office door and closed it, so we could get the privacy *I* needed. "This is how this shit is going to work."

It was after class and we were in her office. I was supposed to be "getting help" with my problems in her Physics 254-A class. Ms. Andrews, or Grace, is one of my college professors I was sexing on the regular. She was bugging out, talking about how she wanted out, but I was not having it.

"Grace, wouldn't you lose your job if the dean of the school found out that you were exchanging grades for sex?"

Her face frowned up as to say "You wouldn't?"

Little did she know, I wouldn't, but she didn't need to know that I wouldn't say anything. It would ruin my plans. "And wouldn't your husband be quite upset if he found out you were getting bent over by a student, moreover, a female student?

"Hmm . . . I wonder how that would make him feel. Me, doing what he obviously couldn't do right and finding out I was doing it better than he ever could." I tapped my chin with my index finger, pretending to think. I watched the hamster on a wheel in her head try to come up with a way out. She didn't have two legs to stand on.

"Ashley, do what you have to do." She tried to act like the power was in her hands. "I will not stand for this any longer. I am feeling very uncomfortable with this situation and I want out."

"Uncomfortable, huh?" I smiled, slyly walked around her desk, and moved close enough to her to whisper in her ear. "It wasn't uncomfortable when you let me bend your ass over this desk yesterday night. You came right in my mouth, and now you sitting here pouting and whining about how you are 'uncomfortable.'" She shivered and moaned in pleasure, as the thoughts of me going down on her from behind trickled down her spine. I was very good at what I did and she knew it.

"Y—yes . . . That's what I'm saying." I had already moved my hand under her pleated, black, knee-length skirt, toward her kitty cat. She started to purr like one as I eased my hand in between her thighs and pried them open with my pinky and thumb.

"D—don't do this . . . no . . . not now." Her voice was sensuous and low. Her fight was growing weaker as I inched my fingers inside her and started to thumb her huge clit.

"Don't fight it," I whispered. "It won't take long, promise."

Her chair was on wheels, so I pushed it back far enough to fit under her desk and to get easier access to her sweet spot. The fight in her was now gone. I got comfortable on the floor, eased her legs over my shoulder, and pulled her closer to me. Moans escaped her mouth as I went in for the kill.

"Uh . . . uhhhh," Grace grunted like a beast. She sounded like she had something caught in her throat. It was an orgasm threatening to blow, I supposed. "That's it—right—right—right—thereeee!" She sounded like a broken record as she came gushing all over my face. Her chest pumped up and down like a horse in a derby. She was trying to bring her breathing back down, but I went in again, not giving her a chance to breathe normal. I was going to show her who I was, again.

I was completely under her large red oak desk, when a knock on the door jarred us from our secret pleasure.

"Ah . . . ah . . . Who is it?" This bitch was about to give us the fuck away with her nervous shit. I squished myself underneath her desk far enough to not be seen at all.

"Professor Andrews," I heard a familiar voice speak through the doors.

"Co—come in," Grace answered with a pleasant, but shaken voice. Either her ass was scared that she was going to get busted or the nut I just gave her had her overwhelmed. I picked the latter, because I was just that good.

I heard the feet of a man come in, shut the door, and walk over to her. She pushed me even further under her desk. The chick had her knee in my throat and I was laboring to breath and not choke. I wanted to jab her in her gut, but decided against it.

"Hey, babe," she spoke seductively to her husband. Yes, her husband was a professor too. I only fucked with the best. No less. Grades weren't the only thing I was getting out of Grace. She was lacing my pockets with money pretty nicely too. I was only going for a couple hundred every so often. I wasn't going to be a greedy extortionist. I needed everything to stay under the radar. I had the get-in and get-out attitude. Laziness will get a sister caught up. "How was your day?" she asked him.

"Good, but exhausting." He breathed out a tired breath. The conversation labored on for about fifteen minutes or so before his tired ass decided to give us a break.

"Okay, honey. I'll be out of here in a little while. Let me finish up some of these papers and I will see you when I get home." I heard a kiss being exchanged, footsteps sloshing across the floor, and then the door closing.

"His big ass needs to be on a crack diet or something," I said, pushing my way out from under her desk and straightening my clothes. I pulled a couple of tissues out of the box on her desk and wiped her juices off of my chin. "I see now why you let me give you the mouth dick."

She shook her head in shame.

"What's wrong?" I sat on the edge of her desk in front of her. I looked in her eyes and saw pain and hurt. "You are feeling bad about doing what we doing?" The question was rhetorical, but she nodded her head yes anyway.

"You are a fifty-three-year-old coward. Man . . . the fuck . . . up." I looked at her like she was sickening to look at.

She hunched over in her chair and burst into tears. She must have thought that I was going to console her or something. That was for her husband to do, not me. She chose to live on both sides of the fence, now she had to learn how to be tough or hop her ass back over the fence. What she didn't know was it was easier said than done. I was only nineteen, but knew all about it.

When I left home for college I thought I was done and over sexing women after fumbling the ball with Antoinette (Tony) , but it was on when I got to UCLA; it all came flooding back again. Now I am living on campus across the country from my family. It's just me and Alex, my twin brother, who was accepted here on a partial football scholarship. I was well out of control within the second year of arriving at college. At first, I tried to holler at some of the young chicks, but they just weren't on my level mentally. I stumbled onto Grace off-campus at a bar on the other side of town. It was a seedy place that most undercover bi-curious women or men frequented. It wasn't a gay bar, but it was a non-limits type of environment. Which meant anything goes.

Liquid Nights was its name and it was jumping every Friday night after midnight. It was a normal night.

"It's Not Right But It's Okay" by Whitney Houston was blasting and it was packed in the place. There was a mixed crowd of all types of men and women in the joint that night. I was sizing up the ladies in a dimly-lit corner as they walked in, trying not to be obvious, but more like copping a feel with my eyes as well. When Grace walked in, she was camouflaged with big glasses, blond wig, and her body was covered in a knee-length black trench coat. She immediately went to the bar for a drink. She looked around a little. I could tell it was her first time. She was a little jumpy as people walked by her. Several ladies approached her and I could see her turn them all away within seconds. She wasn't going to be an easy pull. I knew this only after five minutes of observing her. She had a wall up and I had to be inconspicuous in chipping it away. Homosexuality for newbies is like jumping in freezing cold water; it's a culture shock for the body because it's not used to it, but after a while of swimming around, the body adjusts and gets used to the temperature. I was about to take her into the deep end.

I walked across the dance floor and through a throng of people. A few guys tugged at my clothes, showing interest in me. And why wouldn't they? I was a good catch. I had on some tight silky black leggings, with a chocolate sweater dress that cupped my butt oh-so-right. I didn't have a big bust, but my flowing hair, baby-doll face, and thick lips deflected the attention of most from that region anyway. I had on some shades, but I would lift them and give them a brief glare deep into their eyes letting them know, quickly, that it was hands off of me unless I invited them into my space. I was not a showgirl. I was a show-out girl. Trust. But, don't get it twisted though. Dudes weren't totally off of my list. They just weren't at the top. I had evolved over the last couple of years and knew that I had to keep my options open.

"Can I get me a shot of Hpnotiq?" I sat down at the U-shaped bar and pretended I didn't see Grace across the bar nursing what looked like soft drink. It let me know she was new at this.

"We Belong Together" by Mariah Carey started to play. And I decided to make my move. It was now or never. I grabbed my drink as soon as I saw the last person ease out of the seat next to her. They didn't look too pleased. It was their loss and my gain.

"Hey, how you doing, beautiful?" I sat on the bar stool and lightly rocked to the melody of the music.

"I'm good." She spoke plainly.

"Yes, all good." I smiled. "It's all about you tonight, I take it?"

"Huh?" she questioned.

"You look so beautiful. Most women that come to a club looking as good as you do, know that it's going to be all about them the whole night they are out."

"Well, that's maybe true." She took a sip of what she was drinking and looked around the club again. I took all of her in at close range real quick. She was well put together, for sure.

"Maybe? . . . nahh . . . You got it! All of it!"

"Thank you." She smiled. For an older woman she was gorgeous. Almost flawless.

"So who broke your heart?" I asked.

"No one broke my heart."

"You look like you lost your best friend." I sipped on my drink and stared at her intently.

"No, I don't do friends. They are too much trouble." Again, she spoke in a low monotone. No umph to it at all.

"True that." I nodded.

"Can I buy you another of what you are drinking? What is it that you are drinking?"

"Rum and Coke."

I signaled the bartender and ordered her another drink.

"Thank you." She smiled.

"No problem. There is *plenty* more where that came from," I said, hoping she read between the lines.

After another ten minutes, she finally took her glasses off and I did the same. Both of our mouths hit the floor as we recognized each other in a place like this. All this time we were in class I thought she was giving me funny looks because I was not meeting up with the full requirements of the class. All the eye contact in class was her trying to figure out if she could trust me with her secret. I didn't know. I would have made my move a lot faster. I also wanted to know how she knew about me. But, as I thought about it, I knew the saying "it takes one to know one" was very true in most cases—not all, but most.

***

"Ashley, I love my husband and my job, but I will not tolerate you belittling me." She had the authoritative voice in full effect, but ask me if I cared. "Your little scare tactics don't work on me."

"Sure they don't." I walked back around to the front of her desk, opened my book bag, and pulled out several sheets of paper. I laid them on the desk in front of her and watched her stern face disintegrate right before my eyes.

"Wh—where did you get this from?" she fearfully quizzed me.

"Don't worry about that. Just know that I have copies. Don't make me use them." I grabbed my bag and left her in her office to think about her next move.

Chapter 2

Grace
Uncovered
April 1st 6:40 P.M.

I sat at my desk and put my head in my hands. "How in the hell did she find this?"

I looked at the paper that Ashley had sat in front of me and shook my head. My past was resurfacing right before my eyes. Tears watered up in my eyes as I thought about my past. I just couldn't deal with this then or now. I folded up the papers, walked over to my filing cabinet, and neatly tucked them into an empty folder and closed the drawer back up again and locked it up.

"I will deal with this later." I walked over to my coat, on the back of my office door, put it on, then grabbed my briefcase from off my desk, and walked out of my office with my head held high. I was not going to let some wet-behind-the-ears, spoiled brat, run me. Somehow I have to get some leverage on her to even the score. I know it sounds harsh, me squabbling with a barely legal child that is less than half my age, but I needed things to go back to the way they were before I ventured out on this trail of destruction.

The wind was blowing as I walked across the parking lot toward my car, pulling my Dolce & Gabbana jacket closed with the hand that held my briefcase and fumbling with my lunch bag in the other. I put my finger on the fingerprint reader to open my door. I quickly got in, threw the briefcase on the passenger seat, put my finger on the fingerprint reader to start the car, and pulled off. I looked at the dashboard clock and it read a quarter till seven.

I was still a little emotional fifteen minutes later as I pulled up to the fancy carryout that my husband and I frequented. Because of our busy schedules as professionals, we often had to eat out or bring something home because our days usually started pretty early in the morning. It was the reason he was overweight and why I was beginning to pick up some extra pounds myself.

I walked into the take-out side of Benson's Bistro and ordered some fried chicken, pilaf rice, sweet potatoes, string beans, and a gallon of their peach tea to go. I smiled at the African owner, who knew me all too well. As he slid me my order I put my finger on the fingerprint reader to charge my bank account. I selected the correct account and was done in seconds.

"Have a good day," he said as I turned and walked out of the establishment. I hopped back into my car and head toward my home. About twenty-five minutes later I pulled up to my Tudor-style home in Ingleside and parked my car beside my husband's.

I grabbed my bags of food, the gallon of tea, my briefcase, and struggled my way up our short, cobblestone walkway. I was loaded down with baggage of pain and secrets, but my husband only saw me struggling with the bags in my hands as he opened the door.

"Aww, baby, give me that," he said as he took all the things that cluttered my hands and let me walk in the house freely. I trailed behind him as he scolded me about not calling him on the cell phone from the car.

"I'm sorry, babe." I pouted and kissed him on his cheek before I sat down at our dining room table and watched him go into our kitchen and bring back dinnerware for our meal.

My husband, David, has picked up about eighty pounds since we have been married. He was still handsome in the face, but the extra weight that threw him into 250-pound range, which he picked up over the years, was a complete turnoff for me. We had met when I was in grad school. I was twenty-six years old and he was two years younger. He was this five foot nine, 170-pound, caramel brick house. At a moment's whim he would pick me up into the air and spin me around like a rag doll. We had a whirlwind love affair for about six months before he popped the question. At the beginning of the honeymoon period in our marriage, we were having nonstop sex, we worked out together in between classes, and we both were toned and athletic. He was so romantic and spontaneous to the point where I would literally have to fight him off of me just to get a good night's sleep in.

Now, almost thirty years later, he was getting pretty sloppy, but that was only one of the reasons I was looking for attention in other places. All he wanted to talk about was work. After grad school, we both received reputable positions in both our fields of study at UCLA. Soon both our careers began moving, but his was moving a bit faster than mine. At first, I was a little jealous, but I got over it because I knew David worked really hard for his position. Over the years, his priorities shifted heavily toward his career and less on me. Now, he was just so boring at times. I know I wasn't a beauty pageant queen or anything anymore, but a sister still had it going on.

My Coke-bottle figure was long gone, but I wasn't anywhere near a two-liter shape either. And if a sister ever got to the gallon-shaped size, I will pay someone to off a bitch and put me out of my misery. I was pleased with my dark chocolate skin and thick sister-girl hips. I stood only at five feet six and toted a healthy 165 pounds. It is said as a woman hits a certain age she hits her sexual peak. I was there now—shit, I was always there—but my husband just couldn't keep up. It was like we switched positions and I was now the horny toad. The less he satisfied my urges, the more I looked for means of sexual relief. I had brought dildos and porn to try and curb my savage hunger, but it was to no avail. The dildos would burn out and the porn only made me more curious.

In fact, a particular woman-on-woman scene in a porn flick I was watching sent me over the edge. The more I watched it, the more I wanted to see what it was all about. On one particular Friday night, David was asleep in his office, something he does more and more as time went on, I decided that it was then or never. I had looked up lesbian/gay hangout spots on the Internet and one in particular caught my attention.

Liquid Nights was all the way across town and I knew I wouldn't be spotted by anybody that knew me or what I did for a living. I went in just to be curious, but Ashley spotted me and proceeded to spit her game at me. She had a way with her words and the next thing I knew she had me in the backseat of my car with my ass in the air and my face pressed against my back door, moaning as she made me cum multiple times. The things she did with her tongue and the strength of my orgasms kept me coming back for more. I was now what people called a cougar. More and more I kept doing things irrationally, like sex in my office during breaks in between class and even in bathroom stalls in multiple locations on campus. I loved the thrill until I noticed that Ashley was demanding more and more of me. She would barely come to class, halfway participate when she did show up, and she would leave in the middle of class as if she felt "she had better things to do," as she said. The more she made me cum, the more control she exerted over me. And I didn't like to be controlled. Now she had a secret about me that only a few people knew about me, and that few didn't include my husband. It was something that could ruin my marriage and my career. I wish I knew she was going to be behaving like this, because I would have never gotten involved with her in the first place. I also wondered how she uncovered my secret. I made sure I paid close attention to keeping my past in the past. Now she was threatening me with it and now she had my back against the wall.

I sat in my chair across from my husband and smiled as I watched him devour two chicken breasts, a heap of rice and potatoes, all while slurping down two large cups of tea. The slurping of his tea and the loud burp that followed had brought me back from my trip down memory lane. *Where is the husband that I married? Because the one sitting across from me must be an impostor! I'm beginning to think I'm the reason for his weight gain. Nahhh! He's in charge of his own weight. I will not add that to my list of stress.*

"Honey, don't you think you should have taken your time eating that food?" I asked with a sympathetic tone. He had crumbs on his shirt, making me wonder what the napkin he had tucked in his shirt was for.

"Yes, dear, I know I should eat slower, but I have mountains of work to do on my desk. I needed to cut some time out of somewhere to compensate for the lack of time in the day."

"Honey, I know that seems logical, but at the same time you are cutting time off of your life expectancy as well. It's just not healthy. I can't sit here and watch you eat yourself into a casket." His face flushed from content to depressed, all in a matter of seconds.

"You're right, Grace." He took the napkin from around his neck, wiped his face, and pushed away from the table. Something he should have been doing long before now. "Next week I'll put myself on a strict diet." He got up, removed his plate and mine and casually walked toward the kitchen in the back of the house.

"I've heard that before," I mumbled under my breath.

David walked back from inside the kitchen seconds later, walked up to me, and kissed me on the cheek. "Grace, you've put on a couple of pounds as well. I suggest you start the diet with me."

I wanted to bust him upside his head for that comment, but I let him slide since I had noticed the weight gain myself. "We can even work out together like we used to do," he suggested. The smile on his face was one of genuine love. I saw his eyes glimmer with memories of our beginnings. I take it he too wanted to go back to when we first started dating. He didn't know that was also all a lie.

"Sure," was the only response I could get out of my mouth. I was not ready for this. My opening my big mouth always seems to get me into more undesired tasks. And keeping my weight together is a task in itself.

"I'll be in my office for a little while, catching up on some paperwork. I'll be up later on."

"Well, don't fall asleep at your desk like you did the last time," I spoke as he headed toward his office.

I in turn wiped off the table, vacuumed the carpet around where he and I ate, and made my way upstairs to take a shower. I was exhausted and a nice, hot shower always did the trick for me. I was in and out of the shower within twenty minutes, making my way into my walk-in closet to pull out a bra and panty set to sleep in. In my closet was a mirror that stretched from the floor almost to the ceiling. I posed a couple of times and surveyed the extra weight my husband said that I had picked up.

"It's not that bad." I did notice that I was beginning to grow a mushroom stomach and my arms were getting to be a little bit flabby. I had a plan to indeed work out with my husband. And maybe, we could work on our marriage as well. Our sex life is almost nonexistent; besides, the little bit I do get only lasts a couple of minutes before his big ass is out of breath, huffing and puffing next to me saying, "Damn, baby that was good." So many nights I wanted to roll over and smother him with my pillow while screaming, "Is this good? Is this good, mutha-fucka?", but I didn't, I just let that shit roll off my back like oil and water.

I flicked on the plasma television and found something to watch that would put me to sleep. Eventually I fell off to sleep, hoping my life would be different when I woke up.

Later that night . . .
"Hello," I whispered into my cell phone. My husband was snoring so loud in the bed that you would have thought that we fucked twelve times. He didn't even move when I got out of the bed and grabbed my terry cloth robe off of the end of the bed. I walked down my stairs with a lot still on my mind. I was glad it wasn't Ashley on the phone, but I wasn't completely happy about who was on the phone. I walked down the

hallway and to my kitchen to get as much privacy as I could. I didn't trust David even though he was asleep. All sleeping eyes aren't always sleeping. I knew that from experience, but that is another story for another time.

"Hello Mother." I was a little annoyed that she would call me this late at night. "Is everything okay?"

"No, everything is not fine." She sound annoyed too. "My only child left on this earth has not called me in a while."

"I know, Mama. I'm sorry. I just have been busy. You know I have a very time-consuming job."

"So that is your excuse now. Work." She shot down my excuses for not coming to visit her every time she called. I had an excuse for every call. This was our relationship now. This is what it has come to.

"Look Ma!" My tone was stern. "I don't want to do this."

"What do you mean *this*?"

"The arguing that we do every time that you call me." I sighed. "I have enough stress as it is."

"Your stress is because you don't want to be upfront with yourself. You don't know how to forgive others as well. Especially, family." She confirmed what I already knew. "I can't tell you enough how sorry I am for the way things turned out. What more do you want from me? What more?" I could hear the pain in her voice.

"Sorry, Ma. I'm sorry." I broke down and started to sob. "You're right."

"Mama knows that already." She spoke assuredly. "I didn't do everything right, but I did get some stuff right. I know it because you are successful and you made me proud." I needed to hear those words. She never said she was proud of me.

"Baby, how's your husband doing?" she spoke sarcastically, casting my mood downward again.

"He's a very happy man. Very happy indeed."

"Umm . . . I bet." Another sarcastic remark flew out of her mouth. "So when am I going to meet him? You know, face-to-face?"

"Soon, Mama. Soon."

"Don't you think it's been long enough. What are you ashamed of?" she asked.

"I am ashamed of nothing." I lied to her and myself. "He's a very busy man. His free time is limited."

"So we are still playing Russian roulette, huh?" She laughed. "Baby, remember as a child, you were never good at playing games. Remember life is not a game and it plays for keeps."

"Don't I know it." I spoke lightly, more to her than me.

"I was just calling to check in on you, my child." She was now speaking sweetly. "And your secrets . . . Talk to you soon."

"Okay, Ma." I hung up the phone. My mind was racing a mile a minute. She acted like all of this is my fault when she knows she had a hand in it. I loved my mother like a child should love their mother. I paid her bills and all, but I also have some great resentment toward her. I just didn't know how to deal with it.

I went back upstairs and climbed back into bed and fell asleep as soon as my head hit the pillow.

Chapter 3

David
A Real Man
April 1st 9:30 P.M.

"Ahh," I moaned softly as I came on my stomach. I slouched back in my chair and breathed heavily again, exhausted because this was the second time I had jerked off within the half hour that I had been in here. I watched my would-be liquid children die on my chest as they dried up.

"What a waste." I pulled a couple of Kleenex from off of my desk and cleaned myself off.

My wife thought I was in here working, but that was not the case. It almost never was. I came in my office to relieve myself in privacy. What she didn't know was that I had an addiction to porn.

For most of our marriage I have had this addiction. Most people didn't know that Grace and I were not the perfect couple as we portrayed. She was very adamant about not wanting children. She never gave me a reason why, but she always made me wear a condom when we had sex and she insisted on being on birth control. I was fucked up mentally by this. Her rejection hurt me to the core. It almost felt as if I was not man enough to give her a child. A man almost always wanted to have a prince or princess to carry on his bloodline, but it was out of the question with her. She was unrelenting.

I figured wasting my seed in her or on me was all the same, so I masturbated to porn in private. I know you are saying, "So what!", because having an addiction to porn was not foreign to a married man. It's not right, but it wasn't foreign. The thing is that I was watching man-on-man porn. My wife's rejection and me being tampered with by my father—well, not him per se—but both were catalysts to my weight gain and me now wanting to experiment with men. But what man would want me at my age? The extra weight that I carried was not in the plus column either. I mean, I was a good-looking brother at my age and I knew I could still turn a few heads. My wife's recognition of my weight flooded back in my head and the urge to squeeze off another nut began to weigh heavily on me again. I changed my mind, because with the combination of the amount of food I ate and the two nuts I busted earlier, I would be like a walking zombie at work tomorrow. I needed to quit while I was ahead. I got up out of my chair and made my way upstairs toward my bathroom and got in the shower.

I eased into bed next to my snoring wife. She was so pretty when she slept.

"We would have had some beautiful children," I whispered to myself as I gently rubbed her cheek. "What was wrong with me that you didn't want to have children with me?" I rolled over with my back to her. I wondered if she could tell that I wasn't the man that I pretended to be. *Could she see through the mask that I put on since the day I met her? I wonder if she married me because she felt sorry for me. I wasn't man enough for her and she knew it, but she married me anyway! Now my shit was coming apart at the seams. My secrets were threatening to spill out and expose who I really was.*

I drifted off to when I was back in middle school. I was a very shy little boy and I was not one to be the center of attention. I did my work in class and played football during recess like any other normal little boy at my age. I was twelve and full of energy and secrets. One day in particular my mother had dressed me in my school uniform, blue khakis and a powder blue button-up shirt. I had to admit I felt pretty good that morning as I sat at the table eating my cereal and toast. My oldest brother Wallace had on jeans and a regular shirt, because he just started high school and they didn't have to wear uniforms. My younger brother, Robert was in his last year of elementary so he too was dressed in regular clothes.

As usual my dad said he would be taking me to school since I was the closest to his job, but today it was as if he was rushing more so then usual. He took turns between Robert and me, because his school was in close proximity to my father's office as well. My father was a psychologist and he had his own practice. He would usually take me straight to school without detouring, but this day was different. This particular day we stopped by his office.

On his way to his office he kept complimenting on how well I looked in my uniform and how I looked like a "real man" today. He used that term so much when I grew up. I poked my chest out real proud-like, because I loved my dad and his approval. My dad was my idol. He was everything a "real man" was supposed to be. I wanted to be just like him. Now that I think back, I was really foolish. Anyway, we pulled up to his office and that is when my life changed.

"Come inside with your old man for a second," he said, rubbing my head before unbuckling his seat belt and getting out of the car. "I want to show you something in my office." I was excited, because my dad rarely let any of us come to his office. He was very adamant about separating home and work. He almost never talked about what he did at work when he was home.

I followed behind my dad and admired the way he was dressed too. He was such a well-put-together man. We walked into his office and everything in his office was immaculate. He had the basic stretched-out leather chair that you see patients laid out on television stretched out on, divulging their innermost secrets and pain.

"Hey son, sit right on that chair right there," he said, disappearing into some closet in the back of his office. After a couple of minutes of waiting, there was a knock at the door.

"Come in." My father peeked out of the room he was in and spoke slightly louder than in his regular pitch. A slender man walked in, shut the door, and stood in the middle of the floor. He had these beady eyes that looked at me like he was looking through me. My eyes darted from him to the floor as I fumbled with my book bag, hoping that my dad would hurry up. This guy was freaking me out. A couple seconds later, my dad walked out of the room he was in with a towel in his hands.

"How are you doing today?" My father walked up to the man and hugged him for a couple seconds too long. He rubbed the guy's back and his hand moved down to his buttocks and squeezed it hard. By this time, I was freaking out on the inside because I had never seen two men hug in this fashion, especially my father. I had never seen my father behave in such a manner, even with my mother. They both backed up and my father's eyes shifted toward me. I, in turn, looked at the floor. I didn't know what to do. My eyes watered up and I wanted to run and get the hell out of there. I knew something wasn't right, but I couldn't move.

"Son, won't you to say hi to John," he said, reaching out his hand as to say come here. I walked toward the two men, legs trembling as I walked. "Come on son, he won't hurt you."

For the first time in my life I looked at my father with uncertainty. *What is wrong with him?* I looked up into his eyes, which were glazed with happiness, and wondered.

The guy hugged me as I made my way up to him. It felt uncomfortable, so I quickly pulled out and backward a little.

"Son, don't worry, he won't hurt you. He's a *very* good friend of mine."

I looked at him and then the guy. "O—okay." My mind was racing and at the tender age of twelve I was confused.

"I'm ready," my father said to the guy as he rubbed the guy's bicep and squeezed it. The man walked over to the leather couch and began undressing from the waist down. By this time, my stomach was rumbling and my legs were shaking a little harder. I backed up toward the wall a couple of feet from the front door. My dad was still in the middle of the room watching the guy slowly take off his socks. I knew this because I was watching too, but I was terrified. My father, on the other hand, was like he was in another world altogether. There was even saliva running down the side of his mouth.

"Dad, I want to go . . . *now!*" I was easing my way toward the door.

"A couple . . . more . . . min . . ." His voice trailed off as if he was answering my question and taking in the sight of the man who was now bent over and playing in between his buttocks. I looked at the clock and noticed only ten minutes had gone by, but it seemed like an hour. He walked over to the couch, bent down, and stuck his face in between the guy's buttocks and started licking like a dog at a water bowl. Tears were running down my face and I began to sob as the guy began to moan "oh, yeahs." My father started going crazy: biting the guy's buttocks, smacking it and sticking his finger in his buttocks.

"Dad!" I yelled. His head snapped around like he was possessed and I was wrong for calling him. "I'm going to be late for school." I lowered my tone. I wasn't that in love with school, I just wanted to get the hell out of his office as soon as possible. He got up from in behind the guy and walked over to me. I looked away, because I didn't want to look at him.

"Son." Both of his hands were on my shoulders and he crouched down to be on my level. "You're a real man, right?" I nodded my head, looking at the floor.

"Look at me when I'm talking to you," his stern voice penetrated me. I almost had to force myself to look at him. I was ashamed and confused at the same time. "Do you love me?"

I nodded my head yes. I did; I idolized him. Whatever he said I believed, and whatever he said was right. I didn't argue with him; he was my father and I knew he would never steer me wrong.

"There's something that Daddy wants you to do." His arms started to massage my shoulders. I guess he was trying to loosen me up, because this situation was new to me and it did have me tensed up. "You're a real man, right?" I nodded my head again.

"I need for you to do me a favor," He got up and walked over to his desk and opened a drawer and pulled out something square, metallic and shiny. It looked like a big piece of gum. He then walked over to the guy again and waved me over.

"Pull down your pants," he instructed me. I nervously did as I was told. The other guy turned his head around and a smile came across his face. I stood there shaking and ashamed. The man looked at my father and my father then nodded his head. He then turned around, got down off of the chair and kneeled before me.

"Son, close your eyes and be very still."

A couple seconds later I felt the strange man's hand start to pull on my penis slowly and after a minute or so it was as hard as a rock. I had played with myself before but I had never been this hard. Then, I felt something warm on my penis and my eyes shot open and I saw the guy with my penis in his mouth sucking very hard. Tears were running down my face once again. I looked at my father who standing next to me rubbing the top of my head. "It'll be over soon, son. Just keep your eyes closed." He smiled like he was proud of me; it was the same smile he had when I played basketball, football, and my team had won the game. After a few seconds, my body started to twitch and the guy pulled off my penis and started massaging my penis again. I opened my eyes as I watched white liquid shot out of my penis and all over the man's face.

"Well done, son." He walked over to his desk again and pulled out some napkins and handed them to me and the other guy.

"Clean yourself up and pull you pants up." He looked and me and the other guy. He walked back out the room, to his other room, and after a couple of seconds he came out with his coat and hat. I looked at the clock and only twenty minutes had passed. I grabbed my book bag and stood by the door, not looking either man in the face.

John walked out first and after a few minutes me and my father did the same. We rode to school in silence and before I got out of the car he told me that I showed him that I was a real man today and that everything we did should never be told to anyone, especially my mother.

In the following weeks, my brother Robert would soon join us and the same scene played out, except my father let the other guys put his penis in my brother's buttocks. Neither of us said anything to anybody, because, as my father put it, we were "real men" and real men didn't gossip or kiss and tell.

Years later in high school I learned that the behaviors and things my father made us participate in were wrong and was not accepted in society and I hid my secrets very well from then on. To this day my definition of a "real man" has been blurry. I couldn't share any of this with my wife, because I was so ashamed. This is also why I never let my wife meet my family, especially my parents. My father was a big no-no. I just couldn't stand his presence. I was liable to snap. He was dead to me. And unfortunately my mother was too, because she was an unknowing ally. I wanted to see my mom, call my mom, hug my mom, and share my wife with her. But, I couldn't and strangely my wife almost never asked about them. My father twisted my life and my way of thinking so much. I am surprised that I have gotten so far in life and my career. Or maybe I haven't gotten that far. Maybe I am just marking time. Going around and around in my head.

My wife saved my life and I didn't want my past coming back to mess that up. That was my logic. That was my truth. Take it or leave it.

Chapter 4

Alex
Searching for me
April 3rd 1:35 P.M.

I sat in the college cafeteria looking over the list of
numbers I got off the phone directory online. There
were so many Parks living in California that I just
didn't think I would ever find the info I was looking for.
I had already been through dozens of phone numbers
and I still haven't found out who James/Jerry Parks's
family was or lives. I could only do but so much calling because with class and football practice I had little
time to do anything else. I put my head down in my
hands and rubbed my temple with my thumbs, trying
to focus on my homework before me and the two chili
dogs I had sitting before me. I sipped my soda and took
a bite of my now cold hot dogs and flipped through my
playbook for practice. I had so much to do and so little
time.

"Man, I need some help with all of this." I spoke a
little louder than I should have.

"Excuse me?" I heard a voice from behind me say. I
had been so engrossed in myself that I didn't notice anyone around me. I turned and looked up and saw one of
the school's servers-cooks standing before me. He was
an older guy, probably around my father's age. A little
rough looking, like he had a bad night or something.

"Nah, man, I was just talking to myself out loud," I said looking at him with wonder. He looked familiar, but I just could not place him. He was looking at me the same way for a few seconds.

"Oh . . . okay!" he finally spoke back. "I was just making sure." He walked away and I turned to gather my things so that I could get back to the apartment, get ready for tomorrow, and make some more calls on the apartment phone.

As I walked out the cafeteria I got another glance at him as he was cleaning off food trays. I still couldn't place him, so I kept it moving.

A couple of hours later . . .

I heard Ashley come in the apartment. I was sitting up at the computer in my room doing some studying and searching the online phone directory again. Ashley acted as if she could have cared less about the news we got when we were sixteen, about the one we called Dad. When my mom said that he was not our biological father, I didn't freak out at all, I loved him nonetheless, but that didn't stop me from wondering about my biological father and what he was like. Since my parents never really discussed him, the only thing I have of him is the letter he wrote me before he died. I was hell-bent on finding out for myself. I needed closure in the situation. I wanted to know who the other half of me was, the other side of my family.

I knew he was born and raised here in California, but, again, it was hard trying to track down his family.

I got up out of my chair and walked out into the living room where Ashley was sitting, going through her backpack.

"What's up, Ash!" I must have startled her, because she jumped.

"Oh, hey Lex!" She was a little jittery as she stuffed whatever she was looking at back in her backpack. She was so sneaky that it wasn't funny. I tried to stop being concerned about her shenanigans a long time ago, but being the oldest I can't help being concerned. It's just seems like when we moved out here from Baltimore she started acting weird again like she was when she was home. Her being out late at night, whispering into her cell phone and having large amounts of money stuffed in her dresser drawers. Yes, I was still nosy, but I figure I had to help her stay out of trouble. I couldn't put my finger on it, but I hoped she wasn't out here pimping one of the little lesbos running around on campus. I still can't forget when I found out she was having sex with women.

"Is everything okay, Ash?" I walked up to sofa she was sitting on and sat down next to her.

"Yeah, I'm fine," she looked at me dead in the eyes. The jitteriness seemed like it instantly disappeared. She was still a good liar, I figured. No, I knew. "Why you asked that?"

"I asked because you just seemed a little jumpy a couple of seconds ago. It was like I scared you or something."

"Um . . . Lex . . ." She patted me on the leg and got up off the chair, throwing the backpack over her shoulder. "That's a normal reaction when someone sneaky walks in the room and startles you." Man, she can be a smart-ass bitch sometimes.

"Sneaky?" I looked offended. I knew what I was, though, but she didn't have to call me out, though. "Ash, I was just walking into a room. How is that sneaky?" I stood up as well. She began to walk toward her room. I trailed behind her.

"Lex, just leave me alone . . . all right!" The *all right* had an "I will cut you!" undertone, so I left it alone. She slammed her door and I walked into my room right next to hers.

"Chicks are just plum crazy." I shook my head and laughed.

Ring . . . ring . . . ring . . .

"Hello." I picked up the apartment phone without looking at the caller ID. We didn't have many people calling, so I knew it was my dad, mom, Diana or Li'l Shawn calling.

"Hey, son," I heard my dad speak through the phone.

"Hey, Dad," I said and blew out a breath of frustrated air.

"What's wrong, son?" he asked in a concerned father tone.

"Nothing is wrong, Dad, just a little frustrated, that's all."

"School or football?" he asked.

"That, plus my other half." I wasn't about to tell him I was searching for my biological father's family.

"Oh!" he laughed. "What did she do now?"

"Nothing in particular, Dad, just being the crazy woman she is." I wasn't sure of what she was doing, so I chose to leave out the details, at least until I knew what they were and if I could handle it by myself.

"Get used to it, Lex. They are all a bunch of crazies," he laughed into the phone.

"Well, I'm actually calling about the amount of phone listings you guys were calling for from the apartment phone." My father pays most of the bills for us while we are here. Before we left Baltimore, he made an agreement that he would finance us fully through our second year of college. He would expect us to have a job by the end of the second year and he would cut down his financing to half of what he is currently doing. Ashley was not thrilled with this, being the spoiled little brat that she is. She has been grumbling and moaning ever since Dad called us and told us it was time to start looking. I had no problem with it, though. I knew sooner or later that I would have to be a man and start fending for myself. "The amount of calls has been extremely high the last couple of months. It's only you two in the apartment, right?"

"Of course, Dad, just me and Ash. Nobody else lives here."

"That still doesn't explain that volume of calls on these bills. It's like someone has been going through the phone book or something."

"Well, Dad, Ashley and I both have been looking really hard for jobs. That is why there are so many numbers on the phone." I hoped that was a good enough lie, because I was not a good liar and I had no backup lies.

"Oh . . . okay. As long as you guys are doing what you are supposed to be doing while you are out there. Alex, I'm looking forward to seeing both of you graduate from college in two years, okay." He had such high expectations of us and I can't fault him for wanting us to succeed. I've just been wondering in the back of my mind if his care and love for us was genuine or not. Since, technically we are not his children. He's never given us that impression, but I still wonder sometimes.

"Me too, Dad . . . me too."

"Lex, let me speak to Ash for a sec."

"Okay." I walked to Ashley's door and knocked.

"Yeah!" I heard Ashley yell from behind the door.

"Dad wants you on the phone." As soon as I heard her pick up I hung up my phone.

I walked to the bathroom and started the shower. About five minutes into the shower I figured out where I knew the guy in the cafeteria from.

Chapter 5

Back In Baltimore . . .

Shawn
Loose Ends
April 3rd 8:02 P.M.

"Whew," I blew out a nice strong breath after I hung up the phone with Ashley and Alex. "Children!"

I sat back in my chair, real hard. I was in my office as usual going over bills and such. Alex was the mild one, the one I really didn't have to worry about. I'm sure he has his problems and all, but he knows how to stay focused and keep it moving. Now Ashley, on the other hand, is a whole different story. After I found out that she had a lesbian relationship, I have tried to keep a closer eye on her. I must admit I spoiled her because I thought she may have needed more attention when it came to her reaching out for same-sex contact. It had an adverse effect. She became accustomed to my coddling and now she doesn't want to work for anything. The entire time we were on the phone talking she was giving me attitude and blowing her breath as if I was wasting her time. I just hoped and prayed that she didn't turn out to be like her James. I could have inadvertently triggered something in her that would cause her to act out. I prayed that I didn't, but I knew that it was possible.

On the other hand, I had Alex there to monitor her, and if she did become out of hand I am sure he would report to me any and all odd occurrences.

On another note, Wallace, James's boyfriend, just up and disappeared on me. I was sort of a confidant and counselor to him when he needed to talk. He kept asking me questions about James that I didn't know and some questions I knew answers to, but couldn't divulge because it was giving away the secret of me and James being sexually involved. I don't know why I didn't tell him about us. Well, I did. I just wasn't ready to tell me yet. I was attracted to him and the more I would talk to him the more I would fantasize about him and me together. I have been having steady counseling sessions with my pastor and a licensed therapist and I was making major headway, now that he was gone. I have told Mona about him; well, I didn't tell her he was gay. I just said I was helping him out on a case brought against him. Another lie I would have to pay for, for sure. I am glad he is gone and I don't have to deal with him or look at him. My pastor and therapist both said that I would need to have minimal contact with anyone that was "in the life," to assure that I would stay abstinent. I agreed.

"Forgive me, God," I said as I looked up to heaven. "I need some help tying up these loose ends in my family." I got down on my knees and began to pray.

Chapter 6

Wallace
Remember When . . .
April 4th 9:34 A.M.

It was a pretty normal day as I woke up in my apartment in Culver City. A nice, plush neighborhood that was quiet and laid back just like I liked it.

I laid in my bed on Saturday morning thinking about homeboy from the cafeteria yesterday. He looked awfully familiar. He looked just like a miniature James to be exact.

"Shit! Shit! Shit!" I sat up in bed as painful memories invaded my mind. I threw my dreads in a makeshift ponytail, slid into my slippers, threw on my robe and made my way toward my bathroom. I stopped, turned and looked at my bed. Half of the bed was still undisturbed.

"Baby, you supposed to be sleeping next to me." I walked up to a picture of James and me after we got married, which was on the nightstand on his side of the bed and picked it up. Tears slipped out of my eyes and down my cheek. Touched his face with my thumb and I put it down where it was.

"Maybe, I'm seeing shit. Homeboy doesn't look like my baby. I'm just bugging." I shook my head and walked toward the shower. "But he does look familiar to me, I just can't place him."

In the shower my mind was racing. I had to do something really heavy today. I have been putting it off for way too long.

When James died, I tried my best to keep up a good front and hustle like I normally did. But I was consumed with him. I missed him so much. I would break down in my car a lot. Then I remembered the way I got him was underhanded. It was called karma and it took away my baby. My love and my heart. I lost my thirst to hustle, slowly but surely, when James died. I had no one to live for anymore. I had no one in my life to spend my money on. I had no one to love me anymore. So I sold everything I owned in Baltimore and moved back to California where my "family" was. I had long forgotten about my parents and my brothers. Here I was starting all over again at almost fifty-one years old.

When I moved back here two years ago I thought all I would need was the money that I left Baltimore with to shop and keep me busy, but I was wrong. Loneliness crept in like locusts and I had to find something to do with my time. I finally enrolled in culinary school. I graduated and looked for a job. Since I had no previous experience, I had to take an entry- level position at UCLA's cafeteria. It wasn't a million-dollar job, but I love cooking the food for the kids and it kept me busy. But, I still wasn't completely happy. On top of missing James, I wanted to have a relationship with my family. I didn't know them and almost thirty years has passed. I need my family, but I still had issues with my mom letting my dad put me out and my dad putting me out. I had many questions that I needed answered. I just hope I wasn't too late.

I finished washing myself up and got dressed in some denim Capris and a plain white T. I threw on a plain powder blue fitted hat and some white Rockport sandals. I feed the cats, the ones that belong to James. Mindy and Shaw were the only physical things, besides the pictures and a few pieces of clothing, which I had left of James. I made sure I took good care of them. I jumped into my tan Lincoln Navigator and speed off toward my mom's house.

I drove down the streets of Gardena watching my past fly by as I passed my high school hangout spots that I frequented, and the first place I had sex with a guy. Twenty-five minutes later I slowly pulled up to the block I called home so long ago.

"Home," I breathed out. I looked at the neighborhood where I would watch my brothers run up and down the street and play on. Football, baseball, soccer; you name it, they played it. I was the oldest, but felt like the youngest, because most of the time my father would scold me for not being the "man" that he thought I should be like. He said real men don't cook. I always wondered about the term "real men" as a child. I would hear him and my mother argue all the time about what he thought a "real man" consisted of and how I wasn't living up to it. I would go in the bathroom and look at my genitals and I wondered why he would say the things he said. I had the same genitals he had and looked just like him, so why was I not a "real man"? For a period of time, I tried to be like my younger brothers and run up and down the street and play games like them. I admit I enjoyed it, but my heart wasn't in it. So back to cooking it was for me. I loved to see the smile on my mom's face when I got something right. She would call me "li'l chef man." I felt special, unique.

At nine, I knew I was different. I knew I wasn't like other boys. I wasn't feminine or nothing like that, but

I paid attention in class and liked colors and detail. But, I also liked cars and clothes. I would go to the library and look at the latest car and fashion magazines and marvel at how good the guys looked next to them. There were girls in the pictures too, but I never really noticed them. I paid it no mind then, but now I know that I was born the way I am. I was gay. I wondered if my mom and dad knew before I did and hoped it would go away. That is what I was here to find out.

"Nothing's changed." I looked at all the detached houses that had an array of colors and white picket fences, typical suburbia.

"Let's do this!" I had to psyche myself into this. I just didn't know what to expect.

I walked up the pathway toward the door and stood in front for several seconds rubbing my fingers on the inside of the palm of my hand nervously.

I finally pushed the doorbell. Hoping no one was home. Several seconds passed by; the wind had picked up and tossed my dreads around. I turned around with the excuse I was going to get my jacket that I had left in the car.

"Can I help you?" I heard a couple of steps down the walkway. I turned to see a woman standing in the doorway. My mother was still beautiful. She was noticeably older but she still didn't look the seventy years old that she was. I hung my head low for a second. I was afraid to look back up.

"Wallace? . . . Is that you?" Her voice trembled a little.

"Yes . . . yes, ma'am. It's me." I said lifting my head back up and slowly walking back toward her. Everything in me was shaking as I tried to hold back the tears pushing to spill out.

"Oh my lord . . . my baby. . . . You came back home."
Tears were rapidly falling out of her eyes and down
her face. She held her arms open wide. "Where have
you—? I can't belie—oh . . . my . . . lordy. My baby's
home." She squeezed me so tight that it was hard to
breathe. I hugged her back just as hard as my tears of
pain and anguish fell on her shoulder. It felt like I was
ten all over again and I had passed a test in school or
cooked something just like she would have. A mother's
hug was like water in the desert to a thirsty man. Going
without it for too long was devastating.

I pulled back and looked at my mother. "Yes, Ma,
I'm back." My mother had picked up a little weight, but
she still looked pretty. Madison or Madi as her friends
called her was the apple of my eye as a child. I was still
in love with her looks and how she looked at me right
now.

"Uhhh . . . Thank ya, Jesus . . . Thank ya, Lord!" She
praised God. "You brought my baby back *home!*"

I just continued to look as she went on and praised
God for a few more seconds. I remembered my momma being a spiritual woman as I grew up and church
attendance was a regular part of our weekly regimen,
even though most of the time my father would not be
there with us.

"Look at you, all plump and stuff. I see you been
eating good," she said as she patted my stomach and
squeezed my cheeks, causing me to blush. "Oh, and
look at that hair of yours almost down to your bottom."
I blushed again and looked around to see if anyone saw
me standing in the doorway with my momma in her
robe, scarf, and curlers. I was a tad bit embarrassed.

"Wallace, baby. Come on in baby. Get in here!" She
pulled me in by the arm and shut the door.

"Wallace, I'll be right back." She headed toward the
stairs. "I need to check on your father."

"Yes, ma'am, take your time." I was still a little nervous. I had questions, but I knew she had some as well. I didn't know if I was ready to answer any questions she had.

I stepped into the living room and was instantly transported back to my childhood. The house had not changed much at all. Well, she had a plasma television on the wall, which looked to be about thirty-two inches or so. The picture frames were now all digital, even the ones from when we were kids. I looked on the mantle and saw the picture of my brothers and wondered how their lives played out. It flashed in my head how I had blocked so much out once I left here and headed to Baltimore. You would have never thought I had brothers or a family for all that matters. I guess James wasn't the only one keeping hush about his past. I did the same things. They say you attract who you are and not what you want. I shook my head at that thought. It was ironic now that I looked back. I was the least bit innocent as I portrayed to be. I wasn't just quiet with my mess.

Anyway, David was a little younger than me and Robert was the youngest. I missed my brothers, even though when we were children it seemed that we didn't have anything in common. From looking at one of the pictures on the wall, I could see that David was in a cap and gown. He was a really smart guy as a child. Robert was a teen standing in front of a car by himself. I assumed neither had children, because I saw no pictures of any children anywhere. I looked around a little further and saw pictures of my mom in her Sunday best gathered around a bunch of ladies and various church functions. She looked so happy. None of them had my father in it, which wasn't odd at all. He wasn't a church-type man, but he said he believed in God and that was enough for him. I looked around the room at all the knickknacks my mom had around the house. Angels and crosses were everywhere. I smiled because my mother always had a thing for angels. She even relayed to me that I was her "little angel" at times. I always felt like I was her favorite. She never said it but I felt it to be true. That all changed the day she let my father put me out. I was so angry at her for not fighting for me and for giving me up so easy. Too many nights in Baltimore I would wonder what I did for her to just let me go so easily. I heard her footsteps coming down the stairs, so I sat down on the living room chair and pretended I was looking at a text in my phone.

"I'm back." She walked in the room with a denim skirt and a white T-shirt on. "You hungry, baby?"

"Ahhh . . . Yes, ma'am." I answered back, not looking her in the face.

"Well, come on, Mama's little angel." She turned and headed toward the kitchen. At her age she was still fast as lightning. I was amazed at her speed. I smiled as I got up and trailed behind her. I still loved her nicknames for me, especially that one.

"Sit down while I fix us something good to nibble on." She was always a nibbler, when it came to food, because I have never seen her eat an entire plate of food in one sitting. A little here and a little there was her routine, till this day. It was nice to see she hadn't changed that much.

"So tell Mama, what you been doing with your life." She moved back and forth to the refrigerator to the stove.

"Wellll . . . I—I moved to Baltimore, after I left here." I wanted to say, *when y'all put my ass out on the street*, but I didn't want to disrespect my mother. "And I enrolled into culinary school."

"Wow, my baby a chef?" She turned around from the stove and smiled.

"Well, that didn't happen right away. The money you paid me off with . . . I mean *gave me* . . . I got an apartment and a car, but that didn't last too long so I looked for a job to keep money coming in, but no one would hire me and I had to use an alternative means of employment to get money to pay my rent, car note, and insurance."

"Baby, you aren't a stripper are you, because I didn't raise you to sell yourself out." She looked disappointed.

"No, ma'am, I wasn't a stripper. I was a drug dealer. I sold drugs." I couldn't sugarcoat it at all, she and I was too old for that.

"A drug dealer?" She looked even more disappointed. "Lord have mercy! Are you still selling it? Do you have that stuff on you now?" She put her hand over her heart like Fred Sanford did on *Sanford and Son*.

"No ma'am, I stopped selling it a couple years ago. I moved back here to get my culinary degree and reconnect with y'all . . . My family."

"Thank you, Jesus!" She blew out a breath and turned back around toward the stove to cook whatever she was cooking. "Mama prayed for you out there, wherever you were, because I didn't know where you went when we put—when you left this house."

"Well, Mama, getting put out, moving to Baltimore, and selling drugs wasn't in my plans for my life, but I made due with the hand that I was dealt. It doesn't make it right but, it is what it is."

There was a few seconds of silence in the room, then she started to hum a hymn or something as she threw some toast in the toaster.

"Mama, why did you let Dad put me out the house like that?" I blurted out.

"Wallace, your father was the head of the house and what he said went. I didn't want it to be that way, but I did what the Bible said to do. I had to honor my husband."

"And put your son out on the street." I was angry now. All of the resentment I had bottled up over the years was threatening to spill out. "What kind of honor was in that?"

"You would never understand!" She slammed down the wooden spoon she had in her hand and walked toward me.

"Understand what!" I breathed hard and angry.

"How you could abandon your son to keep your husband happy. Yeah, I understand! "

"Wallace, how dare you come back here with this foolishness? Did you come back here just to throw this back in my face?" She was crying, I was crying. I wanted to reach out and hug her to tell her I was sorry, but I didn't. I wanted answers for all the pain that I was feeling. I wanted to know how she could sleep at night while I had nowhere to go and no one to turn to.

"No, I didn't . . . me . . . I just." I put my face in my hands and breathed hard again. She sat down beside me at the table and rubbed my back.

"Wallace, baby, I can't take back what happened. I can't. You'll never know how it was to watch my first-born walk out of the house and not know where he was going, how he was going to eat and if I was doing the right thing. I prayed to God that he would keep his hands of protection on you. That's all I could do." She leaned in closer and put her head on my shoulder. "Wallace, I loved you and still do. After all these years, I still wonder if I did the right thing. Baby, you're still alive. You're still alive. God kept you for me. Can't you see, Wallace baby. I had to let you go, because I knew God would keep you."

She pulled away and I sat up and looked at her in the eyes. She was smiling. I forgave her. I think. "I'm sorry, Ma. I shouldn't have come at you in that manner. I know you only did what was right at that time."

"Hello! Hello!" I heard someone yelling from the living room.

"I'm in here!" she yelled back.

Into the kitchen walked a tall pretty chick in a purple and white sundress, high heels, and a spiky haircut. She was pretty and she knew it. I was in awe. She walked over to my mother and gave her a hug.

"What you cooking and who is this, Ma?" She sashayed to a chair at the table and sat down and crossed her legs.

"Ma?" I looked at my mother in confusion. I can't believe I had a sister. She must have been born after I left. "I have a sister too?" I smiled because I always wanted a sister.

"Well," my mother cut her eyes at the chick across the table from me. "Not quite . . . This is your brother-sister, Robert or as he likes to be called, Rebecca."

"Excuse me?" I blurted out.

Chapter 7

Ashley
Family Matters
April 6th 1:15 P.M.

I sat in on my bed spread eagle as I watched Grace
as she lectured on my forty-two-inch plasma TV. I had
opted to do class from my room. You see, nowadays
when you're in college you can sit in the physical classroom or you could log on to the classroom at home and
get the lesson from the comfort of your home. It was a
luxury of the times and I partook in it with a few of my
classes. You could see them, but they could not see you.
You could also buzz in if you had questions too.

"Her ass is turning me on," I moaned as I stuck my
finger in myself and swirled around, then I pulled out
to let my partner taste me.

I was doing Grace, but I made sure I had someone
else to return the favor. I liked to get a couple of nuts in
good just like the next bitch.

"Umm," She licked my finger and moved toward my
legs like a cat on the prowl. She was older than me too.
She had me by over ten years. She too was a little thick.

She went in for the kill and went straight for my kitty
kat. I spread my legs as far as I could. She flicked her
tongue on my clit and continued a trail up to my navel
and then she scooped one of my C-cups into her mouth.

My eyes were still on the class that I was attending via Internet. I was so entranced by Grace that I didn't even notice that Ebony had moved up to my neck trying to give me a hickey.

I moved my neck letting her know I wasn't into that.

"What's wrong?" she asked, disappointed. I looked into her eyes and saw that her whole world had revolved around me. I wasn't surprised. I knew that I was a good catch, but she didn't know she was just my hot box (human sex toy).

Without noticing, my eyes wandered back toward the plasma screen without answering her question. Like two magnets trying to get together, I couldn't stop looking at Grace and wondering how I could be with someone in her condition. I mean, I feel really fucking crazy right now even messing with her. It made me wonder if I was who I thought I was or was I just fucked-up like most people or more. I knew her secret and yet I still fuck with her on an intimate level. I'm dumbfounded with myself.

I felt the bed shift and it brought me back to reality. I looked at Ebony as she put on her clothes. She looked at me with anger in her eyes. I, on the other hand, let her get dressed. I was done with her for the day.

"So you're not going to stop me from leaving?" I chuckled as I grabbed the remote to the TV and cut it off. I then got out of bed and walked up to Ebony. And grabbed her in an embrace and started fondling her all over 'til I got to her ass. I squeezed and shook it and got what I wanted and walked away from her.

"Hey, what are you doing?" she asked me as I opened her wallet that I had retrieved out of her back pocket. I wasn't grabbing her butt for pleasure, well not that kind at the time; I was getting my fee out of her pocket. She walked up to me as if she was going to take her wallet back from me. I gave her a look that she knew all too well. She knew she had to pay to play. She backed up and waited for me to finish handling my business. I grabbed what I wanted and threw the wallet at her and watched her fumble and catch it.

I walked to the door and she trailed behind me.

"When I'm going to see you again?" she asked as we got to the front door.

"When I see you." I responded. She looked at me in confusion as she stood with her back to my front door.

"Huh?" she asked.

She didn't get it. I didn't like to be trapped in a box, controlled, or questioned from no one, not even my parents. I only tolerated them for the time being.

"When . . . I. . . . see . . . you." I broke it down like I was using sign language. She could be slow at times.

"Oh . . . okay." She looked down at the floor, disappointed. "Can I get a kiss good-bye?"

"How many times do I have to tell your slow ass that I don't kiss bitches? I don't know where you mouth been. You could be eating shit for all I know. Nah, not going to happen. Now roll out! I got other things to do." I opened the door to let her out and Alex was standing at the door about to put his finger on the door reader so he could get into the apartment.

"Later baby," Ebony said as she walked away. I wanted to bust the bitch in the head for being so reckless with her mouth, but shit I didn't care. Alex couldn't do anything to me either.

I walked back into the apartment with Alex following behind me.

"Ah . . . Ashley, who was that chick?"

I turned around and gave him a menacing stare.

"Ms. Mind Your Fucking Business." I turned and walked into our kitchen. He followed me like he usually did. Men just don't know when to quit sometimes. "Damn, Ashley, why does it have to be all of that? I was just asking you a question. You are always acting like a bitch."

"Did you just call me out of my name?" I walked up to him and pointed my finger in his face. "A-S-H-L-E-Y is how you spell my fucking name. Don't disrespect me again. Don't forget I could ruin your life with what I got on you, you need to be treating my ass right for holding onto your mess." He looked pissed off at the mentioning of what I knew about him. But, I knew him. He wasn't going to do anything.

"Damn, Ashley why you got to be like this? You are acting like a nutcase or something. Your ass need treatment or something." He walked toward the refrigerator and pulled out a soda. I reached my hand out and he instantly gave me the soda. He went back to the refrigerator and pulled himself out another one. I had him trained too. I hated to treat him as I did, but his ass was so nosy that I thought he was going to try and bust my ass and mess up the operation that I had going.

"I thought you said you were done with women after that last chick showed up at Mom and Dad's renewal ceremony."

"You're minding my business again." I narrowed my eyes, letting him know he was pushing me past my breaking point. He knew me very well, so he backed off again.

"Crazy," he let out with an exhausted breath.

"Yep, better know it." With that said I walked out toward the living room and flopped down on the couch, drank my soda and planned my next move. A bitch needs to be ready to roll with the punches. (Yeah, I called myself a bitch, but only I can treat me like that, not anyone else). Not long after I got comfortable, Alex comes in and sits down next to me.

"Ashley, you ever wonder what our father was like and his family?"

"No, not really," Ever since I was told about my father not being my father, I just shrugged it off and lived by the motto "It is what it is." I was neither here nor there with all that.

"You mean to tell me you don't want to know what he was like and all of that?"

"Alex, he dead and all the money he left us is gone. What I need to know about his life for? He dead and gone. Not unless they got some money or something." I laughed. I know it seemed coldhearted, but I liked money. What can I say, I was selfish.

Alex shook his head in a way as to say "What a shame." I didn't care.

"Anyway, I've been doing some research and I think I may have found someone in his family that may be able to tell us about him."

"What are you going do after you find them? I mean they asses might be broke or crackheads or something. I think you may need to leave this mess alone. You got family, be satisfied with what you got." I was contradicting myself, because I was after more myself, money that is. Family; I had enough of them.

"Ashley, it's not that simple. I want to know about family medical history and stuff like that, you never know. You might find out that you get your crazy- ass ways from a family history of psychotic episodes or something. You have been acting like a lunatic lately." He laughed, but I didn't.

"Whatever." I got up off the couch and walked toward my room. "Just make sure you see if they have some money first. Don't even mention my name if they asses broke." I closed my door, undressed, showered, and got in the bed to get me some much-needed sleep. I had big plans for my future.

Chapter 8

Alex
Questions
April 6th 1:33 P.M.

"She must have fell and hit her head, she's just plain evil. I can't believe her attitude has gotten this out of hand." I walked into my room after staring at her door for a few seconds in disbelief.

I walked over to my dresser and pulled out a picture of my girl. I had to hide her picture, because Ashley did know some stuff about me that I didn't want her to know about. Little did she know we had some stuff in common. My girl was an older woman that was about thirty years older than me. I had to sneak around and be with her for fear Ashley would tell her my business. Ashley was just mean like that. I think I was falling in love with her and I didn't want to risk losing her. The conversations we had been having were off the hook, she had wisdom and age and she was bigger than me, so she could throw me around a little bit too. I loved aggressive women, it turned me on to be manhandled by a woman.

I was interrupted by the vibrating of my cell phone.

I hit the answer button and put my phone on the cradle that was hooked up to my plasma television. As soon as I sat it on the cradle my father's face popped up on the screen.

"Hey son." He sounded upbeat and happy. He was in his office at home.

"Hey Dad," I said equally happy. I loved my dad. He was such a good example of what a man could be if he put his mind to it. It made me work hard in my studies and on the football field. He looked a little bit older and I could even see his hair beginning to get some gray hairs sprinkled throughout his head.

"I'm just calling to check up on you and Ash. Making sure all is well."

"Well, Dad, everything is fine. With the exception of Ashley, life is good out here." I smiled.

"What has she been up to lately?" he asked. "She is the crazy twin," he laughed.

"Nothing real crazy, just lashing out and stuff like that." I couldn't tell him that she was out here doing her lesbian thing again. I knew he would call her and confront her. I couldn't afford for her to tell him that I took out a loan to get help with my issue. He was all about debt and money management. The last thing I wanted him to know about was me getting into debt.

"I think she is stressing about one of her classes she had a problem in." I didn't know anything about her class schedule or her study habits. Shit, I hardly saw her with a book in her hand. She was so smart I mean, maybe she was a quick study like she was when we were in high school.

"Did she find a job yet?" he asked.

"I don't know Dad." I shrugged my shoulders. "I try to stay out her way when it came to her business." The incident we just had earlier flashed through my mind making it crystal clear that I really needed to do just that from now on.

"Well, let me call her phone to ask her."

"Hold on, Dad. I need to talk to you about something else first."

"What is it?"

"I need to know about my biological father, James-Jerry Parks." His face became instantly flushed, like he had seen a ghost.

"Hold on." He put up his finger and got up out of his chair. I heard what sounded like a door being closed and then he appeared back in front of the screen again.

"What you need to know?" he asked..

"I just needed to know if you and Mom knew anything about him."

"What brought this on, Alex?" He asked a question with a question.

"Well, I was just curious about this other side of family that I didn't know about. And I also wanted to know about the medical history, so I know what I may or may not be pre-exposed to. You know, like mental illness and things of that nature."

"Alex, I don't think you have anything to worry about, besides I think most of his family has passed away."

"Dad, did you know him?"

"In a way," he fumbled. "But that's neither here nor there. I think it is best that you leave the issue alone."

"Dad, is everything okay?" His eyes seemed like they were watery, like he was about to cry or something. "You look like you are about to cry. Dad, I didn't mean to bring up the past. I just had some questions about him, that's all."

"Sure, son, I'm fine," he sniffed. "I think my allergies are messing with me, that's all. Son, I can't stop you from wanting to know. And I knew someday you would want to know. I just didn't think it would have been so soon. I'm not going to hold you back, if this is what you want, then let me know your progress as it goes along." He shifted in his chair and then looked out of the window.

"Dad, you are my dad. That will not change. I just need you to know that." He nodded his head as a tear slid down his face. "I just don't feel complete if I don't find out about who and what this man was, so I will know more about me and why I'm the way I am. I love you, Dad, for being the best example I could ever have in life. You taught me to confront my issues and just like you did with your homosexuality issues."

"You're gay?" He sat up in the chair like a stiff board.

"No, Dad, I'm not." I shook my head no. "That is an issue I don't have to deal with for sure," I confirmed.

"Oh . . . okay." He relaxed. "Alex, your brother and sister want to say hi."

He got out of the chair while Li'l Shawn and Diana sat in front of the screen. I talked to them for a couple of minutes. Afterward my mom hopped on for a few seconds and told me she loved me and to kiss my sister for her. I hung up and lay back on my bed and thought about my dad and why he wanted to leave things alone. My curiosity was getting the best of me and I wanted to know even more now than ever. It was like he was hiding something and he didn't want me to find out about it. But, then again he told us everything at the table a couple of years back, so I know that that could not have been true. I just wanted to see if I was like this James/ Jerry or not, since I did favor him in the looks department. I want to know what else I got from him. I got up, jumped in the shower and got in the bed. Tomorrow, I start my job at the school cafeteria and I need to be on time.

Chapter 9

Shawn
The Whole Truth
April 9th 4:15 P.M.

"Damn!" I pounded my fist on my desk in anger. I was in my office at my privately owned firm in Baltimore. I swiveled my chair around to look out the window of my office that sat on the twelfth floor at the corner of Charles and Fayette Streets.

"God, are you punishing me or something?" I wasn't really questioning God. I was just wondering why Alex was trying to dig up stuff about James and asking me questions that I knew I still wasn't ready to answer just yet. It was like he was trying to disown me as a father. He said he loved me and I will always be his dad, but will that be the case when he finds out that his biological father was gay and I was one of his lovers? I thought by telling him and his sister that I was bisexual, back when we had that family meeting would be enough and I wouldn't have to give them every detail, but apparently I was wrong. I needed to come clean to both of them fully before they find out and really disown me as a father. All this lying just has to stop. But, how do you tell your children that their mother and father had a sexual relationship with their biological father?

Chapter 10

Fast Lane
Grace
April 11th 7:05 A.M.

I woke up on Friday with my cell phone ringing off the hook. I rolled over to see my husband was gone and that I was alone once again. I should have been up an hour ago, but I would just have to speed drive to work this morning.

"Hello," I answered, barely awake.

"Get up," I heard Ashley's voice demand through the phone.

"I'm up." I slung my feet off the bed, into my slippers and then went to my window and opened them so the sunshine could shine through.

"You're off today," Ashley barked through the phone.

"You know I work Monday through Friday. Why would you ask me that?" I stretched as I made my way to my bathroom to wash my face and brush my teeth.

"That was a demand not a question," she corrected me.

"What? I can't just call out of work. I have classes to teach."

"You can and you will. I'll be waiting in front of my house for you."

"What I am supposed to tell them?" I mumbled.

"Y'all bitches are so dumb. You sure you got a degree? I have to tell you everything to do. Make something up. I don't care, just be here in twenty minutes." Click.

I pulled up to Ashley's apartment with sunglasses on and a hat. I didn't want to risk being seen by anyone I might know. She hopped in and I pulled off.

"Where are we going, Ashley?" She ignored me as she typed into my GPS an address without my permission. She was a bold bitch. I shook my head in amazement.

"Just follow the directions and you'll see when we get there." She reclined her chair and took a nap.

An hour or so later I pulled to a car dealership. When the automated voice said "your destination is on your right" Ashley awoke from her slumber. I pulled the car on to the lot and put it in park.

"You are getting a car?" I asked.

"Yep." With that she hopped out of the car. "Let's go."

I hurried up behind her like a scolded puppy. I felt like clipping her ass just to see her young ass hit the ground, but I held it in. Within seconds we were approached by a tall, slender, black salesman.

"How can I help you ladies?" he asked with a beaming smile.

Ashley pulled out a piece of paper and handed it to him.

"I see you have come prepared." He smiled. "Let's make this happen. Please follow me to my office."

We trailed behind him as he walked. He had a nice ass to say the least. I smiled at the thought of playing with it.

"Have a seat and I'll be right back with the paperwork." He exited his small office.

"So, how are you going to pay for this?" I asked Ashley.

"Don't worry, I got this." She smiled. I looked at her with a confident smile. Man, I wanted to beat her ass. If she didn't have what she had on me I would've busted her in the head a long time ago. *Crazy-ass bitch!*

The salesmen walked back in the office with a frown on his face.

"Ms. Black, you're going to need a cosigner for this car since you don't have any credit. Is your mother going to be cosigning this with you?' He looked at her then me.

"She's not my mother," she shot back at him.

"Oh my bad, I should have known, since she doesn't look a day over thirty-five." He smiled and looked at me. I blushed.

"Look, man, she's my woman." I could tell Ashley was about to explode. "So stop disrespecting me by flirting with her right in front of me."

"Your women?" He still looked puzzled. In this day and age people still aren't comfortable with seeing two women together, especially a straight man.

"Yes . . . My bitch . . . my filet-o-fish. Whatever you want to call it." I put my head down in shame. "*Comprende?*"

It took me a few seconds to get myself together and look back up.

"You ready to get on with the car business, since you filled up on my business?" Ashley asked, mugging the man.

"My apologies," he mustered up with a look of embarrassment. "Let's get back to business."

"Let's!" Ashley said cosigning his last comment. She then sat back and crossed her leg, letting one swing in aggravation.

"No, she will not be cosigning for the car with me." I breathed out a sigh of relief. "She is signing for the car fully."

"What?" I belted out. "You didn't tell me you needed for me to sign for this car when you picked me up."

Ashley turned toward me and smiled. A smile that said "bitch, do what I say or else." "Will you please sign for the car for me?"

"Sure, no problem." I forced out a smile. Man, this bitch was taking me on a fast ride. I was wondering what else this bitch had up her sleeve. He handed me the papers and I hesitantly signed.

"Are you going to put this under your car insurance?" he asked me.

"Nah, I got that covered." Ashley cut me off before I could answer.

I sighed again in relief, because I didn't know how I was going to explain to my husband why we had another car on our car insurance policy.

After signing the lease to the car and exiting the building, Ashley jumping in her brand-new car and speed off leaving me with a simple "later." I have got to get this trick before she ruins all that I have accomplished in life.

"She keeps on fucking me over and I don't even get a good nut out of the deal. This bitch is like a pitbull off its leash. "

Chapter 11

David
Dear John
April 11th 1:05 P.M.

"Brittani, where is Mrs. Andrews?" I questioned my wife's secretary.

"Sir, she called out today." She looked at me like I should have known where my wife was. "She said she had an appointment that she forgot to add to her itinerary."

"You know what, she did tell me that last night. I just forgot about it myself. Getting old does that to you." I chuckled and so did she. I was embarrassed to the fullest. My manhood was being tested once again. *You can't even keep track of your own wife. Faggot ass!!! She probably out getting what your fat, faggoty ass couldn't give her!* I thought to myself.

"I'll talk to you later. Have a nice day." With that I walked off toward the elevator. Once I was out of the building and walking across the campus, I pulled out my cell phone. "Call Grace."

You've reached Grace. I'm not available to take your call at the moment. Please leave me a detailed message and I will do my best to get back to you as soon as possible. Enjoy your day! I listened to the message about four more times as I dialed her phone back to back. Finally, I left her a message.

Hey babe, give me a call when you can. Let me know if everything is okay. It's your husband . . . David.

I hung up and I couldn't help but get teary-eyed as I walked to my office building. I hopped on the elevator and quickly wiped my tears away as I got off and greeted my secretary.

"Hi, Laura, any messages for me?"

"No sir, but you do have an appointment with one of your students in about five minutes."

"Who is it?" I asked, not really wanting to talk to anybody today.

"Alex Black."

"Okay, let me know when he gets here." I walked in my office and shut the door. I threw my coat and briefcase on to my cream leather sofa and flopped down in my chair behind my desk. Alex Black was one of my genealogy students that I had a good friendship with. He was in search of his family he had on his father's side and came to me asking for special assistance. I accepted because I saw the fire in his eyes. The same fire I had at his age. I was a need-to-know person myself, so I knew what it was like to set up a goal and see it through to the end. He was also a football star on campus and I could tell from all the ladies in class that he was highly sought after. For some reason I have never seen him with anyone of the gorgeous ladies on campus and he never even let it slip that he was seeing someone. I was curious to know if he was a switch-hitter or just focused on his school career. I had to admit he was easy on the eyes.

"Professor Andrews . . . your appointment is here," my secretary spoke through the intercom.

"All right, let him in."

Within seconds Alex walks through the door and sits down in front of me, all smiles.

"How are things going, Mr. Black?" I made sure to be extremely professional at all times. You never know who's sitting across from you. And with today's technology a conversation could be recorded with one push of a button on a cell phone and you would never know it. Even though I did show interest in him he would only know it if he put it out there first.

"Well, sir, I think I am very close to finding the people in my family." He smiled a bright beaming smile. It was a beautiful one as well. Made my dick jump. I had to rearrange myself in my seat just so it wouldn't be noticed if I had to get up or something.

"That's good. I am so proud of you for sticking this out for so long." I leaned on my desk with my elbows and my hands clasped together. I looked at him in his eyes and he did the same. I still didn't get a signal so I went in for some evasive questioning. I also had a degree in psychology as well. I wanted to see what his body language was like when he answered.

"So now that that is done, you can probably spend more time with your girlfriend. And you probably can introduce them as well."

"Girlfriend? Me?" He looked slightly offended. "Who said I had a girlfriend?"

"Well, I just assumed that—"

"Well, it's not good to assume, Professor Andrews." He cut me off. "I just need to focus on what is important to me right now, school, football, family, and now a job."

"Oh, so you have a job now?" I sat back and listened.

"Yes, I start working in the school cafeteria today after class. All they have me doing is cleaning up. It's a start for right now." He smiled again. *Wow! He has such a pretty set of teeth. And look at his lips . . . they look . . . soft.*

"Well, Professor Andrews, I got to get to class. I just wanted to give you the progress report and see how you were doing. Are you still going to start the training in the school campus sports arena?"

"Yeah, I plan on it." I smiled. A picture of him in training gear turned me on and I had to shift my dick once again.

"Well, whenever you ready just let me know. Maybe we can train together. You know one hand wash the other." He smiled. If only he knew what I was thinking at that very moment. He probably would never want to see me again. He exited my office and I pulled out my cell phone once again. This time I wasn't calling my wife. I was calling my little secret.

"Hello." I heard a stern and rough voice answer the phone.

"John, I need to come over. Now," I whispered into the phone.

"Cool, I'm ready now." I hung up the phone. I picked up my briefcase and exited my office just as fast as I got in.

"Laura, I have an emergency. Please cancel my appointment and my classes for today," I said, walking to the elevator.

"Is everything okay, sir?" She called out as I impatiently pushed the elevator's button.

"Yes," I said as I entered the elevator. "It will be soon." The elevator doors closed. I exited the building and moved swiftly toward my car on a mission. A sexual mission. Alex had turned me on so bad that I need to see my childhood abuser today instead of our usual day.

I made my way to his house in about thirty-five minutes flat. The trip usually took me about an hour but, I need to bust a nut with the quickness today.

John Parks was the same man that my father was treating and fucking when I was just a boy. He turned me out and my brother and yes, I was still "seeing" him on a regular basis. Yes, it was totally unhealthy on so many levels, but I got used to it and it was a way of life for me now. Nobody knew I was seeing him but me and him. He was twenty years older then me, but he keep his shit on lock. He was in better shape then I was and he could still take the dick like a pro. I parked in my usual spot about two blocks from the apartment house he lived in and walked down to his residence.

I called his phone and let it ring five times before I hung up, letting him know I was outside waiting to get in. It was our little signal that let him know that I was waiting to come in.

"Hey," I said as I walked into his apartment. It was immaculate and everything was in its place. I took off my shoes by the door, then took off my clothes and folded them on a chair next to the door.

"You gaining some extra weight." He smiled. I frowned because once again attention was brought back to my weight and I didn't like to talk about it. I knew I was fat, but I didn't need a reminder. "Don't worry, it makes for better sex. The rougher the better." He smiled. I smiled after a few seconds.

His ass was a freak and at his age I was afraid I was going to break something on him when we fucked. That shit didn't stop me though. I wanted to break something while I was fucking this faggot anyways. He and my father fucked me and my brother Robert up for life. A broken rib or ass bone was the least I could do to him for fucking me up so bad. I walked past a picture on the mantle. It was a woman and a little boy in the picture. I saw it on every trip over here. I asked on several occasions about the identity of the people in the picture, but the only response I got was that it was "none of my fucking business." I assumed it was maybe his wife and son, but he never talked about it and would get extremely irate whenever I asked. I looked at the picture even closer and noticed that the boy had an extreme resemblance to Alex Black, which puzzled me. I made a note to see who it was Alex was looking for.

"Daddy's ready," I heard John yell as I made my way toward his bedroom. He was on all fours and ready to take the punishment I was about to take out on him. I pulled at my dick and my thick eight inches was ready to do some damage. I reached for a condom on his nightstand and entered him with a force that pushed his head and body toward the headboard with a bang. He liked it rough. So rough was how he was going to get it. I fucked him in three different positions over an hour's time and came three times within that hour. I showered and exited his place about fifteen minutes later, satisfied and ready to get in the bed. I shed a few tears on my ride home, because I wanted so bad to end it all. And on so many times I came close to doing it, but for the sake of my wife I kept it moving. Hoping that I would get the help that I knew I needed before it was too late.

Chapter 12

Wallace
I know you.
April 14th 1:03 P.M.

I was serving a couple of kids when he walked in the cafeteria. I tried my best to concentrate on what I was doing and keep an eye on him at the same time. It didn't work. Because instead of putting a sandwich on the student's tray in front of me, I dropped it on the floor next to it.

"Sorry, I'll get you another one." I hurried and grabbed another burger and put it on the tray correctly this time. The chubby-looking girl looked at me and shook her head.

"It's all right. We all make mistakes. Just don't do it again, cutie." I smiled even though she really didn't interest me. My eyes still shifted between her and the James look-alike that was headed my way. She didn't even notice, but she keeps on talking as she slowly walked away. I did a couple of um-hmms so I didn't seem to be rude. She could have been asking to fuck me after my shift, but I didn't hear it. I had a couple of people still in line, so I played it off like I was serving them as he walked up to the staff door, put his thumb on the sensor and opened the door. *He works here now? When did this happen?*

After I had served the last couple of students and before the next rush, I asked one of the other cooks to watch the line while I went to the back and inquired about the new hire.

My boss was sitting in his office with his door slightly ajar as I knocked.

"Come in," he called out. I walked in and noticed the James look-alike sitting in a chair in front of my boss's desk.

"Hey, Wallace, what can I help you with?"

"Uh—uh—uh—nothing, sir. I'll talk to you later." I tried to ease out of the door just as easily as I had come, but I was stopped by the sound of my boss's voice calling out to me.

"One second, Wallace. I'd like you to meet Alex Black, he's the newbie for the floor staff I just hired."

"We've met already," Alex said as he smiled and I walked up to him and shook his hand. He had such a beautiful smile, just like James did. And his hand was so soft. Then I remembered where I knew him from, again. I felt kind of bad for the feelings I was getting for him seeing that I knew his father.

"He's one of our star football players and he has an impressive academic record as well."

"Well, that is awesome. We need someone like him on our team here too." I was smiling hard, almost too hard.

"I am going to need you to show him the ropes and answer any questions he might have."

"Sure, boss." I smiled and walked out of the office.

Within a couple of minutes Alex was out of the office and my boss was showing him his duties. He caught on quick because after an hour or so he was on his own in the cafeteria. Emptying trash cans, cleaning tables, and sweeping floors: He was good at it all. I smiled as I watched him from a distance. He was a strapping guy; though he wasn't huge he was adequate for the job. I could tell he spent some time in the gymnasium as well. Again, I still felt kind of guilty about lusting after him. His father was a confidant in my life after James was killed. Shawn Black was James's lawyer and I grilled him as much as I could about James and how he could have gotten himself into someone killing him, my estranged cousin Tyrone to be exact. I've only been in contact with my cousin briefly during our childhood. He was a cousin on my father's side of the family. On the few occasions we did have together we did bond the best we could. But that was so many years ago. To this day I still don't know how he found me in Baltimore.

Anyways, Shawn and I would meet up a couple of times, over a year's time, to discuss James and how I was coping with his untimely death. He was a real help. He would always just sit and listen and be attentive. Like a real friend should. I could tell by our conversation that James and he were friends as well as lawyer and client. I felt myself getting too vulnerable and attracted to him, so I cut off our little sessions for a while.

A couple of weeks after I had cut him off, I saw Shawn's car in traffic and I followed it to a gas station to apologize for not speaking to him for so long. I pulled up behind the car he usually drives, hopped out of mine and walked up to his. I tapped on the window only to find Alex sitting in the driver side of the car.

"Can I help you?" He asked as he rolled down the window. I was so embarrassed, because at that moment I felt like a stalker of sorts.

"Nah, I'm sorry. I thought you were someone else." I finally said as I looked at the James look-alike. I thought that I was going crazy then too, because like you see on television, all the guys I was seeing started to resemble James in some way.

"You made me nervous," he chuckled. "I thought you were a cop or something. Not that I'm doing anything. Cops are just pulling us over randomly with these unmarked cars all the time." I smiled and looked toward my car.

"I know," I managed to get out. Here I was an almost fifty years old stalking someone for attention. Shawn was a family man and I knew it. I was lonely and clingy and I needed to get a grip. I didn't want his wife to suspect anything that wasn't there and cause problems for him. So I knew from then on I was going to leave him alone.

"A brotha can't even drive his father's car without being paranoid about cops pulling him over for pushing a nice and classy car." He laughed.

"Oh, this is your father's car?"

"Yeah, my dad lets me drive his car from time to time when he's home resting from all his cases during the week. He's a lawyer." Alex smiled when he said that. I could tell he was proud of his father and what he did.

"Mr. Black is your father?"

"Yep, sure is. You know him?"

"Yeah, he . . . uh . . . represented me in a case a couple of weeks ago. That's why I followed you. I thought that you were him. I wanted to thank him for all his work on my case again. He's a very good lawyer."

"One of the best," Alex cosigned my last statement.

"Well, I won't be holding you long. Tell your dad I said thanks again."

"Sure will." I shook his hand and walked off toward my car.

I sat in my car for a few seconds with my phone to my ear pretending I was on the phone. He had no clue that I was watching his every move. I eventually pulled off and made my way back to my home. I cried the whole night and when I woke up I decided that that day would be the day I started to pack, tie up my loose ends in the drug game and move back to my hometown.

That was about three years ago and now I was looking at that same face here again.

After the rest of the cafeteria staff made their way out of the building, everybody spread out and walked toward their cars. I looked around and didn't see Alex anywhere in sight, so I hopped in my car and pulled off campus and down the street. About a block down the road I saw Alex casually walking with his backpack on his back.

I blew my horn and pulled over to see if he needed a ride or something like that.

"Hey, man, you need a ride?" he kind of waved his hand like he didn't, but I persisted anyway. "You sure? It's not out of my way."

He walked over and got in and buckled his seat belt. I was smiling inside as I pulled off.

"So, where to?" I asked.

"I'm about a mile and a half down the street and on the left."

"So you remembered me, huh?" I asked and smiled. I was overzealous and it showed.

"Yeah, it took me a minute but I figured it out." He smiled too.

"So, how is your dad doing?"

"He is doing all right. He still does his law thing. He got his own practice now."

"Say what! That's what I'm talking about. It's always nice to hear nice things about black men these days."

"Yeah, it sure is. I'm going to be on the list soon enough. I'm going to be just like him."

"Now that is good to hear too." I looked over and saw the proud look on his face. "Let me know when we getting to your spot."

"You got about four blocks to go."

"Okay." I nodded my head as I paid attention to the road. "So what are you going to school for?"

"I'm majoring in both genealogy and sociology."

"Man, that is deep. You really are going for it."

"Yeah, I am a nosy person by nature and I love football, but I knew that there is a chance I may not make it to the pro's so, I figured I would use my nosiness as a springboard for my education." He nodded his is head like he was sure about what he was saying. I was sure he was too. He had confidence and pride in the way he talked. Such a turn-on.

"Well here we are," I said as I pulled up into the parking lot of his apartment complex. "So, this is it, huh?"

"Yep, this is where I lay my head."

"You live alone?" I took my turn being nosy.

"Nah, me and my twin sister lives here together."

"Oh, you got a twin?"

"Yeah, but we nothing alike." He chuckled. "But, that's not a bad thing. We even each other out."

"Oh, that's good. You got any other brothers and sisters?"

"Yep, I have three sisters and a brother."

"Wow, I know what your father likes to do." I laughed. He did too. I felt glad that I didn't pursue Shawn when I was in Baltimore. What I thought was there wasn't and I would have felt real crazy when he rejected me.

"It's a long story and you would believe it if I told you."

"Well, here's my number. Call me and tell me about it sometime."

With that he got out of the car and made his way to his apartment building's entrance. I pulled off toward home.

Chapter 13

Ashley
A Bad Bitch
April 17th 1:34 P.M.

I was driving down the palm-filled streets of Inglewood with the top to my convertible down and my hair blowing in the wind. I had decided to skip my classes today and take my new toy for a ride today. The sun was out and I was feeling quite lovely. I had on a sleeveless blue sundress that perked up my C-cups just right.

"This is the shit right here." I turned up my satellite radio player as my anthem played. "Spotlight" by Jennifer Hudson was still a classic even after all these years. She was my favorite singer to say the least.

I looked at my jump off next to me and smiled.

"You having fun, babe?"

"Yeah." She looked like she was scared to death. I would be too if I was in the position she was in. Ebony was a thirty-five-year old deaconess at her parents' church, but she had a wild side. And we know how preacher's kids can be. Off the fucking chain. But, I was far more advanced than her even though she had me by some years. I met her when I started going to her church, Blessed by God Ministries, about six months after I moved here to Cali. She was in the choir and so was I. I was a lead singer for many of the songs and she would stare at me in amazement whenever I did so. I loved to sing and I hoped that one day it would be a career for me, but that was another subject for another time.

One day after a rehearsal Ebony came up to me and asked me if she could have my number so we could work on her voice and a couple of songs she was having problems with. I said okay. I thought it was innocent until she forced herself on me. I was a little shocked to say the least. We ended up getting it on in my bedroom that night and she had to sneak out in the middle of the night to go home. She had a husband and she said she was just experimenting with her sexuality. From then on, she has been my orgasm queen. I told her that her secret was safe with me.

I pulled into one of my favorite restaurants, Benson's Bistro and put the top onto my car up. I stepped out of the car in an all-black cat suit underneath my dress. One would say it was too hot for all of that, but I was working it anyway, with some four-inch pumps to match. Ebony had on some cute tan capris, a frilly shirt with tan open toes wedge clogs. We walked into the restaurant with her leading. She knew I was in charge though.

"Can we have a table for two in the corner?" I asked the greeter as we stood at the greeter's desk.

"Sure, follow me this way." I followed her ass as we walked toward our table. I was so entranced that I almost walked up on her heels when we got to the table.

I pulled out the chair for Ebony and then I sat down myself. I didn't want to be a man, but I played the part as best I could, because as you know by now, I'm a bad bitch.

"Your server will be right with you," the waitress said as she walked away.

"You okay?" She must have saw that I was looking at the waitress's ass as she walked away, because she looked heated.

"Do you really have to disrespect me like that?"

"Like what?" I asked, playing dumb.

She just looked at me with a pissed-off look. "Oh, you talking about that . . . her . . . I was just looking . . . What? I can't admire another chick in front of you?"

"I wouldn't do that to you." she said in a serious tone. I didn't care though.

"I'm not you," I stated. "We are not exclusive, re- member, you have a man."

"That's beside the point," she huffed. "It's just disre- spectful."

"Look, I need you to play your position. I like you, but we not in a relationship and that was your call, not mine."

"I know I said that, but—"

"But nothing," I cut her off. "You had your chance to be exclusive, but you wanted to be a punk bitch about it, so I decide that it is what it is. You not the only one I'm doing and frankly, I like it that way."

She sat back and folded her arms and pouted like a baby. It just proved to me that age is nothing but a number and maturity can't be based on age, because some people's age and maturity didn't always coincide.

"Look, let's just enjoy the meal and our time togeth- er." By the time I said that the waiter had come to our table and we ordered our food.

"I have to use the bathroom," I said, getting out of my seat and walking toward the bathroom. I wanted to eat my food without an interrupted break so I decided to go now instead of later. The restaurant had a U- shaped design and we sat on one end and the bathroom was around the other side.

"Okay," I heard Ebony say as I got up.

On my way to the bathroom, I noticed Grace and her husband sitting in the corner just like me and Ebony had done. I decided to have some fun and walk over to the table to say hello.

"How are you doing today, Professor Andrews?" The look on her face was of pure surprise.

"I'm doing well. And you?"

"Well, I can't complain. Life is good. I'm sorry you couldn't make it to class the other day. I was so looking forward to your lecture." I had to make sure I covered all my bases. I didn't want to be associated with her in any way.

"I'm sorry too." She smirked and looked at her husband. I looked at him too. "I had some personal things to take care of. I had a pain in my behind that I had to get checked out."

"Oh, I hope everything worked out for you." I smiled. She was trying to bitch me right in front of her husband. "Be careful because you never know when those pains come back at you. Sometimes they can get worse and they even can put you in the hospital."

"You got that right," her husband interjected. I just looked at him in pity. He didn't have a clue.

"Well, I got to be going to the bathroom. I was just stopping by to say hi."

I walked off with a satisfied smile on my face and made my way into the bathroom. As soon as I got in the bathroom I went to a stall and locked myself in. I put down one of those toilet seat protectors and took a piss. You never know who's been squatting or what they may have left behind. I wiped myself and was about to pull up my underwear when there was a knock on my stall. I hurried up and pulled up my panties and opened the stall to see who was on the other

"The walls have mirrors on them," was the first thing she said to me.

"Excuse me?" I said in confusion.

"I saw you checking out my ass as I showed you your table." She was the greeter that showed us to our table. She was bold as shit. A complete turn-on.

"So?" I shot back at her.

"I'm bi and I'm on break. I was wondering if you wanted some dessert *before* your meal." She smiled. And put her hands on her big hips.

"Shit yeah . . . I got a couple of minutes."

"A couple of minutes?" she questioned.

"That's all it's going to take. I got this." I flickered my tongue and pulled her into the stall. She had on a short black knee-length skirt that I just pushed over her head as I bent her over the toilet. I pulled out a female condom, because I didn't know this bitch at all. I learned how to give orgasms through the female condom. Again, I was a bad bitch. I immediately went to town and within minutes I had her juices running down her legs and on to the floor.

We finished up and then cleaned up and exited the stall. As we walked out the stall, Grace was at the sink pretending that she was washing her hands. From the look she had on her face I could tell she had heard our little session, but I didn't give a fuck because we weren't exclusive either. I let the waitress walk out first and I followed suit within a minute's time.

I walked back over to the table with a serious look on my face; I didn't want to give away what I just did in the bathroom.

As I sat down the waiter was coming toward our table with the food. It's amazing what a bitch could do in less then fifteen minutes.

"What took you so long?" Ebony was pissed off again. Her ass needed to be on the altar more, because she sure does have a possession problem.

"Excuse me?"

"It's took you almost fifteen minutes to go to the bathroom. That is not normal."

"Neither is licking pussy but you do that shit too, don't you?"

Her mouth hit the floor, because the old couple at the table was staring at us. They heard every word I had said. Their mouths were open too. They shook their heads in shame, but I was comfortable with who I was, but she wasn't. I had to keep her in her place. "For your information I had diarrhea. Is there anything else you want to know?"

She shook her head no and started to eat her food. I did the same.

After the meal, I let her order some dessert while I prepared her for what I was about to ask her for.

"Ebony, I need you to pay my insurance bill on my car until I get a job." I had no intentions on getting a job right now, besides I had two sponsors and a possible one in the greeter I just did in the bathroom. Juggling people and school was a job in itself.

"What?" She almost choked on her cheesecake.

"You heard me." I had a stone-cold face.

"Ashley, I live paycheck to paycheck and you know me and my husband have a joint account. I can't just spend what I want to out of it. He would kill me."

"I know all of that," I said matter-of-factly.

"So how was I supposed to get it then, if I was going to do it?"

"Oh, you are going to do it. You're the head deaconess at church, all you have to do is take out a love offering for yourself once a month."

"Bitch, you have lost your mind if you think I'm going to be stealing from a church. And my parents' church at that." She was a light-skinned chick and her face was almost beet-red.

"Call me out my name again." I warned her. "You know. . . . you never really know that the person you are intimate with is crazy until it's too late. You're in knee deep, bitch, so I suggest you do what I tell you or I could give this info to all the members of the choir at church and your parents." I had slid my HTC Thirst phone over toward her and watched her eyes nearly pop out of her head.

"Go ahead and flip through the pictures. There are plenty." I sat there as she went through the pictures. I saw tears water in her eyes and fall down her cheek.

"Now press the 'phone' button and scroll down until you see your husband's name." Her mouth flew open again. "He got a nice Facebook picture, doesn't he?" I laughed. It was amusing to see the power you had over people when you knew stuff about them that they didn't want anyone else to know.

"Ebony, I didn't want it to come to this, but since it has, I just want you to know what I am capable of. I also got video of our sex session too. Press the 'camera' button twice if you want to see."

She did as she was told and within seconds the sounds of her pleasuring me filled the air. She fumbled to get it to cut off, but heads still turned toward us in the few seconds that she had played it. At this point she was shaking and crying. Our waiter was coming our way as she handed me back my phone.

"Is everything okay?" she asked, mainly looking at Ebony.

"Yes, we are fine," I assured her. "Well, I know I am. I don't know about this soft bitch over there." I shot a look at Ebony.

Ebony simply nodded as she dabbed her eyes with a napkin.

"Well, here is your bill. You can pay it at the greeter's station on your way out."

"Thank you," I said to our waitress. "The food and service was superb."

"Good. Have a nice day. Hope to see you again."

"You sure will."

"So do we have an understanding?"

Ebony nodded her head yes.

"I thought so." I smiled, but she was still a wreck from the neck up.

"It's the price you have to pay for living on both sides of the fence." I schooled her. "Play or get played . . . You just got played . . . Now I'm ready to go." We both got and walked toward the front of the restaurant.

"Go on out to the car . . . I'm going to pay this bill and be right out." She did as I asked and slowly walked outside.

I walked over to the greeter's station to "pay" my bill. The girl I just offed in the bathroom was all smiles as I walked over. I handed her my bill with no money or credit card. She hit a couple of keys on her computer and slid me back my receipt. It was paid in full.

"Later," I said as I turned away to leave.

"Later," she replied back. I turned the receipt over and her number was on the back. I smiled to myself.

"I got me another one," I said as I walked toward my car. We got in and pulled off toward Ebony's house.

"I need the first payment by next week, so don't be late," I said as she got out of my car and walked toward her house. I made it home about a half an hour later and got some homework done.

When I got home I was exhausted. I simply fell on my bed like a log. "Being a bitch was hard work," but I had to keep up with what my father started, well Shawn Black, I don't know nothing about this Jerry Parks guy. I left that up to Alex to figure out, with his nosy ass.

Every since my father told us about his issues with his sexuality and that we weren't his biologically, he started to spoil us. I think he was doing it to buy our love, but he never admitted it. I truly wasn't all that fazed about him being that way, it was a part of life. And I knew firsthand what it was like to deal with that particular issue. I had no room to judge him. Even though we never really talked about it fully and in depth, I knew he wanted to and I did as well, but how do you start a conversation about something like that? I didn't know how. And I never really sat down to think about it.

Times like these when I'm alone in my room and whole house is quiet, I think about what it would be like to not have these feelings for other females and where it stems from. I want to be normal like any other girl growing up and chasing boys, but it didn't work out for me like that. Here I am a spoiled brat/daddy's girl and I do chicks. Screwed up, huh? . . . I will say so too if I was outside looking in, but being in my shoes isn't an easy task and sleeping around with the same sex isn't something you can just give up. I tried and it's not that easy. I even consulted my pastor back home and I was told in order for God to clean up an issue in your life you have to want to get rid of it, he doesn't just take it away. You have to hate it and detest it for it to be removed. I simply wasn't ready to let go.

"Man, life is hard." I got up out of my bed, walked over to the mirror on my dresser, and stared at myself for a few minutes. I was a good-looking chick to say the least. Not perfect, but I could pull a man if I wanted to. I had some hollas from men every now and then, maybe more than I noticed. But I did and that was a start. Before I could stop it, tears started flowing from my eyes and I was bawling. I wasn't as hard as I played it out to be in front of people. I had a heart and I had feelings too. I was angry, but I didn't know who I was angry at more, God, me, or my parents. I wanted to know who was to blame for the way I am now.

"Somebody has to answer for the shit!" I threw myself on my bed and cried myself to sleep.

Chapter 14

Alex
Me and my Baby
April 19th 10:35 A.M.

"How was your day, babe?" my girl asked me over the phone in a sensual voice that I adored. I was laying in my bed in my boxers and nothing else. I was a little ripped in my chest and abs. Nothing spectacular, but just enough to show off or pull my shirt off and get a couple of hollers.

"It was good, baby girl."

"I love it when you call me baby girl." She giggled. "It just does something to me." The *something to me* was low and she dragged it out sexually. I was horny so I pulled out my dick and started playing with it.

"Keep talking to me like that . . . I need to squeeze one off real quick."

"Sure, baby. What you want me to say?"

"Anything . . . just moan." I grunted as I tugged on my manhood.

"Like thissss," she hissed, "Ummmmmmmmmm. And, uhhhhhhhhhhhhh."

"Yeah. . . . Yeahhhh. . . . Like that," I was feeling the pressure building up and my balls were tightening. "Keep on doing—" I couldn't even finish my statement before I was spewing all over my stomach and chest.

"Ahhhhhh." I sighed. My chest heaved up and down. "Nothing . . . like . . . a . . . good nut."

"You got that right honey." Baby girl giggled into the phone. "I wish I was there to give you some hands-on loving."

"I know, baby. I'm just not ready for that step yet." No, we haven't been intimate yet. I just wasn't ready to go the next level with her. Some things have changed about me and I wasn't ready to expose it just yet.

"Baby, size doesn't matter to me. I can work what you got. Believe that." She laughed. I felt some kind of way when she said that. Women always are saying that mess, but when it get down to it, her girls and the whole neighborhood will be know about your "issue" before it's all said and done.

"Don't worry, baby girl. The time is coming."

"Okay." She sounded disappointed. I hate to make her wait because of my issues. But it was what it was. I needed more time. I was just hoping she would wait it out with me until I felt more comfortable.

"Look, baby girl. I gotta go. I got practice and then work in about an hour. Can I call you back later?"

"Sure, daddy. I will be over my mom's house looking after my dad for a few, but hit me up." With that she hung up and I walked to my bathroom and took a shower.

While in the shower, I thought back to how I first met my baby. It was something else I tell you.

I was in an Omega Sigma Tau fraternity fund-raiser for homelessness. They were raffling off dates to some very fine ladies. It surprised me that the crowd of ladies was mixed with all ethnicities. I was just happy to be asked. A brother did have it in the looks department and it didn't hurt that I was on the football team either. I was a good catch nonetheless.

I was won by a successful Asian doctor in the crowd who was battling it out for me with another Latino woman. I was overflowing with pride as they went back and forth. My testosterone was in hyper-drive. I even did a couple extra poses to make the ladies go wild, and they did.

Anyway, the next day the date was set for me and the foxy, hot Asian chick and it was a mess from the jump.

First, the restaurant that she picked was a seafood spot that I didn't know about until I got there. I am allergic to seafood by the way, except for fish, that is. The menu only consisted of that and steak, so I went with that. I only ate red meat occasionally, but I decided to let it slide and do the meat and potatoes thing.

Second, I never thought this was going to be a serious, serious date. But homegirl had only one thing on her mind—dick. Don't get me wrong, she had a banging body, but I wasn't for a relationship just yet. School, family, football, and work were my main focuses right now. Adding a relationship would only further complicate things. I had enough of that dealing with Ashley and this whole James Parks research business. My plate was full enough.

Homegirl had feet like an octopus and I constantly had to push her feet from in between my legs. Her ass had actually palmed a part of my thigh trying to find my dick. I was floored. The chick had talent for sure. And I hadn't been laid in a minute. All kinds of sexual thoughts were flowing through my head, but I calmed myself down by thinking about the time I saw my grandmother naked once when I opened her bedroom door without knocking. That did the trick every time.

"So why are you playing hard to get?" she said, attempting to get her foot in between my thigh again.

"I'm trying to find out if the myth is true about you black men."

"Huh?" I looked at her in shock. I wasn't dumb. I knew the myth. I just thought that myth died out a long time ago. It wasn't a family restaurant but, I did look around and see who was in an earshot of our conversation. Thankfully no one was paying us any mind.

"Don't play dumb, you know what I want. I paid good money for a good time." She smiled and then leaned over the table and whispered, "Me love you long time." At that moment, I felt very dirty and used. Any other brotha probably would have jumped at the chance to bang an Asian chick and a doctor at that. If you were good in bed, you could be set up for life. But that wasn't my MO. I wasn't looking for sex. When I decided to be in a relationship, it would be for love and mutual compatibility. Not a hook-up.

Our conversation was interrupted by the loud vibrating of a woman's purse at the table closest to us.

"My phone is vibrating," She looked at us with nervousness all over face. She was alone at the table.

But, I knew better, it couldn't have been a phone, because her purse literally started moving toward the end of the table. She looked on in horror as her purse fell off the table and her contents emptied out on to the floor. A large dildo fell out onto the floor and she scrambled to get all of her contents back into her bag. She immediately rushed out the restaurant in embarrassment. I felt sorry for her. She must have been mortified. I know I would have been super-embarrassed.

My date and I were close to the window. I was facing it and her back was to the restaurant window and I could see the lady from the other table standing outside smoking a cigarette.

"I am going to take a smoke, I'll be right back," I told my date, got up out my seat and walked away from the table before she could get a word out. The truth is, I didn't even smoke. But I did carry a pack of cigarettes, just for instances like these. I had to be on my A-game at all times.

"Are you okay?" I said as I walked up to the lady from the restaurant. She was puffing away.

After a few seconds of looking at me she spoke, "I'm fine." She still looked embarrassed. I wondered why she would keep that kind of thing in her purse anyway, but I didn't question it. The freak in me understood it clearly though.

"You have nothing to be ashamed of." I spoke with sincerity. "Everybody has an extremely embarrassing moment and that was yours. Just be glad it wasn't your mother or father it fell out in front of." She laughed and so did I. I looked back into the restaurant to see my date on her cell phone and paying me no attention. My guess would be that she was trying to find a replacement for the dick she wasn't going to get from me tonight.

"Aren't you on a date?" she asked me as she looked back into the restaurant and looked at my date.

"Sort of." I shrugged. "She won me."

"Huh?" She looked puzzled.

"She won me in an auction at a charity event my fraternity had yesterday."

"Lucky her." She smiled.

"Well . . ." I looked away and blushed.

"I'm sorry for being so forward, but a sister is too old to be holding back. My clock is ticking honey." She laughed. I did as well. I looked at her for a few seconds and noticed that she was an older woman. But she too was gorgeous: High cheekbones, tall legs and firm breasts. Our eyes locked and from that moment I knew that I would talking to her again. Again, I wasn't looking for a relationship, but a new friend definitely wouldn't hurt.

I didn't go back into the restaurant and from that day on, we talked almost every day. That was a couple of months ago and we have been getting closer everyday too.

The next day was Saturday and it went by fast. Practice was only two hours long and then I was out of there. I showered, chatted with a couple of the fellas and made my way over to the school cafeteria. I was looking good today too. Some blue linen Capri pants and matching shirt did a brother all right in this hot weather. After work, I planned on catching the bus to one of the addresses I wanted to spy on just in case Ashley was right and my "father's" family was a bunch of lowlifes or something like it.

After work I decided to go home and get some rest, I didn't feel like doing a whole bunch of traveling after I left work. A brother was tired.

Chapter 15

Grace
Constant Reminders
April 23rd 5:21 P.M.

"Hello." I picked up my cell phone and sluggishly answered it. I was in my office not doing much of nothing at all. I had just finished instructing my last class. I was mentally and physically exhausted. I had so many decisions to make and none of them were easy.

"Hey, baby. How are you doing?" my elderly mother asked. I didn't talk to her much, but this was the second time in a couple of weeks. I hoped she wasn't starting anything new, like calling me everyday. She reminded me too much of a past that I did not want to remember, but now was being taunted with it daily, by others and myself. Alberta Candace Jones was my mother's name. Most people called her Candace because she didn't like Alberta or Berta, which is what close family called her.

"I'm still alive." I blew into the phone. I was exasperated and heavy-hearted. I wanted to fall on the floor and cry, kick my feet and scream as loud as I could. But, I was an adult and that would have been childish. I tried to pretend that I could deal, but I was about to break any day now. I just knew it.

"Grace, what's wrong?" She was so sweet, but I just couldn't pretend like everything was okay.

"You already know." I was stone-cold serious. There was a long pause, like there always was when we talked or didn't talk about the obvious. I was fucked up for life and she was privy to all the facts. Yeah, she knew every fucking thing.

"Baby—baby—I—"

"Save it. Before you even start with your excuses about how you didn't know and all that shit." Mothers know when their children were being tampered with and abused. She just paid it no mind because she was getting what she wanted out of the deal. My uncle, who was also her brother-in-law John, was the nastiest pedophile in California. He took that shit to a new low. She would let this bastard molest me for some fucking liquor, which he would buy her by the gallons, to the point where she would pass out. She was on welfare and she would make sure the rent was paid and that food was in the house, but her ass was a stone-cold drunk. She couldn't keep a man because of it. My father left her ass because of it. He never touched my older sister, Sherry, but he made it a point to babysit me and sent my mom and sister on trips to the movies and other places like that. His ass was staying with us because his wife put his ass out. I overheard him and my other uncle talking about how he was molesting his own son, Jerry, as well and how good it was. My stomach lurched and churned roughly as I thought about it as if it was yesterday. I was always sneaky as a child and I would always creep downstairs and listen to the conversations the adults were having on the porch. I knew too much about adult stuff at eleven years old.

He didn't stay with us too long, because he was a "crazy paranoid muthafucka" as my mother would call him in a drunken stupor.

"I'm sorry, Mama. I'm just having a rough time right now." Tears rolled down my face. I just wanted the ground to open up and swallow me and take me away, but I knew that was not going to happen. Well, not just for me. If anything that shit would take a couple hundred unwilling people as well with all the quakes that have been happening lately.

"It's all right, baby. I know what ya mean. Your past has some way of sneaking back up on you at the least appropriate moments. I was just calling you to see if you going to be putting any flowers on your sister's grave. This weekend makes the fifth year she been gone. I miss her so much." Mother starts to sob into the phone and I get a little misty-eyed myself. Five years ago my cousin Jerry who changed his name to James and Sherry were brutally shot and killed in a murder-suicide in Baltimore. To this day we don't have the reason why, just the burden of going to her grave. She had a son that she brought back to California. My sister was very smart and had the potential to be the best. She had a good career in law. But when she moved to Baltimore to get away from my drunk of a mother and to start fresh, she got caught up in some foolishness and ended up getting pregnant. She never told us who the father was and we never really asked. She was just as screwed up from my mom being a drunk and all the changes I was going through myself.

"Mama, I got to go now." I tried to rush her off the phone. She had just taken me back further then I wanted to go in history and added some more stress to my already overloaded plate.

"You gonna go?" she asked.

"I'll try." I hung up the phone abruptly. I wanted to but I sincerely couldn't. I just couldn't handle going to a graveyard and talking to somebody who was dead, because I felt like I was close to it or I needed to be. Everything I was living was a lie and the truth was trying to drag me out kicking and screaming. Everything I said was a lie and now breathing hurt. I couldn't and didn't know how I was going to go on if the truth came out. Would my husband accept me for me in the condition I was in? Shit, if Ashley could then I knew he could. That shit puzzled me too. She was not only a psycho, but her ass was fucked-up in the head as well.

Makes you wonder how her home life was and her parents. They had to have some disorders and dysfunction going on. Shit, you born with that kind of crazy. I laughed but it wasn't anything funny about it. I was still so curious about how she got the information. Only a handful of people knew and I kept that to a complete minimum. I didn't even want to know half the time, but she knew and she had the proof. So here I was at her beck and call and couldn't stop her if I wanted to. I like the peace-filled life I had before I met her and messed it all up by being vulnerable and letting my guard down. My regret is too little too late.

I got up out of my office chair, closed my blinds and left for the day. I was going home and prepare a meal fit for a king for my husband, because I didn't know how long I would have him.

"Hello," I said, answering my cordless phone that was on the wall. I was running around the kitchen a little. Everything in my kitchen was marble and stainless steel and I loved it, even if I didn't cook in it as much as I wanted to. I was preparing a couple of baked chicken breasts stuffed with shrimp and crabmeat and a nice sauce drizzled over the top. I had baked potatoes and asparagus for sides and some corn bread muffins.

"'What are you doing?" Ashley asked with a smug tone. I was so sick of her.

"I'm fixing dinner for me and *my* husband," I said with some sass.

"Oh really, what you fixing for *your* man?" she countered. By this time I was getting a real attitude.

"It doesn't concern you. Shouldn't you be studying or something?" I asked. I had the phone in between my ear and my shoulder while I took the corn bread out of the oven.

"I am studying," she laughed. "I'm studying your husband as he walks his fat ass in the house."

"What?!" I quickly placed the tray of muffins on the counter and did my best to run to the front window. Sure enough, my husband was getting out of his car and walking up the driveway. "Where are you at?"

My breathing changed to a heavy pant as I walked briskly back to my kitchen to pretend like I was still cooking. I had a couple of seconds because of my husband's weight.

"I'm in my car waiting to come in for dinner."

"You can't come in," I blurted out.

"I can and I will." She laughed. "A sister sure is hungry. I'll be in in a couple of minutes. Oh and I might want dessert afterward. If you know what I mean." I heard her laughing as I hung up the phone. This bitch has lost her mind. All I want to know is why.

Seconds after I hung up off the phone my husband walks in the kitchen.

"Hey, babe. What do I owe this honor?" He had a silly smirk on his face. I couldn't blame him because I rarely cooked.

"Oh, it's nothing special. I just wanted to cook for my man." I smiled, trying to cover up the anguish on my face. I was going to have to put on the act of my life.

"Wow, I never saw this coming. Am I dying?" He burst out into laughter. I chuckled slightly trying to find something in me that would make me laugh as hard as he was, but there was nothing in me to laugh about at all.

"No, babe. Go wash up while I set the table." I kissed him on the cheek as I walked into the dining room to set the table for three. How in the hell I was going to explain to him Ashley was coming in to eat was beyond me. All this lying and hiding was taking its toll on me for sure.

"Oh, honey we will be having a guest coming to join us for dinner," I called out down the small hallway that leads to his study and our small first-floor bathroom.

"That's great, honey," he said as he came in the dining room and sat down.

I walked back into the kitchen and prayed to the lord god that Ashley would get hit by a car or something before she got to our house. I needed a serious miracle right now. The chiming of the doorbell told me that I was on my own. I couldn't even blame God for not answering my prayer. I was asking for a lot. I slowly walked to the front door. I had to walk past the dining room and living room before I got to the door and I took as much time as I possibly could. I straightened up a flower arrangement and picture on the wall before I got to the front door. Shit was just that bad.

I stood at the door and sighed for another second before I opened the door. Ashley was dressed in a calf-length denim jumper and a white shirt underneath it. She looked innocent, but I knew better than that.

"Hello, Ms. Ashley." I perked up my tone just in case my husband decided to come to the door after me. "I'm so glad you could make it." The smile on my face was that of the Joker in *Batman*. I was smiling so hard my cheeks were shaking like the muscles were about to give out. I let her in and waved at a neighbor across the street. I wanted to scream for help, but decided against it. It was of no use anyway, because I couldn't begin to explain my situation to any one and not have them looking at me like I had two heads.

I closed the door and showed Ashley to the dining room. I let her seat herself and I made my way to the kitchen to get the food and take one last breather before I walked back into the dining room. I made several trips back and forth before everything was finally set out on the table.

We had a large dining room table with six chairs to match. One chair on both ends and two chairs in the middle. I sat on one end and David sat at the other end. Ashley sat on my left and in the chair closest to me. I filled both their plates before I sat down to eat myself. I only baked in glassware and my nervousness showed up several times when my metal spoon clanked the side of the glass as I served the food.

"Is everything okay, babe?" my husband questioned me with a frown.

"Yeah, I think I'm just moving too fast. I know how you like your food . . . hot." I smiled and then looked at Ashley.

"You're right about it." He laughed. "My baby treats me like a king." He looked Ashley's way.

"I bet she does." She smiled back. "Because she sure gives her students the first-class treatment as well. She bends over forward for me all the time."

"What?" My husband drops his fork on his plate and looks at me. All kinds of shit flooded my mind and body, so much that I almost slide out of the chair and onto the floor.

"Oh. . . . my bad. . . . I meant she bends over backwards for me all the time." She laughed and looked at me.

"Oh . . . okay." He laughed as well and picked up his fork and began eating as well. I was beyond mortified. If that was her way of letting me know she wasn't playing, it was now well understood on my part.

"So I take it you're one of my wife's favorite students, because she's never invited anyone over for dinner. Ever."

"Yeah, you can say that. I was having a little trouble in her class and she was more than willing to help me after class." All the while she was saying this; her bare foot made its way up my skirt and rested in between my legs. She was impressive, because she never missed a beat while talking and eating. I, on the hand, had completely loss my appetite. And conversation was the last thing on my mind.

"Wow, babe. I'm so proud of you for taking special interest in your student's academic well-being." He smiled and continued to eat his food.

"I do what I can," was all I could manage to get out.

I noticed that David was finishing his food so I decided to get dessert ready. I slid my chair out and made my way into the kitchen to get the Bundt cake I had baked.

"I'll be back in a sec. I am going to get dessert."

"All right now." My husband smiled. I loved to see his smile, especially when I cooked. "I'm going to sleep good tonight."

I walked into the kitchen and grabbed a few dessert saucers and a cake knife to serve. Ashley snuck up on me as I was rinsing the knife off in the sink.

"I'm ready for dessert now." She grabbed my behind and squeezed it, causing me to jump and yelp a little.

"Look! Stop it before my husband catches you." I scolded her as I turned back around. She backed up a step and looked at me. I was afraid of what she would do next. But I stood my ground and kept the serious face I had.

"Okay, but I am getting impatient so I need you to get rid of him fast, so I can get the dessert I really want."

After Ashley left and my husband went off to bed, I got restless and decided to go do some shopping and the only place I knew I could spend a couple of hours to myself and not be disturbed. That was at the all-night Wal-Mart. Yes, I love to shop.

Even at eleven o'clock at night Wal-Mart was thriving with shoppers as if it was eleven in the morning. I grabbed me a cart and made my way over to the ladies department to see if they had some cute shirts that I might like to wear. A sister had to keep up appearances and my style always had to be unique and flawless. I know what you're saying. Wal-Mart is nowhere near Neiman Marcus, but I found out that if you mix and match clothes from different outlets then you can come up with a style all your own. High-priced clothes aren't always the best, despite what people say.

I walk around a few racks, found some cute tops and a nice blazer that would work well with something I already had at home.

"Grace?" I heard someone call out. I turned to see who it possibly could be that I knew and was up in the Wal-Mart at such a late hour as me. I turned to see someone from my past . . . someone I hadn't seen I such a long time.

"Heyyy," I squealed like only a woman could do as I almost ran over to the only best friend I ever had. I was so shocked to see her. "Oh . . . my . . . goodness! Girl, you look *good*!" I huge and squeezed her as tight as I could.

"You too, girl." She kissed me on cheek and pulled back.

"Reeby . . . Reeby. . . . Reeby." I shook my head in disbelief. It had been some time that we'd seen each other. "Turn around so I can get a good look at you." She did so and she didn't have a hair out of place. Everything was in place like it always was when we used to hang out. It was a short time but our friendship was a fast one and we bonded like Krazy Glue.

"Girl, let me see you too." I turned around in same style she did, but I was a little disheveled because I practically ran out of the house after all of the drama I endured moments earlier. "You are looking good *too*."

"So how long has it been?" I asked her.

"Girl, I haven't seen you in over thirty years."

"Wow, girl that is a long time," I said, amazed at all the time that went by. I had to admit that we both still looked good even after all these years.

"Yes, it is. So what have you been up to in all this time?" she asked with her hands on her hips.

"Well, I'm married and a professor at UCLA." I smiled hard. I was proud of my life spite the drama. "And no children."

"Married?" she asked. "Really?" she asked like I wasn't supposed to have a man.

"Yeah, girl and he's fine." *Was fine!* I wanted to add, but I left it alone because I was long from perfect myself.

"And chile we both crossed children off our list a long time ago." She laughed and then glazed over. I was instantly reminded of my molestation: The reason I couldn't have children. But we both had that in common. That is why we were so close so long ago. We had a lot in common.

"So what about you? You find that special man?" I asked with a smile. Hoping she did. We both vowed to find a man that would fit our needs and love us unconditionally. Our traumas as children lead us to look for good men because of the behavior of one man toward us. You know . . . like anyone that has been abused.

"Well, girl I got me a little something on the side. It ain't serious yet, but he got potential." She laughed. "I'll keep you posted."

"Let me get your number so we can hook up and hang out," I asked as I whipped out my cell phone.

"Sure girl. I likes to hang out." She giggled. I called out my number and she punched them in. I did the same with hers.

"Look, I have to get home so I can get ready for work tomorrow. But I promise I will call you when I get some time to hang out."

"Sure thing," she agreed.

"Give me a hug so I can be on my way." I reached out to hug her one more time before we both went our separate ways.

I smiled the whole drive home. I feel like friends that you can rely on and relate to is a necessity in life. It is always good to have someone to talk to and confide in and never have to worry about it coming back to bite you. I was so glad to have my best friend back in my life.

Chapter 16

Wallace
Spoiled Rotten
April 26th11:35 A.M.

It was a windy Saturday evening and I was back at my mother's house. It took me a couple of days to get used to the fact that my brother was now a full-fledged woman. That shit is wild. I haven't see him since he was sixteen, but I never remembered him being feminine in any way. We weren't around each a whole lot as teenagers, but I don't think I would have missed this by a long shot. It was puzzling to say the least.

It was just me and "her" in the house. My mother had some kind of church function she had to attend and my brother/sister always sat and cared for my father while she was gone. I decided that I would come over and help since we haven't seen each other or talked in such a long time. Let's just say a brotha had some questions.

My father, who was sick with Alzheimer's and some dementia, really didn't know who I was when I had first came over today. My dad was in the bed. In pajamas. He was thin, but not frail. He had moments of clarity. Like when he looked at me and asked, "Where your ass come from? You ran off like the sissy you were." I looked at him and felt my hand ball up involuntary, but I unclenched it and simply nodded my head. There was multiple medication bottles spread out across the dresser and I spotted a box of adult diapers in the corner.

"This nigga is in bad shape," I mumbled to myself and turned to walk out of the room and back downstairs.

"Baby, where you going?" My mother followed after me as I made my way down the steps and into the living room.

"I'm going to sit down here for a little bit." I sat down on the sofa. "I'm a little tired from work this week." It was partially true but I went with it. I really didn't work that hard and I was in good shape for my age.

"Your father didn't mean what he said up there." She sat down and rubbed the top of my head. "His mind is leaving him and he probably didn't even know who you were." I looked at her and shook my head. She was still in denial about the mean old bastard, but I let it slide.

"You're probably right." I kissed her on the cheek. She got up off the sofa; she made her way to the coat closet, put on her coat, and then made her way out of the door. I went into the kitchen to fix me something to eat.

I sat at the table for about twenty minutes eating and thinking: thinking about James, James's look-alike, Alex, and now my transsexual brother.

"Man, this is some mess. I should have stayed my butt in Baltimore for all of this drama." I picked up my dishes and put them in the dishwasher and it automatically started itself. It scared the shit out of me when I did it at my own home. This new technology was something else. Everything was high-tech and almost everything ran on electricity. Electricity was an eighty-percent source for powering cars now too. Gas was steadily declining.

Anyway, I was getting lonely down here and I wanted to see what led my brother to becoming a woman. I was trying to form the questions in my head as I walked up the carpeted stairs and made my way into my mother's room.

"Ohhh! Shit!" I belted out as I watched my brother/sister going down on my father's manhood with his mouth. I immediately turned and sprinted down the stairs, slipping and falling down a couple, but I quickly regrouped myself. I got up and made my way into the kitchen to find something alcoholic to drink.

"What the *fuck!*" I yelled to no one in particular. My mother didn't have anything but cooking wine. I wanted something stronger, but this would have to do. I found the biggest glass I could find, poured me a glass and sat down to try and erase the memory of what I just saw. I have never in my life seen something so disturbing in all my life.

"Don't judge me," my sister/brother said as he walked in the kitchen. He was switching and all that. He looked and sounded like a real woman. I got up out of my chair and leaned up against the kitchen sink with my arms folded. I didn't want him anywhere near me. I had run into transsexuals before but I never indulged in it. I was a gay man and that is what I wanted. If I wanted a man that dressed like a woman then I just would have gotten a woman. Point-blank. "You don't know anything about me."

"You got that shit right!" I looked at him and shook my head.

"Your own father? . . . mannn . . . that's . . . that's . . . that's some fucked-up shit. Nah, that's some sick shit."

"You don't know shit about shit up in this bitch," she fired at me as she went to the refrigerator and pulled out a bottled soda. She walked back over to the table, pulled out a chair and plopped down like the lady she was. "Your ass had the easy way out your whole fucking life. Your ass left this bitch and never turned back. And when you was here, you was up underneath mother dear," she huffed. "Father never got a chance to *spoil* you."

"What the fuck are you talking about?" I reached over to pull out a chair. My lower back was hurting a little from the fall on the steps. I pulled it as far back toward the sink as it could go. I wasn't scared. I was still a little grossed out by the sight I had just seen. "You got shit all screwed up if you think I wanted to be spoiled by that mean bastard."

"You don't even know what I mean do you?" she posed.

"Yeah I know what you mean. His ass never treated me like he treated y'all. You and David got the easy end of the deal. He loved y'all. Y'all could do no wrong. Me, on the other hand, I wasn't man enough for him."

"Just be glad you weren't man enough for him." She laughed and threw back the soda she got out of the refrigerator.

"What?" I asked, perplexed.

"When I said he spoiled us, I meant he molested us. Well, he watched us get molested."

"Hell nahhh," I waved my hand at him, shooting down his claim. "His ass wasn't a faggot by a long shot. You are making that shit up for sure."

"Look at me, Wallace. He wasn't the father you thought he was." Tears rolled down her cheek like a running faucet. "Do you think I just woke up one day and said I want to be a woman? That shit was forced upon me by him and his lover. You don't know half of the shit me and David went through while you was in Mother's care."

"What? That can't be true." I shook my head.

"It's very true." She wiped the tears from her face.

"When?" I asked.

"When we were kids." She sat the soda down on the table and looked at the floor a minute. I had a feeling this was going to get deep. Maybe deeper than I wanted it to go. My opportunity to get up and leave passed as she began to tell me stuff that blew my mind.

"Well, you know Dad used to drop us off to school in the morning?"

"Yes, I remember." My school was nearer to the house so I walked most of the time.

"Well for a long while everything was good and we would get to school and that would be it. Around the time I turned eleven, Dad started taking us to school earlier then usual. You remember?"

"Yes, he said traffic was getting a bit heavier and he wanted to leave out earlier to ensure he would get you guys to school on time and that he would get to work on time." My dad made a habit of us eating breakfast in the morning as a family.

"Yeah, that was a muthafuckin' lie to the fullest," she growled. "His ass was taking me and David to his office and letting John suck David off and fuck me like I was his wife. Dad would just sit there and jerk off to it all."

"Ohhh, shit." My mouth was on the floor.

"That's not it." She shook her head from side to side. "He said that we were being 'real men' every time we finished and that men should never kiss and tell. Real men . . . fucking liar . . . I hate his ass."

"Damn that some messed-up shit." I rubbed my temples, trying to process what I just heard. "Does Mom know?"

"Nah, she doesn't have a clue to my knowledge."

"Well . . . ahhhh . . . I might as well tell you about me too." I looked her in the eyes.

"He did this to you too?"

"Nah, but that didn't stop me from being attracted to men."

"You're gay?"

"Yes I am.

"So what's up with David?" I asked.

"Well, his ass is married and he's a college professor at UCLA."

"Really?"

"Yeah his ass hit the books and got out of Dodge not long after you left us here. He's married to some shady chick he met. He didn't even invite us to meet her. Never did. David's ass didn't waste no time marrying her ass and getting the fuck away from this house." She chuckled.

"Wow, I had no clue all this was going on." I brushed my hand through my dreads. "So I take it he's not gay."

"You and I both know ain't no man straight after his father's lover gives him a blow job for years. This shit ain't rocket science. His ass is in the closet or he on the DL. I feel sorry for the chick. Whoever she is. Plain and fucking simple."

"True," was all I could get out. I guess I had to make a trip to see my brother since we do work at the same school.

"So why did you just up and leave us?" she asked.

"I didn't just up and leave. Our father gave me an ultimatum. Go to regular college or get out."

"Whatttt!" he looked surprised. "I thought you just said fuck all of us and split."

"Nope, I got shown the door by my father and mother." I knew what my mother said the other day, but I still think a mother should speak up for her child. It was too late for any of that now.

"So what made you come back here now?"

"Well, I was married to someone that got murdered and I just couldn't take living in Baltimore alone any more. So I decided to come back to find his family and see why he got killed. I knew the who, but not the why."

"Really." Her eyes softened. "That's tragic."

"One of our cousins did it. Can you believe that?"

"Who?"

"Tyrone," I said as all of the pain and hurt of losing James flooded back into my heart. It was like a river's dam with water pressuring it to burst. "Fucking Tyrone!" I banged on the table with my fist, causing Rebecca to jump a little.

"Stop playing. Did he get locked up?"

"Nah man. It was a murder-suicide type of thing." I sniffed back some tears. I was reliving it all again, so I got up out of the chair and threw some water on my face.

"You going to be okay?" She had gotten up and walked over to me and put her arms around me as I leaned over the sink.

"I'll be fine," I said as I slowly eased from under her arm. I didn't want to be offensive. I just wasn't comfortable in that area as of yet.

"You need to stop doing what you're doing with Dad." I looked her in the eyes.

"It's just not natural. You need to get some help for that too."

"Stop judging me!" she almost yelled. "I know all of that. And I will stop. That was the last time I was doing *that* anyway. I don't need no lectures."

"Sorry," I said as apologetically as I could. "It won't happen again.

"One more thing?" I looked at her intensely.

"Sure," She flipped her flowing hair back over her shoulder.

"Are you all woman?" I needed to know what I had already assumed.

"Yep, the magic stick is gone." She smiled. "Snip snip." I cringed a little at the thought.

"So you are really a woman down there, huh?" I darted my eyes downward.

"Yes, the doctors made me feel and look like a real woman down there. Plumbing and all works like the real thing. Minus the babies and all that. A man would never know the difference."

"Wooooow," I was amazed. "Ain't that some mess."

"So have you . . . you know. Been with any men?" I was digging too deep, but this was something I always wondered about transsexuals.

"Yes, I have," she boasted proudly. "And they didn't know.

"Not a clue." She added.

"Isn't that dangerous? To lead men on?" I was a little angry at the fact that she didn't tell her partners the truth.

"Yes, it is." Her face became serious. "But, you don't know what it is to be me or in my shoes. I was forced into this. It was forced on me. There are no rules. I make this shit up as I go along. I want love just like the next person. But who in their right mind would accept me in this condition? Who?"

"Do you think you would have made this change if you had not been molested?"

"Well, the things that were done to me all those years ago were not natural. I didn't know who I was after that. I was so confused about everything. Who I liked. What I liked. I attempted to kill myself several times, but I was unsuccessful. I wasn't even given a chance to really get to decide what I wanted or what the world accepted. My ass could have been the president of the United States, but that shit got erased because of my molestation. I don't know what other molested people did. I just know that being treated like a woman by my molester all that time changed my mindset. I felt like it was what I was supposed to be. And so that was what I set out to be. Now I am a 'her' and nobody will accept me because somebody else decided for me. And as you can see all gay people weren't molested. You are personal witness to that. To this day, I have no solid answers. In fact, I have more questions than answers. Did that answer your question, because I'm still confused?" She laughed a little but it sounded off.

"I guess." I shrugged. That shit was too deep for me. "It's one big mess, I tell you that."

"That it is indeed." A tear slid out of her left eye.

I was silent because I knew that I couldn't even think of something appropriate to say to comfort her. Few seconds of silence went by and we sat there looking at each other. I decided to break the silence so I could get out of there.

"Okay, now that we are past that. Come and give me a hug. I missed you." Rebecca came over and squeezed and hugged me like the man she was. I hugged her back since she was my brother. In any form he was in.

After a couple more minutes of chitchat and all that I took off for home. I had Sunday all to myself and I planned on seeing if Alex wanted to hang out a little.

Chapter 17

David
A Small World
April 30th 2:55 P.M.

"Ump . . . ump . . . ump." I was in my office looking out the window at all of the students walking to and fro. I loved my job and my wife. You would think I was happy and satisfied, but I wasn't. I had been ducking and dodging my past like I was trying to run across a busy six-lane highway. I hadn't been home to my mom's house in so long. I just couldn't do it. There were so many secrets behind that front door, that I just couldn't bear it. My mom was there taking care of my sickly father and I didn't want to go and pretend that everything was okay and it wasn't. I was liable to go in there and try to kill him or something. *Man, he screwed me up!*

My younger brother, Robert, is now a full-fledged woman and that shit blows my mind every time I think about it. I avoided him like the plague, I was just afraid of what he might say or do. I still wasn't comfortable with a man dressed up as a woman. He was my brother and yes I loved him. It just brought a reality to the fact that our childhood was far from normal. Visions of John penetrating my brother on my father's counseling sofa filled my head. He was thrusting him so hard that my brother would whimper in pain. John would always make me watch as I had "to learn" how to do him the same way. My father sat at a distance with his manhood in his hand as he watched his lover destroy our futures for sure. *How could a father be a party to that type of abuse?* He should have known the ramifications of these acts, being that he was psychologist.

I sat thinking for hours on end as a college student on the San Francisco shore pondering and rationalizing on how he could be so heartless. I was still clueless. The fact that I am still "seeing" my molester should tell me that I am in need of serious help. But I was not willing to bare all of my personal business to a stranger. After a while of thinking like such, it let me know that my father too must have felt the same way as I did. These personal issues we have are hard to talk or think about and sharing them just seems like too much. The stares of the knowing party would surely kill me alone. I wouldn't know if they were thinking less of me or trying to help me, so I risked neither. I would carry them to my grave, hoping that my grave didn't come to me before I was ready.

Tears flowed freely as I grabbed some tissues off my desk to blow my nose and dry my eyes.

"Life." I blew out a strong breath as I pushed up out of my chair and out of my office door.

"I'm going to grab something to snack on," I told my secretary as I walked to the stairwell. I decided that I would indeed try to exercise more, so the steps were my new best friend.

I walked across the campus, waving to a couple of students that I had come to know over their years at UCLA. Most of them were men, touched men, to say the least. *I wonder if they knew about me and my secrets.* I shrugged my shoulders and kept it moving toward the school's cafeteria. I rarely ate here for their lack of taste in their food. And I felt a little more comfortable off campus on my lunch breaks. I could talk on the phone to who I wanted to, mainly John, and not worry about being listened to. My wife was known to pop up from time to time and I just couldn't risk being caught in a compromising situation. The less she knew the happier we were, so it seemed. I've been noticing some changes in her over the last year or so. She was becoming more distant and I wasn't fighting it. I had my assumptions, but I knew it was mainly my weight and my busy schedule at work. I guess she finally gave up trying to get some attention from me. I had to admit I didn't have the first clue on how to please my wife physically or emotionally. I tried but I would always feel like I was coming up short on my end. Her distance was my safety net right now and I am going to use it like my life depended on it. The further away she was the less she could see I was falling apart at the seams.

On campus there are numerous eateries and such, like Subway, Taco Bell, Chipotle, Starbucks Express, and KFC, but I choose the cafeteria. I walked into the cafeteria to a small line and an almost empty eating area. I walked up the assembly line–style buffet and proceed to wait my turn. I knew I shouldn't be eyeing the full meal type food, but my stomach growled for more, so I went on with it.

"Give me a cheeseburger and some of those western fries. Oh, and throw in one of those apple pies as well," I said, looking at the selections I was picking out and others I was tempted to pick out as well.

"So I finally get to catch up to you," I heard a voice speak, but didn't recognize it. I looked up and saw a face that I thought I would never see again. My mouth hung open for a few seconds before I was bumped by the next person behind me. I looked at them and continued to stare at my long-lost older brother.

"Wallace?" I asked like I still wasn't sure. I mean, it looked like him but older and he had dreads too.

"What's up David? How you been?" He smiled like he was happy to see me. I was happy to see him too. I waved the next couple of people in line around me so I could get the answers to the questions he asked me out of my mouth.

"I'm doing well. And you?"

"I'm making it," he replied.

"That's good." I had so many questions I wanted to ask him, but I knew he was at work and the line behind me was getting a little impatient with the conversation that was going on. There were two other workers working with Wallace, who was at the beginning of the line.

"Look, I'll be sitting in the cafeteria for a little bit, I know you have to work, so I catch up with you later," I said, moving toward the cashier.

"Cool, I'll see if I can get a small break so we can chit-chat a little more before you leave."

"Okay." I walked to the cashier and paid for my food. I sat down by a window seat so I could get a view of the trees and the nature that surrounded the cafeteria. I looked at the squirrels and birds that frolicked around the trees, lawn and bushes. They were so carefree and they played as if they didn't have a care in the world.

"To take your place would be very wonderful," I mumbled to a squirrel that ran along the window ledge outside of where I was eating. He stopped and paused to clean himself quickly before he scurried off to play again. "But, I know that would be too easy for me. I have to live out the life that I have to the best of my ability."

After about fifteen minutes of time had lapsed, Wallace made his way over to the table where I was sitting with a big ol' smile on his face.

"Stand up, man, and give me a hug." The hug was brief, but I could tell it was genuine by the strength behind it.

We sat down and I just sat there looking confused, because I didn't know where to start or what to say.

"So you not going to ask me where I've been for all this time?"

"Well, it crossed my mind, but I was still in shock about seeing you after all this time."

"Don't worry about it. I completely understand." He laughed. "I was at Mom and Dad's house and Robert—I mean Rebecca—told me that you worked here. I just didn't know where to find you." I flinched a little when he said my brother/sister's name. I think he noticed, but said nothing, because I noticed how he slightly cocked his head to the side in bewilderment.

"Oh . . . no problem," I said as my eyes darted around the room real quick. I didn't know who I was looking for, I just did it. "We would have eventually met up anyway since you work here and all."

"True." He nodded.

"So you a big-time college professor now?"

"Yeah, that's me." I smiled a fake smile. I wasn't too proud of my position here at UCLA at the moment. Mainly because my closet door with all my secrets in them was creaking open at a steady pace.

"You don't sound too enthusiastic about it."

"I know. I'm just a little drained that's all." I shrugged a little. "So what have you been up to while you've been away?" I never really got to ask him why he left. One minute he was there the next minute I was watching him and his bags disappear down the street.

"Well, little of this and a little of that. Some ups, some downs . . . you know . . . life." He rubbed his hands through his hair letting me know he was just as uncomfortable about his past as I was.

"So you married, divorced...got any kids?" I was hoping I had some nephews or nieces I could spoil since I didn't have any children, but then again I didn't need that to be hung over my head as a constant reminder of my shortcomings.

"Not married . . . widowed." He looked down at the table real quick like he was hurt by what he just said. It must have been recent.

"Sorry about that. She was a good woman. I'm sure."

"A good man," he corrected me. I stammered a little.

"You're gay?" I asked. I almost smiled. Not because he was gay, but because I didn't want to be the only one at the table in that condition. . . . If that makes sense. It also makes me wonder how he got that way too. *Did Dad and John tamper with him as well?*

"Yes, I am." He said it like he was proud. "Been that way all my life." Everything in me was screaming to ask him if we had *everything* in common. I held off not wanting to give up my secrets in the first few minutes of us being reunited. I still didn't know if he had a motive or if he was here to genuinely rejoin the family.

"So I hear you're happily married."

"Yes, my wife works here with me." I smiled.

"Cool. Any kids?" he asked.

"No we don't have any kids." I said sadly. "We both have been too busy working on our careers to have any."

I knew that was a lie, but I went with it hoping he believed it.

"Well, it is what it is." He smiled. "I can't wait to meet her."

"Sure. We'll exchange numbers before I have to get back to work." He looked at his watch real quick. My eyes darted around the room real quick again. I saw Alex cleaning up and emptying some trash.

"So when was the last time you went by to check on Mom and Dad?

"I've been meaning stop by the house to check up on Mom and um. . . . Dad, but I've been so busy this semester. How are they doing?"

"Well, Mom is going strong. It is Dad that I don't think is going to make it much longer." He frowned a little.

"I'll have to plan a trip for me and my wife to go visit her real soon." I intentionally left my dad out, because he could rot in hell for all I care.

"Oh . . . okay." He nodded.

"Hey, Professor Andrews. What are you doing in here? You almost never eat in here." Alex walked over and smiled.

"I know. I wanted a quick snack and I didn't want to go off campus. Traffic is usually a mess around lunch-time."

He then turned his attention toward Wallace. "Hey, Wallace, how do you know the professor?"

"We're brothers," I spoke up before Wallace could.

"Woooow. . . . Small world, ain't it."

"Sure is," Wallace and I both agreed.

"So how long have you known my brother?" I asked.

"We were friends of a friend from back in Baltimore, where I was before I came back here," Wallace interjected before Alex could say anything.

"Oh . . . okay." I nodded. *I wonder if they were fucking too.* I knew asking that question was out of the question. I didn't need to bring attention toward myself.

"Well, I have to get back to my office." I pulled out my wallet and gave Wallace my card. "I'm sure you two need to get back to work as well."

"Yeah, you sure are right about that." Wallace agreed. "Give me a hug again before you leave." We briefly hugged again and I made my way toward the cafeteria doors.

Chapter 18

Ashley
Warnings
May 4th 10:50 A.M.

I sat in the congregation in my church waiting to be
called for my solo. I looked around at all of the people
in my church. We had about 150 members easily. It was
testimony service and I watched person after person
pop up and give their thanks for what God had done for
them. It was nearing the end and one of the mothers of
the church stood up. She was always so quiet and she
hardly said a word. She decided that it was her turn before it was time for praise and worship to begin.

"I wanna thank the lawd fo' one mo day in the land of
the livin'. He don' brought me a mighty long ways now.
As I look around this here church, I can say I am truly
blessed of God. I got's me most of my facilities that still
functioning properly in this here body of mine. The
Lawd been good to me, hear me!" A few people clapped
and a few '*praise God*'s' rang out in the sanctuary.

"The Lawd has never left my side. He was with me
when my husband left me. He was with me when my
son moved away. He was with me when the doctor
they . . . they diagnosed me with that lung cancer. He
was with me when my son was murdered. He was with
me when I prayed and prayed to him for a healing in
my body." By this time she was shaking side to side.

And a couple of people in the congregation started to raise hands and wave them.

"God ain't *never* left my side. I stand before ya today five years healed. I'm not talking remission people, I'm talking bout cancer-free. I went back to them doctors and they couldn't find a cell in my body that was infected wit' that there cancer. I'm here to tell you that God is a healer and a keeper."

By this time the organist was playing to her testimony and a couple of people were standing and trembling and speaking in tongues.

She continued, "When you think that you done lost everything and there is nobody around remember my testimony today. God ain't ever gon' leave ya nor forsake ya. Praise the Lawd! Praise the Lawd! Praaaise the Lawdddd!"

By this time the whole church was up praising God. I stood up and clapped my hands and praised God too. It was no denying that the service today would be a spirit-filled one.

At the end of service, everyone was socializing with one another and talking and hugging the pastor for a few seconds. I was talking to a couple of the choir members before I made my way outside to head on home.

"Baby." I felt a tap on the shoulder. I turned to see the mother who got everybody riled up this morning.

"Yes, ma'am?" I asked, wondering what she wanted with me.

"Can have a word with you in private for a second?" She was so sweet-looking. But curiosity was getting the best of me, but I knew it had to be something about my solo I did today. I got personal accolades all the time. I walked away with her at ease.

She pulled me into the bathroom and locked the door.

"Baby, I got's a message from the Lawd for you in a dream." Her eyes were as stern as a cat on a mouse getting ready to pounce.

"Huh?" I got a little nervous.

"Me?" I pointed to myself.

"Yes, Ashley, baby. God don't make mistakes."

"Okay," I said, folding my arms and waited for her to fill me in.

"Baby, I know you may not know me well and I have never said as many as two words to you, but pay attention to everything that I say to you and listen good."

"Okay," I assured her.

"I had a dream that you was getting yourself into some heavy mischief and the outcome was not pretty. Ashley, baby, listen to me when I tell ya. The same thing happened to my son and I regret it to this day. I had a dream about my baby and I didn't pay God no mind and he ended up dead over some foolishness that I could have prevented if I only heeded to God's warning and told him what God had told me." Tears spilled from her eyes and down her cheeks. "I thought my baby was innocent and that God must have had the wrong child on his mind. I was such a fool."

I stood there and pondered all that she was saying to me. I had to admit she was scaring me real good right about now.

"Ya hear me, baby." She shook me with her hand on both of my arms. "Take heed to the warning. Take heed! God chastises those he loves. Whatever you're going through let God know all about. Don't end up like my son and lose ya life, Ashley."

She hugged me real tight and exited the bathroom. I stood there scared out of my mind. After few more seconds of me washing my face with water, I exited the bathroom. And walked out the church and jumped into my car.

I had to admit the whole ride home I was speechless and confused. I tried my best to shake it off by sleeping, but I woke up to the same uneasiness that I fell asleep with.

"Who is this lady?" I asked myself as I got up and walked over to the computer and logged onto the church's Web site. It had a list of all of the members of the church and their numbers. This was a volunteer kind of things, so if you on the list you signed a waiver giving permission to have your info on the site.

"Mother Bella Jones," I read out loud as I wrote the number down. I wasn't going to use it just yet, but eventually I planned on it. I went back to my bed and laid down. I had a big decision to make.

Chapter 19

Alex
Some Things in Common
May 4th 11:30 A.M.

"So where are we headed?" I inquired as I hopped into Wallace's Maybach. It was Sunday and I was in the house for a little while after I came home from the gym. I was supposed to be in church, but I skipped this Sunday. Wallace had called me asking me if I wanted to hang out.

I was a little hesitant about it at first since he had a criminal record and a brother didn't want to mess up anything I had going for myself with school, work and all. I had spoken to my baby girl for a minute before I left letting her know I was going to be hanging out with a coworker. I looked pass his past and I knew from working with him and talking to him that he could not be a bad guy, so I agree to hang out for a bit.

"Well, I kind of need some company while I track down some info on a lead to my dead lover's family. I just don't feel like going alone."

"Okay." I nodded my head unsurely as he pulled off and merged into traffic. *His lover? Was he talking about a man or a woman? It must be a woman because he doesn't look gay. Then again, you never know.*

"You don't have a problem with that do you? I'm sorry for springing this on you. But, as old as I am, I am still leery of certain situations and people. I am not trying to put you in harm's way. I just need someone with me and I can't trust anyone right now but you."

I felt honored and confused at the same time since we weren't family and we weren't that close. I wondered why he didn't choose one of his brothers. "Why didn't you ask Professor Andrews?"

"Well, we're just getting to know each other again and frankly I trust you more with my info and life, than him. You could have easily asked me about when I said 'lover', if I was talking about a man or a woman, but you didn't and I noted that as a trustworthy friend's trait."

"Wow," was all I could get out. I was a very easygoing person to get along with I had to say. If you told me something or I saw something and you wanted me to keep it hush, than it would be that way unto you gave me permission to release it or I died. Yes, I was nosy and extremely curious, but I had mental storage like a camel and I loved keeping secrets. At times, I would want to tell people, other people's situations, but I didn't because I knew what comes around goes around. I like my secrets being kept as well.

"Your secrets are safe with me." He smiled and turned on some jazz as we hit the highway to where we were going. I paid attention to all turns, exits and landmarks just in case something went down and I had to backtrack or come this way again.

Twenty-five minutes or so we were pulling up in front of a house that looked like it was in some type of ungated retirement community.

He put the car in park and pulled out a piece of paper with some things scribbled on it. "You ready?" he said looking at me like he was afraid to go in. I knew then that even grown men have fears. It's like they just never wanted to talk about them.

"Whenever you are," I assured him.

"Let's go." We both exited the car and made our way to the front door.

I watched Wallace hesitantly stand in front of the door he was here visiting. Finally he knocked and after few seconds an older guy opened the door.

"Can I help you?" He was dressed in a brown terry cloth robe and some slippers. He was noticeably muscular and fit.

"Yes, are you John Parks?" Wallace asked.

"Who wants to know?" He looked defensive and took a step back. I looked at Wallace's waist and saw what looked like the butt of a gun. Something I didn't notice before. Then all of a sudden being here felt like a bad idea. I didn't know either of these men well and if anything happened to me no one would know but them. I could kick myself. *With my nosy ass.*

"My name is Wallace. I just needed to know if you are the father of Jerry Parks?" My mouth hit the floor when he used my biological father's name. *What in the hell is going on? This nigga is gay? And so was my father? It explains why Ashley is the way she is genetically. But damn, did I have that shit and didn't know it? I liked pussy for sure. I know this, but was something in me lurking to come out and I don't know about yet? Was I bisexual and didn't know it? What the fuck is going on?* Then it clicked in my head old dude was on my list to call, but he had no address listed, just his phone number. I found that to be odd. I'm kind of glad that I came now. I was getting info without letting Wallace in my business.

The old guy looked Wallace up and down for a few seconds and steps back out the doorway and invited us in. "Yeah, he my son. Come in." I knew for sure I had to keep my mouth shut about him being my father until I knew what Wallace's motive was.

We walked into the apartment and he instructed us to take off our shoes and then he let us sit down inside his living room. He sat in front of us in a recliner while me and Wallace sat on a nice leather love seat and waited for the old guy to speak. The old head did look like my father, but he had beady eyes and looked to be nervous about something.

"What you wanna know about my seed?" He looked at Wallace.

"Well . . . uh. I need to know what he was like growing up and as a teenager."

"Why can't you ask him all of that?"

"Well, sir he was . . . uh . . . murdered five years ago. You didn't know?" Wallace smirked with a puzzled look on his face. It was a look that said "damn you are his father and you don't know your son is dead."

"I haven't seen him since he was a little boy. He and I parted ways a long time ago." His left eye twitched a little and he shifted in his seat as well. He seemed nervous about something.

"Oh," Wallace breathed out dejectedly. "You never talked to him or anything like that since?"

"Nope, sure haven't." It was like he didn't even care. He didn't even know his grandson was sitting in front of him and I wasn't sure if I was going to tell him just yet. I need to be careful, because dude looks crazy.

"You want see a picture of him when he was little?"

"Yes, sir." Wallace brightened up and beamed a radiant smile. He must have really loved my biological father. My grandfather got up out of his chair and walked over to his fireplace and grabbed a picture off of the mantle and handed it to Wallace. Wallace smiled as he held the picture in his hand of my father as a boy. I smiled too because I favored him a little as a child too.

"Here you go," Wallace said as he handed the picture back to him.

"Naw . . . you can keep it." he said pushing the picture away. "Seems like he meant a lot to you."

"Yeah he did," Wallace solemnly spoke. "Do you know if his mom is still alive? Did he have any brothers and sisters?"

"I don't know if that bitch is still alive. We were only married for a little bit and I only fucked her ass once, so unless she married someone else he ain't got no siblings."

"So who was fuckin' who?" the old man asked out of nowhere. My eyes were as big as saucers. I know old dude didn't just ask what I thought he did.

"What?" Wallace asked, offended. "That's all you got to ask me about your son?"

"No . . . did he take dick good?"

Before I knew it, Wallace had rushed the old dude and put the gun to his head. "Muthafucka, your ass is pushing me to kill you. Ask me another question like that and I will put your thoughts and memories all over this chair, carpet and walls. You hear me?"

I watched in terror as the old dude just sat there and smiled.

"Wallace . . . man don't do it . . . he's not worth it." I said as I cautiously walked up behind him. I didn't touch him for fear that his reflex might make him shoot him by accident or something. I didn't want to be a part of any of that. Wallace's hand was trembling as he still had the gun to my grandfather's head. After a few seconds Wallace pulled off of him and backed away breathing really hard.

The old dude just starts laughing out of nowhere and laughing hard too.

"What hell is wrong with you?" Wallace asked him as the old man continued to laugh hysterically now.

"Come on, Wallace, let's get out of here, this dude is insane." I pulled at his arm, hoping he would listen. He looked pissed. I thought of Ashley. *That shit must run in the family!*

"You right." He tucked the gun back in his waist. Then all of a sudden he rushes old dude and slaps him unconscious with the butt of the gun. We grab our shoes and exit the apartment.

"What the fuck was that?" Wallace asked me as I got in the car and buckled my seat belt. I shrugged my shoulders, because I didn't know either. I was confused. I had more questions then I started out with. We pulled off and headed toward home. I crossed old dude off the list and moved to the next person on the list. *So both my fathers are gay. Ain't that some mess!*

I got in the house and collapsed on the sofa. I was extremely tired and confused. Ashley was nowhere to be found. It was so quiet that I practically heard my thoughts wound up in my head. Everything was spinning and moving.

Was Wallace and my biological father James really that close? Was Wallace and my father, Shawn, messing around too? What was really going on? And where in the hell was Ashley? Her ass has been MIA since she had gotten that car. She has been in and out of the house like a crackhead. And where in the hell did she get that car? She didn't have a job. Her ass could be stripping for all I know. This is too much for me to handle. And to top it off I just found out my biological grandfather was gay with a side of lunatic. Wow God! What kind of mess is this! Both these fucking families are messed up.

Ring . . . Ring . . . Ring

"Hello!" My voice was filled with anger.

"What's wrong, Lex?" My father inquired.

"I just have a lot on my mind that's all," I breathed out.

"Let me guess, Ashley is in one of her moods again."

"No, actually she's not." It wasn't a lie because if she was I didn't get to see it. She would be in her room most of the time she was at home, when she was at home. I barely got to see her for a hot minute before she was gone again.

"So what's the problem then?"

"Well, I ran into one of your old clients, Wallace, and we—"

"You saw Wallace? He's out there in California? What did he talk to you about?" He cut me off with all of these questions.

"Well, Wallace and I work in the cafeteria together at the college and I did run into him when we were in Baltimore once. He thought I was you when I was using your car one Saturday in the summer."

"Oh . . . okay," he said letting up.

"Sooo . . . What did you guys talk about?" he slammed me with another question. I was beginning to think there was something between them, but could I just come out ask him directly?

I bypassed it for now. "Well, he mainly asked how you were doing. He kept on rehashing the fact that you were such a good lawyer and friend."

"Really? Wow, that is great." I could almost hear him smiling.

"Yeah, it was much of nothing, but I did get to find out that he was dating Jerry/James Parks. And that they were very serious from what I can tell."

"Really, that's something. I guess you learn something everyday."

"Yeah and come to find out, he is looking for James's family too. He is trying to find out what James was like growing up and all and why someone would murder him."

"Oh . . . okay. Be careful out there and while you are with him. He does have a history."

"Oh . . . ah . . . Dad. I got one question for you."

"Sure, son. Shoot."

"I was wonder if Wallace one of the guys you slept with?"

"What? Me and Wallace sleeping together? Son, Wallace and I didn't have that kind of relationship. It was purely business. Client-attorney relationship only."

"Okay, Dad."

"Son, did he tell you something like that? Because if he did, it was a lie."

"No, Dad, I was just asking, because you never really say anything about it. You just said that you had an issue with homosexuality. I was wrong for asking. I'm sorry. It was none of my business anyway."

"Son, you do have a right to ask me anything you want to. I want you to be comfortable with asking me anything you want to. I'm not promising you that I will be comfortable talking about it all the time, but I will do my best to be as up-front as possible."

"Thanks, Dad." I smiled, because I knew then that there wasn't anything going on between them. I just needed to calm my nosy ass down. Some things just need to be left alone. And my dad's sexuality was one of them.

"Look, Dad, I got some studying to do and some plays to go over so I will hit you up later."

"Sure thing, Lex. Get a good night's sleep." With that he hung up the phone.

The next day . . .

"Hey, baby." My baby gave me a kiss on the cheek as she walked into my apartment. It was rare for me to have a girl over the apartment. I was private when it came to that kind of stuff. I also didn't want anything sexual to jump off. I had goals set. I wanted to reach them without complications and sex only complicated things. I was a freak by nature, and keeping it together was not an easy feat. Beating off did relieve some of that pressure though. It wasn't the same as a women's womb, but it helped. I just didn't want to get too used to using my hands to the point that a woman wouldn't be needed. That wasn't the reason that my baby was over here though. I was lonely. Ashley was out for a while and I really had no friends besides some football buddies. They were all football, all the time. I just wanted to talk. I didn't want anything in particular; just to be around someone. At least that's what I told myself. Things got a little heated a while after we sat down on the couch in the living room. I turned on the plasma television and put in my favorite movie, *Basic Instinct*. Sharon Stone was the shit in this movie. I know for a fact that she was an undercover freak outside of the role in the movie. She was too good at playing the part. Anyway, when it got to the part when she crossed and uncrossed her legs I felt my baby's hand moving toward my manhood.

"Whoa!" I pushed her hand away.

"What's wrong, baby?" She sat back a little. She had a disappointed look on her face.

"Nothing, I'm just not there right now. Don't get me wrong you fine as ever. I'm just not ready to take it there."

"Oh, I thought my age was getting to you or that you were gay or something."

"Gay? . . . nah. I just don't want to mess up a good thing." She smiled.

"Okay, I'm cool with that. I understand. That don't mean we can't fool around." She winked. "I even got my buddy in my bag. We could do some things. Definitely."

My mind flashed back to when my mom caught me in the basement with those two chicks and I smiled. That was really good experience for me. I told my mom that it wouldn't happen again, but I'm grown now. A little bit wouldn't hurt. And this would be the safest sex possible, because there would be no intercourse or juices exchanged. Before I could agree or disagree she had leaned over and started to kiss me on my neck and my ear and fondled my pecs. I was groping her breasts and licking her neck. She was inching toward my manhood again and I pulled her away just in time. I still wasn't good about that area just yet. She started to unbutton her blouse. When the front door open and Ashley flew in like a bat out of hell.

"Damn, Lex. This is what you been doing when I'm gone?" she grilled my baby and then me. She was dancing around like she had to take a piss, but she still got one last smart-ass remark out. "Getting pussy and dick juice on the couch is not a good look Lex." With that she shot into the bathroom. I was so embarrassed that I couldn't even look my baby in the face. She just excused herself and left my apartment.

Chapter 20

Shawn
In Need
May 4th 4:30 P.M.

"Shawn, was that Alex or Ashley on the phone?" Mona asked me as she handed me a glass of lemonade. I was in the backyard in the gazebo that I had built last summer.

"It was Lex," I answered as I sat up in the stretched bamboo lounging chair and matching ottoman. Mona smiled and then kissed me on my forehead. "I called him to check up on them since it's been a couple of days since we've talked."

"Is everything all right out there?" she asked as she turned slightly to go back in the house. "Yes, everything is fine. He's just a little overwhelmed with school, football and work." I hoped.

"Humph! . . . my babies are such hard workers." She smiled really hard. "We trained them well you know."

"I know. I was just a little worried that's all." I was more worried that they would find out that I was sleeping with James. But I knew I was the only living one that knew about that, besides Mona.

"Baby, let them live . . . they are going to make their mistakes. It's just up to us to be there when they need us." She patted me on the head.

"I know . . . I know." I said as she walked off back toward the house and into the kitchen.

"Shawn, what is your problem?" I asked myself out loud. *Those kids love you and they are not going to stop. You think that if they find out that you were sleeping with James that they are going to hate you or disown you? Or is the fact that you were interested in Wallace and even he didn't know about it?*

I laid back all the way back in my chair as tears streamed down my face. The truth was the fact that I was still hurting from my past. I was still scared that I was going to mess up again and fall on my face again in front of my whole family. I prayed day and night that I would not go back but, forward. And it seemed like at times I could slip up at any moment, but I didn't. I looked at the faces of my little ones every morning. That's what kept me going, that and the prayer and Bible study that I had incorporated into my daily life and family.

"God help your son . . . I am in need of healing." I got up and got on my knees and prayed a little while longer, then got up and went to bed waiting on an answer from God.

Chapter 21

Grace
Getting a Little Closer
May 8th 1:33 P.M.

"Can I speak to a Grace Andrews?" an unknown caller asked.

"Speaking." I oozed professionalism.

"This is Mercy General Hospital; we have a female patient here in the ICU. Her file says you are her next of kin so we called you. She is suffering from liver failure and we need someone to come down here to make some decisions on her behalf. She coherent, but lightly sedated."

"I'm on my way," I said, hanging up the phone and rushed around my office to get myself together. "Lawd, not now!" A couple of tears ran down my face as I thought of losing my mother. I knew this day would come. I just didn't think it would be so soon.

I raced out of my office and nearly knocked over Ashley as she was about to come into the building.

"Sorry," I said as I continued walking, she followed.

"So what's the hurry?"

"I have a family emergency. I don't have time to talk right now," I said as I crossed into the parking lot structure to get to my car. She kept on following. She didn't get the hint.

"Anything I can help with?" she asked.

"Certainly not." I kept walking until I got to the elevator and pushed the button. "I don't need any company. And don't you have classes to attend?" I asked all in one breath.

"Only had one today and it's over. So I needed something to do. That's why I was headed to your office. To see if we could hang out." She wanted something and she wasn't fooling me. *This bitch is such a spoiled brat!*

"Look Ashley, I don't have time for this shit. You bugging the hell out of me," I barked.

"Oh, really?" We were standing on opposite sides of the car. "I think I need to call your husband and bug the hell out of him. Let's see if he likes what Ashley has to tell him about his wife."

"Fine!! Get the fuck in!" I yelled. I put my put my finger on the door reader and pressed start button. After a few seconds of reading my fingerprint the car started and I pulled off, out the garage and toward the hospital.

I pulled into the hospital parking garage and looked at myself in the mirror. My mascara was running a little so I reached over to the compartment next to me to get me some Wet Ones to just clean my face up altogether.

"Is everything okay?" I heard Ashley ask me. I ignored her for a few seconds pondering the questions. I mentally went down my list of drama in my life and concluded that being all right was far from me at this moment. I wanted to run from this situation and all of the things that were plaguing me right now. During the drive over to the hospital my husband kept calling my phone. Good thing it was on vibrate and I didn't have to explain anything to Ashley on why I was ignoring his calls. Even though if I didn't have it on vibrate, Ashley would think I wasn't answering my phone because of her. Truth is, my husband knew very little about me or my family and it was the same way with him. I have never met anyone from his family and neither him mine. I know what you are saying: That's not realistic, but it was in our world. I guess we were both desperate for attention when we started dating. It was off to the justice of the peace and then it was done. He never asked to invite his family and I never mentioned mine. It was kind of like we got each other and we knew that family was a touchy subject for both, so we kept it quiet. Now I was about to lose a very important part of mine and I had no one to help me with it.

"I'll be fine," I said, patting her on her leg. We got out of the car and made our way toward the exit.

I stopped right before we went into the hospital entrance. "Ashley, can I ask you something?"

"Sure."

"Look, we about to go in and see my mother. I would appreciate if you kept our relationship between us. She is going through kidney failure and I don't want to excite or agitate her in any way. Okay."

"I promise." She smiled and then placed her hand over her heart and held the other hand up as if she was pledging allegiance. And that moment I saw the little girl in Ashley. The pure, innocent child that probably was sweet as pie. It also made me wonder why she was acting the way she acted. It has to be a reason for her behavior. I would hate to think that she was acting this way out of pure evilness. "I know I've been quite the character, but I will honor this request and keep it cool while we're in here."

"Thank you," I said as politely as I could.

With that we walked into the hospital. We walked through the small hallway that was actually a full body scan. No weapons of any type were accepted in the hospital, library, post office or school in the whole country, except for law enforcement. National security was this country's first priority at all times.

We walked up to the shielded reception desk and scanned our identification cards, letting them know who we were before we could even speak to anyone. There was an instant background check done every time your identification was scanned for any government facility. Warrants, traffic tickets, child support, etc., everything was flagged and if you weren't on the up-and-up you would be quarantined, searched again and then the proper authorities would handle the situation accordingly from there. And it only took a few seconds for anything to come back, so there was no running and getting away.

"Thank you for visiting us. Your room number is 434C. Visiting hours are over at 8:00 P.M. Sharp. Have a pleasant visit," the lady behind the counter with a headset spoke before we were allowed to get onto the elevator. A pleasant visit was all I could hope for. We rode the elevator in silence.

My mind was on my past. What I been through and how I got to where I was at this moment. I didn't know what to expect when I got to her room but I straightened myself up and pushed forward as the elevator doors opened. We walked down the hall and counted down the rooms until we got to the one that my mother was in. I pushed the door and walked in. My mother was in the bed with a couple of tubes running out of her.

"Hey, Ma," I whispered as I leaned over her. She was breathing slowly, but steady. She stirred a little in her bed and then her eyes fluttered open.

"Hey, baby." Her voice was a little on the weak side. A tear slid out of my eye and down my cheek. "You came!"

"Mama, of course I did. You're my mother." I didn't visit her as much as I did and when she told me she was have kidney problems I kind of pushed it off, when the doctor said that my mother would be fine on the medication she told her to take. I wasn't being the child that I was expected to be. I was supposed to take care of her in her time of need, but I was still mending. I thought that not seeing her would punish her, but it took away from the time that we needed to be together. It's amazing what you see when you look from the outside in. All of the things we think we are taking out on people, for things they have done to us, hurts both parties in the situation. And here I am in the hospital close to losing my only relative. I was so angry with myself. "I love you." It was the first time I said it to her and really felt it. I hope it wasn't because of the state that she was in that made it feel real, but you don't miss or treasure something until it's taken or almost taken away from you. Like right now as I looked down at my mom in this hospital bed. The beeping of the machines around her only made it worse, so much so that I had to take a seat next to her to keep my shaky legs from collapsing from underneath me.

I still had my hand on hers as I sat.

"Who is the young lady you brought with you today?"

"Oh . . . she a friend of mine." I darted my eyes to Ashley really quickly then looked back at my mother.

"Baby, you changed your mind?" she asked me with wonder in her glazed eyes.

"No, Ma . . . I haven't changed my mind."

"Ma, have you called Aunt Bella to let her know you're in the hospital?"

"No, I don't want her to know." She was a little sour in tone as she said it.

"Why Ma?" I asked.

She looked at me with a "you already know" kind of glare. I knew all too well, so I left it alone.

Before I could get another question out an Asian doctor walked into the room with an electronic device. "Hello, I am Dr. Hang." He then started to scan my mother's midsection. It looked like a wand that is used by police when they are arresting someone, but this was one that the doctor used to scan over her body. In this day and age there was almost no more need for large scanners in hospitals anymore. A simple wave of the wand and doctors could tell you what was going on internally in you in minutes.

"How are you doing today?" he said as soon as he finished.

"I could be better." I spoke up, seeing that my mom was in the hospital. A "fine" was not the order of the day. I was a wreck inside and I knew it.

"Well let me get to the point of my calling you here. Your mother's kidneys are failing and it is to the point of no return. She has only a few weeks left to live."

"Huh?" I muttered. "I mean—how?—she didn't—" I stammered. "Mama, you told me that everything was fine. How could you—" I instantly got light-headed and room began to spin.

"Miss, you okay?" The Asian doctor rushed over to me and caught me before I almost tumbled out of my chair.

"Yes—yes—no—I need some water . . . water please." I swooned again. He propped me back up in the chair. I saw Ashley leave out of the door. I assumed she went to get me some water. A few more minutes went by and Ashley came back, handed me a bottle of water and rubbed my back. It was feeling so good. I almost forgot where I was. She was so gentle at times. Flashes of our lovemaking popped into my head and I quickly pushed her hand away. I didn't want anyone thinking I was doing a chick, especially my mother.

"Baby—I—I—I didn't want to burden you and your new life." Tears were running down her face. I got up and hugged her as tight as I could.

"Mama, you're not a burden. I was being selfish and I let the mistakes you made raising me control and rule me." I squeezed tighter. I didn't want to lose my mother.

I heard the machine beeping and then it got louder . . . and started make a funny noise, causing me to jump off her. I forgot she had some tubes in her and I might have inadvertently pulled one out or something. But it wasn't me. The noise continued as the doctor raced to her side again checking the machines. I backed up with panic on my face. Ashley stood back by while a couple of nurses rushed in to assist the doctor.

"She's flatlining!" I heard a nurse yell out. "Get her out of here."

"Nooooooouu!" I cried out as a few nurses tugged and pulled me out. I wasn't an easy pull so they struggled. "I'mmmm . . . Not Going. Any . . . where." A big male nurse came and helped the other nurses pull me out of the room, while the doctors worked on my mother.

Ashley silently walked alongside of me as they ushered me toward the waiting room.

"I'm very sorry, but you have to wait in here," the male nurse said to me with a sympathetic look on his face. I am sure that I was not the first person to be dragged out a hospital room by him. "They will do all they can to save her."

I practically fell in the chair and sobbed deep and hard. I was a mess.

A few minutes later the doctor walked into the room with a look that was all to known.

"She didn't make it? She didn't make it?" I yelled out as I got up and ran up to him.

"No ma'am. I'm sorry I just couldn't save her. It seems like she just gave up." he said softly and solemnly.

"No!" I bellowed out without a care. Then the whole room went black.

I awoke minutes later by the help of some old- fashioned smelling salts. My hair was a mess and I was still in the waiting room, but they had my legs propped up on another chair. Ashley was fanning me. She had look of compassion and sorrow. She had been silent the whole time we were here and I was proud of her for being a lady of her word.

"Is my mother really dead?" She simply nodded her head. "Mmm," I moaned as my bottom lip began to quiver again. I took the tissue that Ashley had handed me and covered my mouth as I sobbed and rocked. I wasn't ready for this.

I so wanted to tell her I'm sorry for blaming her for my molestation. It really wasn't totally her fault. I had a part in it. A real big part in it.

Me and Ashley sat in silence as an hour went by. I then decided that I needed to go home. I was in no condition to drive so I let Ashley drive me home. I hoped my husband was home so I could get him to take Ashley home. But when I arrived home he was nowhere in sight. I was so out of it that against my better judgment I let Ashley sleep on the couch downstairs. I drifted off to sleep and was awakened by Ashley in between my legs lapping at my pussy.

"I thought this would make you feel better," she said as she went back to work on giving me some release. It didn't last long because not too long after she started pleasuring me, I heard my front door slam and footsteps moving around downstairs.

"My husband!" I pushed her off of me and onto the floor. Hurting her was the last thing on my mind. How was I going to explain to him that she was in my bedroom . . . naked? She scrambled her clothes and ran into the closet. I positioned myself in the bed to play like I was asleep. I heard him sloshing up the steps and into the bedroom.

"Hey, baby," I rolled over and stretched like I was sleeping good. "How was your day?"

"It was good." He smiled. "I stopped by your office today and was told you were gone for the day. They said something about a family emergency."

"Oh . . . uh . . . yeah . . . My mother died." It rolled off of my tongue like I was telling him it was hot outside.

"Oh, baby," he cooed as he sat down beside me and grabbed me into an embrace. I played into like I was going for an Oscar. "I'm so sorry to hear that."

"It's okay. It was her time." I said it without as much as emotion as I should have, but I was more concerned with him finding a naked Ashley in my closet.

"Anything I can do to make you feel better?" he asked, rubbing my back.

"Well . . . there is one thing." I seductively got up and began to unbutton his shirt and then his pants. I needed to distract him as best as possible. And this was the only thing I could do. I pushed him down on the bed and began to massage his manhood with all my might.

"Close your eyes baby. I am about make you dream big." A big smile crossed his face and he did just what he was instructed to do. I said it loud enough for Ashley to hear and I was hoping that she got the clue. Sure enough as soon as he started moaning she started creeping out of the closet and toward the door. She was now fully dressed and moving quickly. By the time I finished my husband off, I had heard the front door open and close letting me know that she was indeed gone. I let my husband explode all over my face and then I collapsed beside him glad that I got away with yet another day of lies.

Chapter 22

David
Birds of a Feather
May 8th 2:09 P.M.

"Where are you?" I called and called Grace's phone, but it kept going to voice mail. I just stopped by her office and was told that she was gone for the day. And that it was a family emergency. I wondered what kind of family emergency she had since I was the only family she had. I mean I did hear her talk to her mother on the phone every now and then, but that was it. I never met my mother-in-law and or any of my wife's family and neither she mine. It really wasn't a topic of interest for either of us.

I was sitting in my office and it was almost time for me to get ready to head home.

There was a knock at the door.

"Come in," I called out.

"Hey sir, I was just stopping by to see if you still wanted to head to the gym with me for a quick workout like said you would."

"A workout," My mind and libido instantly thought about sex. Mentally I had saw him naked and I was stroking his dick to a full thick length and then swallowing him whole. He didn't know the things I wanted to do with his dick and his balls. I'd bend him over and toss his salad like I was a vegetarian.

"Professor. . . . Professor!" He waved me out of my daze. "Are you going?"

"Yeah . . . I mean, Yes." I corrected my grammar. "Can you give me a minute to get myself together. I will meet you out front in a few minutes."

"Okay, sir." He had so much respect for me. Always had good manners every time he talked. You could tell he had a good upbringing. Almost feel bad for wanting him sexually. I just couldn't help it. I was weak. I presented this confident and in-control man in front of my peers and my wife, but when I get to myself all I feel like is a ho. I am still fucking my molester and pretending to be happily married. When deep down inside I wanted to be with a man. Married to a man. But, my wife was a cover-up, a good one at that. She didn't know she was being used and all these years of being married I was faking it big-time.

I got up from behind my desk and went into my closet and pulled out my gym gear that was being used for the first time. I literally had to blow dust off of it. I had no intentions in gaining this much weight or any at all. I had slacked up and was complacent with myself and my secret life so much so that I slipped up and let myself go.

"I'm ready." I patted Alex on the shoulder as I exited my building.

"Good, because I'm ready to get this." He smiled as he picked his bag off the ground. We made small talk as we made our way toward the gymnasium.

I flashed my identification, as did Alex, and we made our way toward the locker room. I was following him because I had only came here in the beginning of my career here and they had done some remodeling and construction over the years. I was stealing peeks at his butt as he walked. He definitely had a tight end. I smiled to myself.

We made our way into the locker room and my
heart almost burst out of my chest. There were men
everywhere. Small, tall, dark, light, but all muscular.
But what mostly caught my attention was that some of
these men had no shame. Some were absolutely naked.
I mean nothing but flesh. My dick rose and it was hard
to contain and conceal. My eyes were bouncing off of
asses to dick and from dicks to asses. I bumped a few
people as I followed Alex through the locker room. I
almost wanted to keep my eyes closed for fear of a man
catching me staring and whipping my ass.

"Hey, professor," I heard an unfamiliar student yell
out. But he too was naked, so I just waved and quickly
turned from him to keep from staring at his huge dick.
Man, these men just don't know. I know I wasn't the
only one in here like this . . . you know . . . down-low. I
saw a couple of the "children" as we exchanged quick
glances, letting me and them know what "we" were and
some were in attendance as well.

"Professor, you can take this locker right here next
to mine." Alex smiled. Again, such a beautiful smile. *A
handsome, young man. Ump!* "I hope you ready, because I gets it in when I exercise."

We undressed out of our regular clothes and put on
our gym gear. I tried my best to get a peek at his pack-
age, but he was turned away from me, so it was not
going to happen. I so wanted to see what he was working with. If he was hung I don't know if I could contain
myself in his presence without coming on to him and
if he wasn't I probably still would want to take it there.
But, again I didn't even know he was gay or not. I mean
he didn't give off any signals but I knew that was very
misleading. Down-low ain't got no signals until they
got a dick in their mouth or you got theirs in yours. It's
just that simple. You don't know. But I wasn't going to
press up on him just yet. I was patient.

Over a period of about an hour and a half we worked out on every possible machine: Squats, push-ups, jogging, weight , and crunches. You name it we did. I got to see his ass in every way possibly imaginable. I was horny as hell by now.

I got kind of excited when we finished. I was glad we were done exercising, but I was even more excited that we could take a shower together. I had to get a look at his dick.

Well, no such luck. He was evasive in the shower too. I could kick myself I was so horny now. I knew exactly what I needed to do now.

We exited the gym and I dropped him off with quickness and made my way over to John's house to get some much need release. I was going to put a hurting on his ass tonight for sure.

I pulled up to my usual spot, parked and made my way toward his door. I knocked on the door and within seconds the door swung open like it was being kicked down. John didn't look like himself. He looked warn and tattered.

"Everything okay?" I asked as I looked up from kneeling down and taking off my shoes.

"Hell fucking no." He spoke with ferocity. He was a bitter old man but not this nasty. Something or someone must have really pissed him off. I was now having second thoughts about being here. I didn't want to be caught in no shit for a quick nut. This muthafucka has a gun or two up in here and I know it. He always bragged about them, but I never saw them and I didn't care to. I had to admit I was a punk in the worst way. Nobody had to tell me it. I knew it.

"What happened ?" I inquired not really caring. I wanted to hit him off and be about my business.

"I had a visit from some soft-ass muthafucka who wanted to know about my son. He said he wanted to know how he was a kid growing up and all that shit. I told his ass to get on. What I should have told him that his ass was a fucking momma's boy and that's why I fucked his ass." He laughed. But it was a twisted laugh. I was now looking at him like What the fuck? He did his son the same way too. This muthafucka was a serial molester. I was dumbfounded. He made me wonder how many other people he messed up like he did me and Robert.

"Always up under his momma. His soft-ass didn't do nothing but color, draw and read books. And his ugly- ass momma worked all the time, leaving me with him all the time. I had shit I wanted to do and I didn't want to be tied down to no sissy kid and a nagging wife." He flopped down in his recliner and grabbed his bottle of liquor that was next to him and threw it back, taking a long gulp. "When are you going to get a job? She would constantly ask me. I ignored her most of the time. Getting a job was the least of my problems. Her ass trapped me with that 'I'm pregnant shit' so I had to marry her ass. Shit, my mother made me do that shit. Told me I had to do right by her. Huh, her ass didn't even know who my fuckin' father was. How she gonna tell me what to do?" He swigged another gulp of liquor and threw the bottle against the wall shattering it. It caused me to jump. I looked at John like he was a whole 'nother person. But, again I was delusional and just now seeing him for who he is. A gay lunatic.

"Wowwww," was all I could get out. I just stared at him as he continued to mumble some obscenities out of nowhere. As crazy as he was at this moment I still wanted to get a nut off in his ass.

"Look John, I'm sorry about all of that but you know what I came here for," I stated plainly.

"Yeah, I know what you here for." He got up and staggered around the room for a minute like he was looking for something.

"You looking for this." He pulled out a 9 mm gun and pointed it at me.

"Uhhhhhh," my mouth was open so wide I could catch flies. "Nahhhh, man. That's not for me." I was backing up, trying to get myself to the door.

"What you backing up for? You running out on me. I thought you wanted to fuck me?" He laughed a wicked laugh. "Changed your mind?"

"Look, John . . . come on, man. . . . put the gun down." I was shaking a little bit. "It's not what you think."

"Yes, it is, bitch . . . you think I'm crazy. Like all the rest of these muthafuckas."

"Nah, man . . . That's . . . that's not me."

"So you don't think I'm crazy?"

Yeah, bitch you gone! I wanted to say but I kept lying to him to ease his mind.

"Would I be coming here all this time if I thought you were crazy?" I asked turning the tables on him. I saw his hand go down like a bell went off in his head. "I've been with you all this time because you cool peoples." I was lying to him with all I had. Shit we were birds of a feather. We just had different crazies, that's all.

He walked up to me and put his head on my shoulders and cried.

"My son's dead," he said as he lifted his head off my shoulders. I saw pain in his eyes.

"I'm sorry to hear that." I didn't know what else to say. "He's probably in a better place now."

"You think?" His head cocked to the side in wonder. I just hoped his ass didn't snap and shoot my ass up in here. To prevent that I went for a hug and eased the gun out of his hands. He willingly let it slip from his hand into mine relieving my worry.

"Let's get you into bed." I had no intentions of fucking him tonight or anymore for all that matters. I slowly walked him to the back of his apartment to tuck him in and get the hell out of there. Sure enough as soon as his ass hit the pillow he was out. I got my shit and got the hell out of there as fast as I could. I made sure I took the gun he had with me, because you never really know when you gonna need one. His ass won't remember it anyway.

I pulled up to the house fully exhausted and ready to hit the bed. I saw Grace's car in the driveway so I knew she was home. I was hoping I could get some play tonight, since my horniness materialized once again as I pulled up to my house.

I walked in the house, hid the gun in my office real quick and made my way up to the room. I was greeted by my wife, a lovely blow job and the sad news of her mother's death . And I must admit she put a nigga out for the night with the job she did on me. She said it was to comfort her, but I got what I needed out the deal as well.

Chapter 23

Ashley
Chip Off the Old Block
May 8th 5:04 P.M.

I got out of Grace's house just in time. I had just to got a call from home girl from the Bistro to come hook her up again with that good head game. I felt bad for Grace and losing her mom and all, but I wasn't putting my plans to the side just because she was grieving. I had goals to meet and I still need her.

When I got in the house Alex was in his room with the door closed as usual. I put my ear to the door to be what he was for a moment: nosy as hell! I heard him on the phone talking about baby this and baby that. It was about time he was trying to get some pussy and leave my business to me.

After few more seconds I lost interest and walked away toward my room. I was in need of an orgasm, but none of my girls were available.

I scrambled around my room trying to find me a vibrator or something to get me off so I can get a good night's sleep so I can get through my day full of classes tomorrow.

I found me a small massager, stripped out of my clothes, turned on some music and stretched out on a towel on my bed. I was just about to put the massager to my clit when my phone began to ring.

"Hello." I was a little pissed.

"Hey pumpkin!" My father called me my pet name. "What are you doing?"

"Studying," the lie came out so easy. I couldn't believe I was a grown women still lying about pleasuring myself. Shit his ass probably does too. "Gotta keep these grades up."

"That's good, Ash." My father was such a sucker sometimes. He believed everything I told him.

"How is Mom, Diana, Shawn and Brittany?" I was trying to avoid him asking me about work or getting a job as much as possible.

"They're all doing well." he noted. "I was actually calling to see if you had gotten a job yet."

Damn! I can't catch a break to save my life.

"Dad, I been trying," I said in a sweet baby-girl voice that melted his heart every time. I was a daddy's girl for sure. Seeing that we had some stuff in common, he was always a little less stressful toward me than he was toward Alex and the other kids. He knew that I was wrestling with my sexuality too, so I could use that against him from time to time just to get by or anything I needed. In this case, more time to look for a job or pretend to look for one for all that matters. "It's been so hard Daddy. You know . . . I—I . . . been struggling with . . . you know." I paused for effect and then kept it moving toward my finale. "I just don't wanna get out of bed at times. I'm just so tired of all of this! I can't do it anymore!"

"Ashley, I know what you are dealing with. Believe me, I do, but you got to move on and press forward past your issues. Don't let them get you down and when they do, call me, so we can talk about it. Okay?" It gets him every time. I smiled to myself. *People be making it easy,* I thought to myself.

"Okay, Daddy."

"So, with that said. I will need you to find a job in the next three weeks, because that is when I am cutting off the spending money I was sending you to tide you over."

"What!" My mouth fell open.

"Is there a problem?" he sternly asked.

"Daddy, didn't you just hear me when I said I was going through?"

"Ashley, that's just an excuse. You're an adult now. It's time to step up." He countered. "Life goes on, so you need to get through whatever you're going through and find a job. It's called multi-tasking. It's not foreign to you because we made you guys do it when you were home. All you have to do is apply it now. Alex is doing it just fine and so can you."

"Fuck Alex!" I said before I could get a hold of my temper. I was in full effect right now and nothing was stopping me. "I'm Ashley . . . your little girl . . . your pumpkin." By the time I got to "your pumpkin" I was mellow again for effect.

"First, Ashley . . . Watch your mouth when you're talking to me. I'm still your father. And second . . . you'll always be my little girl." His voice was as soft as a kitten's meow. "It's time for you to get on your own two feet and get your own. I can't be there for you all the time and this is the only way you are going to learn of to provide for yourself. Get it?"

"Yes, I get it, but—"

"But nothing . . . one month and then you are cut off." He cut me off.

"Okay, Daddy." I agreed like I was defeated and he was the winner. I got two extra weeks before I would need to find a job. I was the winner. He just didn't know it. Men ain't got nothing on a woman.

"Look, Daddy, I got to go and finish studying, take a shower and get into bed so I can get my day started early tomorrow."

"Sure, pumpkin. I don't wanna interrupt your flow. Don't forget to call me whenever you need to talk."

"Oh, I will, Daddy. Talk to you later." I hung up the phone and looked into the mirror on my dresser at myself. "You's a baddddd bitch." I laughed and fell back on my bed ready to finish what I had started before I was interrupted by my father.

Knock . . . knock. . . . knock.

"Yeah," I called out to Alex on the other side of the door. I was interrupted from my pleasure once again.

"Can I come in?"

I blew out a frustrated breath before I answered. "Hold on." I went to my closet and pulled out a satin purple robe and tied it around me as tight as I could and went to my door and opened it.

"What?" I stood in my doorway with the door halfway open. I needed to nip this in the bud and get back to what I was doing: Me.

"Can you come out into the living room for a moment? I need to talk to you about some stuff."

"Can it wait till tomorrow?" I huffed. "I'm busy."

"Come on, Ash. Give me a break with all that evil mess and come out here." He looked sincere so I did what was asked of me and made my way out of my room and flopped down on the couch. I grabbed an apple out of the fruit bowl on the table and started eating it. I still planned on getting a nut in my room after this talk. I usually get the munchies afterward, so I killed two birds with one stone. He sat across from me as he began to talk.

"First, Ash, can I ask you where you got the money to get the car that is parked outside?"

"Here we go again. All up in my business." I rolled my eyes. *This is shit getting old.* "Does it really matter?"

"No . . . but I'm concerned about your well -being. You're my sister and I don't want to see you get hurt or anything like that because of some foolishness." He had the most sincere look on his face. I had to admit he was always protective of me. Even though I gave him hell most of the time. You know . . . typical female, never pleased.

"I got a boyfriend and he paid for it."

Alex looked at me real hard and then burst out into a laughing fit. I just stared at him like he was crazy until he got himself together. You would have thought I was one of the queens of comedy the way he was laughing.

"Yeah. . . . okay. Ash . . . for real, you don't have to worry about me asking you another question. That was a good one though. Boyfriend . . . hahahahah." He laughed for a few more seconds and then moved on.

"You finished?" I asked seriously.

"Yeah, I am. I also wanted to tell you that I ran into this guy who I think is our grandfather."

"Okay?"

"Well, he was on some real crazy madness and I couldn't get any info out of him about our birth father. I'm still working on finding others, especially his mom . . . I just haven't been able to locate her. I think she may have changed her name back to her maiden name or something, because Parks isn't her last name. I have been through my entire list and came up empty. I might go back and talk to old dude to see if he would let up some info that he has about her. That might be a big mistake because that dude was certifiably crazy."

"Yeah . . . okay. Do what you got to do. Just remember what I said, let me know about them if they have any money. Other than that, leave me out of it. Like I said before, I'm fine with the family I have already." With that I got up, grabbed me a bottle of water from the refrigerator, some Chips Ahoy and made it back to my room to get it on. But before I got it on I sat back and thought about what Alex just told me. He said old dude was our grandfather and that he was "off his rocker." In the back of my mind I thought it may be true that I may have some mental issues, but that was something I would have to worry about later on. Besides, I don't think I'm *that* crazy . . . just a little wild.

Chapter 24

Shawn
. . . Remember?
May 8th 8:23 P.M.

"Mona, do you think I spoiled Ashley?" I asked my wife as we sat in the living room. She was on the love seat and I was on the sofa which was diagonal to each other. The kids were outside playing in the yard. I had just got off the phone with Ashley about an hour ago and was wondering where I went wrong with her. Mona was reading a book, which she did most of the time, while I had the newspaper. We looked like an old married couple.

"Why you ask that?" she momentarily looked up from her book and asked.

"I think she is acting out and up over there in California."

"What makes you think that?"

"Well, the conversation I had with her earlier wasn't a friendly one. It seemed like I was talking to James on the phone." Her eyebrows raised and then she looked at me really hard.

"Huh?" She put the bookmarker in her book to save her place and then put it on the coffee table in front of her. "She can't be acting like James because—" She paused mid-sentence. Like she was going back down our history with James and then she finished her statement. "Okay . . . What are we gonna do about it?

"We?" I asked bewildered.

"Yes . . . she is *our* daughter."

"I know Mona . . . I just think that it is my fault she is like this."

"How so?"

"Well, my mom did the same thing I did to Ashley when I was a child."

"You losing me." She cocked her head to the side. "What are you trying to say?"

"My mother knew that I was being molested and she tried her best to shield me from it by taking me on trips and simply putting it, spoiling me."

"Okay?"

"Mona, my mother made my situation worse by not dealing with it, but covering it up. I went buck-wild. . . . remember?"

"Yeah . . . you are right about that." She smiled.

"I did the same thing to Ashley and now lord knows what she has gotten herself into out there." I sat back in my chair and rubbed my now-throbbing temple.

"So what are you going to do about it?"

"I need to pray first. I am going to need some serious help with getting this situation rectified. I am going to need to be as up-front as possible about James and all the mess he put us through and I need to do it soon before it's too late."

Chapter 25

Wallace
Snooping
May 10th 2:23 P.M.

Here I was again on another Saturday afternoon daddy-sitting at my parents' house. My sister/brother was with his best friend. And my mom was at a church function again. I was dusting and cleaning around the house, but that was very little. My mother was an expert cleaner and she made sure everything was in place most of the time. I had to find something to do besides stare at my father, because he had little conversation for me and I didn't have much to say to him either. There was still resentment there and I guess we both knew it. I just didn't know why he had it for me. I really didn't care that much either. What kept flowing through my mind was the fact that he basically turned Robert and David out. I still was stuck on stupid about that.

I was wondering if my mother knew. I had no idea how to tell her or evidence to show her if I indeed had to be the bearer of bad news. I left my father upstairs in his own shit literally and figuratively.

"I didn't come back for all of this." I frowned my face up in the bathroom mirror of the mini-bathroom next to the kitchen. I was overwhelmed with James's past and now my family's secrets were seeping out as well. I had to make myself busy so I decided to go down to the basement and see if I could find some of my old stuff that was packed away.

I opened the basement door and a cool air hit me and caused me to breathe in and out really strong. Like a smoker take a breath after a puff on a cigarette. I began the descend down the steps and I remembered that the basement was broken down into three rooms: laundry, my father's home office, and storage. I walked past the first door and then the second one and got to the last one. I opened the door and felt on the side of the wall for a switch to turn the light on. I rummaged through Christmas boxes filled with ornaments, cards and various other ornaments. Then I came upon the boxes with the names of all of us children: David, Robert, and then me. I only had one box and I pulled up an old rusty metal chair out of the corner of the room and sat down with me and my box full of memories.

The first thing I saw when I opened the box was my chef's hat that my mother had brought me with I was eleven years old. I pulled it out and tried it on for wear. It was too small. I didn't have dreads at the time when I first got it. I smiled because I also saw the apron that my mother had brought me as well. There was a tear on the side where my father tried to snatch it off of me, when he saw that I had it on.

"Only sissies cook," he barked at me. I held firm to the apron with all my strength. I was about to give in when my mother came to the rescue.

"Ronald," she pleaded with her eyes as she spoke to my father. His gripped loosened as he stared at my mother and then at me. I had on a pitiful frown that I hope with get him off my case.

"Okay." He let go and moved on toward wherever he was going to before he spotted me. I looked up at my mother with a sparkling smile that made her kiss me on the forehead. It was my thanks for her rescuing me once again. You see I didn't hate my father then. I was actually confused by his constant prodding me to "man up." In my mind I was like "It's just food, dammit!" but he saw it a whole different way. I still didn't understand. I sifted through the box some more and found a composition notebook that I used to write recipes in as a boy. I opened it up and found my favorite recipe of all: oatmeal cookies. It was my mom's own secret recipe. I smiled as I remembered the time she gave this to me. She said it was a secret and to tell no one. Come to find out her recipe was the same as anyone else's. She made me feel special no matter what went on in the house. Don't get it twisted my mom was just as good to my brothers, just in their own way. My mother knew how to spread the love evenly. Thinking on the secrets and turmoil that is going on right now made me think that kept secrets were like time bombs threatening to take a family down and maybe a few bystanders as well. I didn't know what to expect next or what else was going to be exposed. After a few more seconds of rummaging through the box I decided to take it with me when I left. I'm sure she wouldn't mind me taking it. After all it was my things.

I gathered up the box, switched off the lights and made my way back down the hall toward the stairs. When I stopped and looked at the door that led to my father's home office, I knew it was unusual for me to be nosy, but I had to see why my father was so secretive with his psychologist practice.

I sat my box down and peeked up the steps for a few seconds. My mom said she didn't know how long she was going to be gone, but I didn't want to be caught in a position of disrespect for my father's privacy. And I didn't want my mother to be disappointed in me, even as an adult. I heard nothing so I twisted the knob that opened the door. I grabbed my box in one hand and felt for a light with the other. Once I found the light I made my way in fully. I closed the door behind me, sat my box on the floor and looked around his makeshift office. Brown and white boxes were scattered about with names and dates marked on each one. A big brown desk with a lamp on it and an old television sat on a stand with a VCR attached to it.

"What are you looking for Wallace?" I asked myself. I had no clue. I just looked. All those years of my father coming home and spending hours and hours down here had made me curious as a child. Now that he was out of practice, I figured what could the harm be to just take a look at all of the crazies my father tried to help. I sat down in a chair and just looked at all of the boxes.

"He sure did help a lot of people," I mumbled to myself. I pulled my hair back into a ponytail and started opening box after box.

Paranoid, delusional, out of touch with reality, schizophrenic . . . these were some of the terms I read on some of the files my father had in boxes. There were files so thick I know my father had to have been treating some of these people for years.

After about a half hour of looking I became bored with it all and decided to get back upstairs just in case my father needed to be fed or something. I bent down to get my book off of the floor and what I saw made me drop to my knees and inspect it a little further to see if I was seeing what I saw.

"John Parks?" I pulled out a box with the name I knew all too well on it. "My father treated him too?"

I sat the box on the desk and opened up the top to see what was in it. In the box were folders filled with papers and VHS tapes. I was confused because in the other box I looked through I saw only folders.

"What's up with that?" I wondered out loud. There were at least twenty tapes in the box with dates on them. I didn't know if I had time to look at the tapes or what was on them, but I knew it had to be important for it to have been taped. I didn't want to risk my mother or Rebecca walking in on me so I packed the entire John Parks box into my box and placed the box in the trunk of my car for when it was time for me to leave. I didn't have a VCR at home because they were so obsolete, so I had to find one or somebody with one that I could trust. I sat in my parents' house for another hour before my mom came home. I kissed her good night and exited the house in hurry.

The next morning I called Alex to see if he knew of anyone who had a VCR or a device that could read VHS tapes. I hit the jackpot when he said he had one. I asked him if he could come over and bring it with him when he came. He reluctantly said yes, because I told him it was extremely important.

Chapter 26

Grace
Grievances
May 13th 2:13 P.M.

I sat in my mother's living room and looked around at my past. Putting together my mother's obituary was hard work. My aunt Bella was making it a lot easier with the help she was giving. I didn't want to put too much pressure on her because she was up in age too. I had just suggested she go home a little while after she came to help me sort through some pictures and stuff. She wanted to put certain pictures in the obituary that I didn't want. I got frustrated with her, but she kept telling me that the truth will make me free and that I should come to grips with my past before it ruins the rest of my life. I wanted to tell her it was already too late, but I know she would have been convincing me otherwise. I still wasn't trying to hear all of that. Truth is I just I want to be alone. I had some grievances with myself, my momma, and John.

My mother still had pictures of me as a child up around the living room. Looking at them made my head hurt. There is nothing like the truth staring you in the face at every turn. I wanted to throw all of the pictures of my youth in the trash, because they were painful reminders. I got off the chair and walked over to the mantle over the fireplace and picked up the picture of me, my mom, and my sister, Sherry. I was about eight in that picture. It was right around the time John came to stay with us for a little bit. It wasn't long after his arrival that my life as a child took a drastic turn.

"No!" I yelled out and threw the picture across the room. I picked up the next picture and did the same. Before long I was just throwing stuff everywhere. I didn't care as I took my grievances out on the inanimate objects in my mother's living room.

"Why me God!?" I hollered out. "I just wanted to be normal!" Tears rolled down my face. My makeup was now a mess, so I sluggishly walked to the mini-bathroom next to the kitchen. I ran some water and grabbed a bar of Dove soap from the shower caddy and started to scrub my face. Minutes later I grabbed a washcloth and patted my face dry.

I was now looking at the real me, no makeup. After all these years I saw the old me for the first time in a long time. I have been putting on makeup for so long now that I forgot how I looked without it.

"There you are." I looked at myself in the mirror. "You've been hiding all this time." An image of me as a child popped up in the mirror. I quickly turned away again. I thought I was losing my mind. I gripped the sides of the sink and shook my head from side to side wildly as I held it down toward the bowl. I didn't want to look up again. I didn't want to go back. I didn't want to remember. But that was all I could do lately... in the classroom, my office, on the drive to and from work, and even in the bed with my husband.

"You're gone! You're gone! . . . you're gone! . . . get . . . out . . . of . . . my . . . headddd!" I grabbed and pulled at my hair as I fell back against the wall and slid down like gravity was pulling me down. I then began to bang my head against the wall as if I was trying to beat the memories out.

The last bang on the wall sent one of my mother's thick ceramic masks that were hanging on the wall careening down, knocking me out cold.

I awoke about an hour later to a splitting headache. I weakly pulled myself up off of the floor by grabbing onto the sink and pulling up. I looked in the mirror to see if I had any damage to my head. Thankfully there was no blood shed. But I did feel a lump though.

"I can't believe I just acted like that." I spoke softly to myself. "Girl, get yourself together." I opened the medicine cabinet and pulled out a bottle of Aleve, so I could get rid of the splitting headache I now had. I walked into the kitchen and pulled out the pitcher of water. I grabbed a glass from the cabinet, sat down, threw two pills in my mouth and threw back the water like it was an alcoholic beverage. I rubbed my temple to try getting some relief right now, but it was to no avail. I heard my phone ringing in the living room, so I walked as fast as I could to get to it.

"Hello," I answered. It was my husband.

"Hey, baby." He sounded a little down. "Where are you?"

"I'm at my mom's house," I said solemnly as I could. I was going for as much sympathy as I could get.

"I . . . I thought I was supposed to go with you?" he huffed into the phone. He sounded disappointed. "Why didn't you wake me this morning so I could come?"

"I'm sorry, baby," I spoke as sweetly as I could. "I just wanted to do this alone." A couple of days before he asked if he could help me with the arrangements and be the support I needed in my time of grief. I told him yes, but the night before I sexed him so good that I knew that he would sleep well through the night and the morning. I snuck out of bed and quietly got myself together and snuck out of the house without his knowledge. I was wrong for it, but I just wasn't ready for him to meet any of my family. What little I had anyway.

"But you're my wife," It sounded as if his feelings were hurt. "You shouldn't be doing this stuff alone."

"I know . . . it's just that . . ."

"I'm your husband," he sharply cut me off. "When are you going to start treating me like the man of the house?"

"Baby, you are the man of the house," I said, a little shocked that he had given me such attitude. "And I wasn't alone, my aunt was here for a little while and she helped me a great deal. I will be home shortly, so don't worry. I will more than make it up too you, daddy," I whispered the last part and added some seduction when I said *daddy*.

"Well," he breathed out an exhausted breath. "I'm going to the funeral, if you like it or not. I want to at least see what your mother looked like in person, instead of the pictures you show me, even if I have to sleep in your car. "

"Okay, baby . . . whatever you want. I'll see you later." I pressed the end button on the phone and sat it back down on the table in front of me. I looked at all the damage I had done to the living room earlier and shook my head.

"It still ain't as messy as my life is right now." I shook my head, got up and started to clean up the mess I made. I made mental plans to do the same for my life. No matter the cost. I left my mother's house and made it back to my house in about an hour. I was exhausted, but I still did what I said I was going to do for my husband. I made it up to him and the smile that was now across his face, as he lay in the bed naked, let me know I had done a good job indeed.

Chapter 27

Shawn
 Apologies
May 14th 3:01 P.M.

I sat on my living room sofa and just stared at James's obituary. To this day Mona still didn't know that I had gone to his funeral. She still thought that I was glad that he died. Well, I wasn't glad he died. When I actually looked back over the whole situation; he actually saved my life. If he had not dragged me out of the closet like he did I probably would have ended up getting worse and sloppier with my down-low lifestyle. It may not have been the conventional way that for it to have been done, but it worked. I was now saved and free.

James and I had a lot in common and I really didn't see it until now. He and I both had been the only child who both struggled with our sexuality. It may not have seemed like James was struggling with it, but I knew he did. Most men and women who struggle with homosexuality just want to be normal.

"I'm sorry, James." I started to cry like a baby. "Man, I owe you so much. I didn't see it then, but you were crying out for help and I was too wrapped up in my mess to see it. Hurt people, hurt people. You were hurting man. You must have been hurting bad."

I started to wonder how his mom must have felt to bury her only child. I started to imagine my mom standing over my casket and my wife and kids doing the same and the grief that his mother must have felt on that day overtook me as I sat on the my sofa all alone. I cried so hard it soaked my shirt.

"What can I do to make this right? I got to make this right. For James and my kids. . . . his kids."

I got up off of the sofa and went into my office to make a few calls and track down some info that I had sitting in front of me all of this time.

"I'm going to get this mess done and over with. Now!"

Chapter 28

David
Threats and Promises
May 15th 12:03 A.M.

It was late at night and I was in bed when my phone started to ring. I quickly grabbed it and looked at it to see who was calling me. It was John. I eased out of bed and crept downstairs to avoid waking my wife.

"Hello," I answered in a hushed tone as I made my way into my house office.

"Where the fuck have you been?" he barked. "I've been calling you and you been ignoring my calls."

"I've been busy," I tried to explain, calmly. "This semester has been quite a busy one and—"

"Fuck that shit," he yelled back. "Your ass ain't never been that busy before. What you think I'm crazy like all the rest of these muthafuckas?"

"Nah . . . nah . . . that's not even it." I was lying, it was the whole truth and nothing but the truth. I didn't need to tell him that to escalate the situation even further. "My wife lost her mother and I've been helping her deal with that."

"Yeah . . . uhhhh huh! I bet." He calmed down a little. "So when you coming back over?"

"Coming over?" I acted like I was confused.

"Yeah, muthafucka . . . Coming over to fuck me like you do on the regular. You ain't forget how to do that shit did you. I thought I trained you well." He laughed out loud.

"I don't think it's going to be a good idea for me to see you for a while. My wife will be on leave for a minute and she will notice."

"What's that got to do with me?"

"Nothing, I'm just saying that I can't right now."

"Well how long then?" *Forever, bitch*! is what I wanted to yell out, but didn't know his state of mind right now. Then again, I did know. He was nuts. And I don't know why it took me this long to see it.

"I don't know when." I said it as sweet as I could. I had to be nice as possible.

"David . . . what you take me for? A fool?" he asked.

"I know when someone is trying to avoid me. I'm old but I damn sure ain't senile. I got my shit together."

"You sure?" I blurted out by accident.

"Oh, so you do think that I am crazy like all these other muthafuckas."

Silence.

"No response huh? I knew it. I treated you good all these years and this is how you do me. You just like the rest. But I can show you more than I can tell you. You gonna regret this, muthafucka! I mean that!" Click!

He hung up in my ear. I was floored and nervous at the same time. I don't know what John is capable of doing. Man, I should have cut him off a long time ago. I went to bed scared to wake up tomorrow. I didn't know where this dude was going to pop up. He was liable to do anything. Even at his age.

Shit! I huffed lightly as I cuddled close to my wife.

Chapter 29

Grace
The Big Bang Theory
May 17th 11:12 A.M.

I was dressed in all black with a veiled black hat to match. I stood in front of my full-length mirror in my walk-in closet. A tear slid out of my eye and down my check.

"Hey, babe," he walked up behind me and slid his hand around my waist and pulled me in an embrace. "It's going to be okay. We got each other. 'Til death do us part . . . remember?"

I looked at us in the mirror and burst into a loud sob. I was mourning my mom, but myself as well. *Today might be the day.* I couldn't help but think that the picture I just saw in the mirror could all end today. "I . . . I know, baby." I turned around, with his arms still around me, kissed him on the cheek. He lifted my veil, pulled me in and kissed me long and hard. For a few seconds, my mind was taken off of my drama and on my husband. I didn't deserve him and I knew it. *He probably would be better off without me*, I thought.

"Mmm baby, we got to go. The family car is waiting on us to go." I pulled away and looked into the mirror to make sure my makeup was still intact. My mind flashed to Ashley for a second. She had been missing for a minute. I hadn't even noticed that she hadn't called me or anything. I breathed in a breath of fresh air. At least I didn't have to worry about her for a while.

I pulled my veil back down and grabbed my clutch purse off of the bed and made my way down to the car that was waiting on us. My husband was already outside waiting by the car as I exited the house. I sucked in another breath of fresh air as I walked down the walkway toward the car. My husband opened the door and helped me in and then got in himself. We pulled of toward my aunt's house and then toward the funeral parlor.

My aunt kept on giving my husband funny looks like she wanted to ask him something. I gave her a look back, daring her. I needed her to mind her business. My mother had given me power of attorney over her final affairs but I gave most of the duties to my aunt since she was around my mother more and knew what she liked better than me.

After about twenty minutes we finally pulled up to the funeral parlor and made our way in. Fresh flowers, cold air and death filled the air. There were already people there, but I didn't know most of them. I had been gone for so long and I was older.

My aunt was in front of me and she stood at the casket to view my mother first. She sobbed a little and leaned in to kiss her on the cheek and then she walked away and sat down on the front row. It was my turn. My legs began to wobble and moans escaped my mouth. My husband had his hand around my waist. "M—M—Mamaaa." I took a step closer, but it still seemed like it was so far away. My body did another dip, but my husband held me tight and wouldn't let me fall.

"Come on, baby . . . You can do it," he coached me. I shook my head from side to side. All of the good memories of my mama flooded my mind and now I was looking at her cold hard body.

I knew there was a line forming behind me, but I didn't care, because this was my mama. I heard a couple *who's thats* but I paid it no mind. I finally made my way to the casket. And that's when the waterworks really began. She looked so good. I know you hear people say it, but she really did: just like she did when she was alive. My aunt had dressed her in a pretty pink dress. Her hair was in pin curls. After a few more minutes of sobbing and moaning I made my way to my seat next to my aunt. My husband stood there for a few more minutes and then he came back to sit with me.

But who I saw in line a few minutes after the line died down made me go from sad to rage in all but a few seconds. My hands started to shake. My aunt grabbed my hand, probably because she though I was emotional about my mother being dead in front of me, but I was past that as of now.

John Parks, you sick bastard. What are you doing here? I thought as he glanced over toward the family row I was sitting on and then walked toward us. I looked at my aunt, and then at my husband, who was locked in a trance as well. I didn't know what to do as he walked over and shook my husband's hand with a wicked grin on his face. He then leaned in to embrace me. This muthafucka was so old he didn't even recognize me or maybe it was the veil that I had on, but I knew who he was all too well. I want to fuck his ass up on the spot. His musty ass looked the same. Like a child molester. I watched my aunt get up and hug him as well. She didn't seem shocked at all. *Maybe her ass is in shock that he showed up to the funeral too.*

Rage in me built up as the service went on. They read the obituary, but both my husband and I were not paying attention. Every time I glanced at him he was looking at John. That shit puzzled me, but I brushed it off as nothing but my mind playing tricks on me because I was so furious right now. Then they called for people to say a few words and guess who popped up. John's simple ass. I was beyond rage now. My husband had my hand and I squeezed it so hard that he had to let go and wring it out.

John went on and on about the good person my mother was and how she was always willing to give him anything he asked. I was seeing red and as he stepped off the podium I charged him like a linebacker.

"You sick *bastard*! How could you show up here?" I hit him with all that I could as he fell into my mother's casket, almost knocking it over. I was feeling real good right about now as I watched him stagger a little dazed, but I quickly went in again knocking him to the ground. There were people trying to pull me off of him, but it was to no avail. "You . . . " Punch! "Sick" Punch! "mutha" Punch! "fucka" Punch! I was whooping his ass real good, almost oblivious to the fact that it was my mother's funeral. I was sitting on him like a kid in a playground fight.

"You"—punch—"fucked"—punch—"up"—punch— "my"—punch—"life." After a few more minutes, I was sheer exhausted when I got up off of him. I looked around a little embarrassed at my actions, to see my husband and aunt still sitting in their seats like it was a stage play. I brushed off my dress and went back to my seat like the lady I was. A couple of men I didn't know helped John's ass out of the room, while he yelled, "Who in the hell was that crazy bitch!"

That pretty much ended the service for me. My aunt and husband had to help me to the family car after pallbearers wheeled my momma out. I silently asked God and my momma for forgiveness for showing out at her home-going today.

We buried my mother right next to my sister. I kissed her grave as we walked back to the car, after they lowered momma into the ground. Before we got into the car, my aunt walked up to me and squeezed me real hard. "Baby, I'm having a family reunion-birthday celebration in a week or two. I'm telling you, not asking you to come, so you can be arounds ya family. We shouldn't have to have someone to leave us to get together. Ya hear?"

I saw the pain in her eyes as she stared at me for a few seconds. "Oh, and don't be afraid to be yourself either when ya come."

"Yes, ma'am." My husband was standing right there so ducking this event was almost impossible.

We all got in the car and in silence we rode back to my aunt's house for the repast. My husband and I declined to go in. I was exhausted and I guess my husband was too. The look on his face was a blank one, one of confusion.

"You okay, baby?" he asked as he pulled me toward him and embraced me. "What was all that about at the funeral home?"

"Huh?" I acted confused.

"Joh—I mean the guy at the funeral. You whipped his ass. Why?"

"Honey, I really don't want to discuss it right now. I am so tired. I just want to crawl into bed and sleep." My head fell on his shoulder. I was more than done: mentally and physically. My moments of molestation swirled in my head like a merry-go-round. One incident after the other. *I can't do this much longer.* It seemed like the ride home was shorter then it was when we left. I slowly crept up the stairs and into my bedroom. I stripped off my clothes and fell onto my bed in sheer exhaustion. The truth was barreling down on me like a full-fledged army tank.

I blinked back tears as I went over a pivotal point in my life. I was like seven or eight when "it" happened.

I was in my room playing like I usually do. My momma was passed out on the couch like she usually was after she had her fill of liquor. So was my uncle John.

I had no friends to play with and my sister was over a friend's house spending the night. I was all alone in my room. So I thought.

"You look so good," I told myself as I looked in the floor-length mirror on my wall next to my dresser. I had on an old dress of my sister's. It was pink with small silky-type flowers on it and it had ruffles on the sleeves and the bottom. I had some of her clips and her hair extensions in my hair. I was the big girl my sister was, in the mirror, that day. I twirled and twirled. I was singing Cyndi Lauper's "Girls Just Wanna Have Fun" into a hairbrush like I was a professional.

I was interrupted by a clapping of hands. I had an audience I didn't know about. I was completely caught off guard. I froze like an Eskimo.

"You really look good." He smiled a mischievous grin.

"Th—thanks." My voice quivered and shook. He was looking at me like I looked at a happy meal that had just been placed in front of me. I didn't know that my life would be changed forever after this day. He walked in and sat on my bed.

"Can you sing it for me again?" he asked so nicely. I didn't know what was going on. I felt it was wrong, but he was my uncle so I figured it was okay. I trusted him. He was always so nice to me. "You look *so* good doing it."

I obliged and began my childish rendition of the adult song. I did all the dance moves in the video as best I could. He smiled the whole time. When I finished, I sat down beside him on the bed. I felt ashamed, like what I was doing was wrong: Dancing in front of a grown man.

"That dress really fits you."

"It's my sister's old dress." I was a little big for my age and it fit snugly. "I was going to put it back when I finished." I lied. I had taken the dress from an old box in the basement and tucked it in the back of my closet for safekeeping.

"Don't worry, it will be our little secret," he reassured me.

"Okay," I said as meekly as I could. On the inside I was ecstatic that I could keep what I found. In exchange my uncle would ask me to let him "do things." I felt it was wrong, but I did it to continue to get to do stuff I like doing. That shit fucked me up for life. Because pretty soon he would make sure my mother stayed liquored up and then he and I would be free to "play around." Me wanting to be a big girl turned into me being a full- fledged woman. I was doing all the things that a child should never do. He started making demands that I now know was molestation. I felt it was my fault that it escalated to the point of no return, so I never said a thing.

That is until later on in high school when things escalated and me and my mom would get into it about my life. She thought I was headed down the wrong road and I felt like it was what I wanted to do. In the end, I just did me and she accepted it. The fact that I told her that her drinking and bingeing and not paying attention to what company she had in her house, namely, Uncle John, didn't hurt either. She was so overdone with guilt that she kept quiet most of the time. It wasn't completely her fault, but it wasn't completely mines either. Me prancing around the house like I was at a young age in front of John didn't help either. I was a little extra with it. I see it so clearly now. I was a willing participant. I blamed others for something that I already wanted. I was flawed mentally way before John entered the picture.

"Dammit!" I punched my pillow. "It's too late to say I'm sorry. It's too late for me to take back the blame."

Chapter 30

David
Sob Story
May 17th 3:04 P.M.

I sat in my home office, confused by today's events at the funeral. My wife wasn't herself today at all. I mean I know we all express grief differently, but she went all the way off and then some. The sad thing is I was glad that she had jumped on John at the funeral, because he was making me a nervous wreck. I just needed to know why she did it. It had to be something strenuous for her to attack him at her mother's funeral.

I pulled out the gun that I had in my waistband and put it on my desk. I had carried it with me to the funeral, because I just couldn't be sure if John was following me or not. I made a mental note to carry it everywhere I went now, after seeing him at the funeral. I was dumbfounded at the fact that he had showed up at my wife's mother's funeral. I wondered how they were connected.

My mind was racing a mile a minute. My phone started ringing.

"Hello," I answered still puzzled.

"Who was that bitch that jumped me at the funeral? Your wife?"

"Ahhh . . . yeah . . . why?"

"Because that bitch whipped my ass and don't know who the hell she was or what I did to her. But I tell you what. Her ass fights like a man." He laughed. "I haven't had my ass whipped like that since I was a boy. You ain't got nothing to worry about when I come to her protecting your soft ass." He laughed again. "You gots you a good- ass fighter on ya hands."

"Yeah," was all I could manage get out. I was glancing through my wife's mother's obituary and something had caught my attention and I couldn't really pay attention to what he was saying. "I—I gotta call you back." I hung up the phone without getting a response from him. I didn't need one.

I walked up to our bedroom with the obituary in hand.

"Babe. . . . babe . . ." I shook my wife lightly so I wouldn't startle her.

"Huh? . . . huh?" She rolled over. Her eyes were swollen and red. I figured it was from all that crying she did at the funeral. "What's wrong?" She must have seen the puzzled look on my face.

"I was reading the obituary and I didn't see your name. All I saw was your sister's name and a Thomas Jones. Who is that? You never mentioned you had a brother."

I was looking at her intensely. She stared back at me for a few seconds. Her eyes began to water and then a couple of tears fell down her cheeks.

"It's my deceased brother . . . he died when I was eight. A car accident. He ran out into the street and got hit by a car. He was instantly killed." She cried harder now.

"So why wasn't your name mentioned?" I asked. "Well, my mom never forgave me for it. That's why I haven't been to see her as much as I should and why I kept you away from my family. It was too hard to bear. She practically cut me out of her life and she instructed my aunt not to put me in the obituary since I let her only son die. I was supposed to be watching him, but I was doing what I wanted to and let him run into the street."

"I—I'm sorry." I felt a tear run down my face as I got up off the bed. "Go back to bed. I'm sorry I brought it up."

I wandered back downstairs feeling really low. I was sorry I brought up such a painful memory like the one she just told me about.

Chapter 31

Ashley
Caught Up
May 23rd 9:30 A.M.

"Ashley, where are you going?" I heard Alex ask me as I was headed to the door. I turned around to see him standing in the doorway of his room with a smirk on his face.

"I'm going to hang out with a couple of my friends." I smiled as I continued my way toward the door.

"Be careful out there. And be good."

I looked back toward him. "I've always been good. I got this . . . remember that." I boasted.

He shook his head and went back into his room. I laughed, threw on my shades and left apartment. I hopped in my car and made a beeline toward Ebony's place. While driving, I thought to myself.

I got to leave Grace alone for a minute. That situation is weirder than most; almost unheard of in most settings. But, it was real, so I took advantage. I was that bitch that did things most would shy at doing. This crazy-bitch thing is taking its toll on me. It was getting to me. I really had some issues that I need to get help for. No joke. A sister was warped I tell you. I wasn't totally gone, but a bitch had her moments of insanity. I believe everyone does from time to time. It was just that my shit was on blastoff for longer periods of time than normal.

I pulled up to Ebony's apartment and watched as she ran out of the house and straight toward my car.

"Whef!" She blew out a tired breath as she hopped in my car. "I hate doing this behind my man's back and in front of the lord." She buckled her seat belt as I pulled off.

"Okay," I nonchalantly said.

"I had to tell him I was going to choir rehearsal. I don't like lying to him." I saw a tear slide down her face.

I was stopped at a light so I looked at her and said, "Well it's partially true . . . You would want to make sing tonight when we getting down tonight." I laughed. She didn't find it funny.

"So where are we going?" she asked with her hands folded on her chest and her mouth twisted.

"Don't worry about that. You'll know when we get there."

I was all giddy and ready to have a very good time.

After about twenty minutes of driving, I pulled up to my destination with a huge smile on my face. It was a detached Victorian-style house. I wondered how homegirl could afford all of this but I was one who minded my business.

"Let's go." I looked over at Ebony whose mouth was still twisted. "I'ma need you to get your shit together while we in here. Don't be fucking up my mood. Feel me?"

"Yeah . . . okay." She opened her door and got out. I did the same.

We walked up to the door and I called Monique so she came to the door and let us in.

"We're here." I dialed the number and ended the call all in a few seconds.

The door swung open and Monique stood before us in a sheer negligee. Everything was hanging out: titties and ass. I looked over at Ebony and her mouth was open just as much as mine.

"Come in, ladies." Monique turned and sashayed down a small corridor and then turned toward us as we walked in and closed the door. There was some music playing but I didn't know who it was. It was soft and sensual though.

"What's going on?" Ebony leaned in and whispered in my ear. "Why are we here?"

"Bitch, you about to get fucked up if you don't stop asking questions," I spoke out of the side of my mouth and made it look like I was being seductive to Monique. I wanted to bang Ebony in the side of her neck for asking so many damn questions. If she didn't know by now that I was in control, I was going to have to cut her loose and let Monique step in her spot. Monique was the chick I met at the restaurant spot. I don't know why Ebony didn't recognize her, because she chewed me out about looking at her ass. She wouldn't know I was looking if she wasn't looking too, which made me think she was paying attention to her surroundings like she was supposed to be. I made a mental note to check her ass when I dropped her off later.

"Y'all ready?" Monique asked as she walked back by us and up some stairs. She had on high heels that made her calf muscles look fabulous. "Come on upstairs."

We both did as we were told. I let Ebony go ahead of me. I didn't want any surprises and shit. I wasn't ready to get my ass beat or anything like that. If somebody had a head start if something popped off and it was going to be me. Pussy ain't worth dying over.

Finally we walked down a small corridor and into a large room with a huge bed canopy bed with really thick beams. Everything in her room was pink: the carpet, pillows, comforter, paint, and window curtains . . . everything. The bitch must have even dyed the muthafuckin' cat pink too. Her fluffy ass scurried out the room, because she must have known that she was the only pussy that was not going to get fucked tonight. I shook my head at that mess. Some people take shit too far.

"Take yo shit off," I turned and looked at Ebony who, shockingly, was all smiles. She was a weird-ass girl I tell you. I started to undress and Monique started to gyrate and swing around her bedpost like she was a second-hand stripper. I almost laughed when she slipped and fell off the bed and rolled on to the carpet, but I didn't. She played it off by crawling on her hands and knees toward Ebony, who was naked by now, and she crawled up her body like she was a mountain and started to lick her body all over. Then she made her way up to her mouth and she started to tongue her down real good. My pussy was throbbing and twitching like a man's dick. I looked over at the bed and saw a couple of dildos and vibrators all stretched out in an assorted variety. *This bitch is a full- fledged freak*! I picked one and pushed the others to the side. I spread my legs as far as they went and started to fuck myself with the dildo that had an electronic stimulator for your clit. It was a high- tech orgasm dynamo. Monique and Ebony were now on the floor in a sixty-nine position moaning and sucking like there was no tomorrow. You would have thought Ebony was unmarried and without a child the way she was sucking on Monique's pussy and tits.

"Ahh . . . ahhh . . . ahhhhhh," I moaned as the toy did its job in seconds and gave me the orgasm that made my legs go limp for a few seconds. I didn't even notice that Monique and Ebony had gotten up off the floor and onto the bed where I was.

One was doing my tits and the other was sucking my womb. My moaning escalated as I drew near to another orgasm.

"Yes . . . baby . . . yesssss." I hollered out in ecstasy. Monique got off the bed again and I watched her put on a strap-on dildo.

"Get on all fours," she instructed Ebony. Ebony crawled over top of me and started kissing me on all fours while Monique positioned herself behind her. You knew when Monique had hit Ebony's spot when her head flew back and she started to buck. I was still a little weak from the last orgasm, but I still managed to get one of Ebony double-D's in my mouth and suck like I was breast-feeding. We were all moaning and Monique was fucking Ebony like she was a real man and Ebony was her bitch.

"Yeah . . . yeah . . . yeah . . . yeah . . . yeah . . ." Ebony was stuck on repeat as Monique punished her. Ebony had started to kiss me again as she neared her climax. She climaxed then she collapsed on me. I rolled Ebony off of me, took the strap-on dildo from Monique and fucked her like she fucked Ebony a few seconds earlier. We all took turns on each for over two hours before Ebony and I ended up showering and leaving to go home.

"You have fun?" I asked as I pulled off toward the highway. She had that look on her face. The look I hated. Regret.

"It's too late to be feeling sorry for what you have done now." I shook my head. She was on the verge of messing up my day with her guilt. "Did you enjoy yourself?"

"Wellllll . . ." She stammered. "Yeah, I did."

A big smile came across my face. I didn't let her know I was getting paid for letting Monique fuck her. Homegirl gave me three hundred dollars too. Ebony didn't need to know all that though. She got something out of it anyway.

Twenty minutes later we pulled back up in front of her house.

"Can you give me one more orgasm before you leave?" she asked with pleading eyes.

"Baby girl, I'm tired. Maybe tomorrow." I was tired and I did have classes in the morning.

"Pleaseeee," she begged.

"Where are your son and husband?"

"He's at work. He works nights at Wal-mart. My son is over my husband's mom's house." Her eyes were pleading me to give in.

"All right, but just one and I'm gone." *A bitch's job is never done*, I thought to myself. I parked my car and we made our way toward her house. She opened her door and we walked in. All the lights were out but I followed her as we made our way to her living room.

She flicked on the light and sat down on the sofa. She unbuttoned her pants and pulled them down to her ankles. I went in for the pussy like it was a piece of watermelon.

"So this is what you call choir practice?" I heard a male voice say from behind us. We both jumped up and were staring down the barrel of a 9 mm gun.

"Ba—ba—baby . . . What you doing home?" she asked the dude, whom I assumed was her husband. I had only saw him one time and that was at a distance when he was picking her up from church. I did make sure I took a picture of his tags when he pulled off, so I could get the info I needed on him to move my plans to pimp her along. "I thought you were at work."

"I ain't fuckin' another dude that's for sure." He mean-mugged me. I mugged him back. I had a lot of balls for a bitch that was staring down a gun. I was scared as shit on the inside though. I wasn't ready to die just yet.

Baby, stop what you're doing, because it's not going to end well for you. The old lady's voice popped into my head. *Oh shit!* I muttered to myself in fear.

"It's not what you think." Ebony tried to explain. I shook my head in disbelief.

"So this bitch wasn't just up in between your legs licking your pussy?"

"I don't love her. I love you," she pleaded with her hands held out in front of her, stretched out toward him like she was trying to hug him. She must have forgotten that her pants were around her ankles, because she tried to step toward him and fell face-forward onto the floor. I shook my head again.

"Pull your shit up." Her husband pulled her up to her feet with one hand and with the other hand he still had the gun pointed at mc. I noticed he had a silencer on the end of it too. So if he did kill us no one would know he did it. "So you getting my moms to watch our son while you doing this chick?" he asked. I thought the question was rhetorical, but she still nodded yes.

"What this chick got that I don't have?" he asked her. Tears and snot ran down her face. And it looked like she was starting to hyperventilate too.

"I'm sorry. I didn't mean to . . . It was just—just—she made me do it," she stammered and then blurted the rest out. He cocked his head to the side in wonder as he looked at me and then at her.

"You made her do this?" he asked me. This dude must be dumb too. I can't make her like having sex with other women.

"Dude, you got this all twisted up." I spoke with authority. "I'm not a magician. I can't make her like pussy. And as far as I was making her do this; I don't have access to your apartment . . . she does. I think you need to be a little smarter about this and ask yourself a few questions. I was just a supplier in this here situation. The middleman per se."

"What you trying say? I wasn't pleasing my wife in the bedroom?" *Bingo! I think he's got it.* I wasn't going to say it though. I had checked this guy's past; he has a record. And I didn't want to be added to his list of offenses: murder.

"I think you need to ask her that. Not me. I'm going to take my leave while y'all discuss what y'all need to discuss." He thought about it for a few seconds and that gave me an opportunity to try and walk out of this apartment with everything intact.

"Baby . . . please forgive me . . . I was wrong for doing it. It was a big mistake," I heard Ebony say as I sneaked past him as he kneeled down before her.

I was at the door turning the knob, when I heard what sounded like a gun click next to my ear. I turned to see it pointed right in between my eyes. "Bitch, where you think you going?" I saw him raise his hand and the pain of the butt of the gun hitting me in the head let me know this may not end too well. Then the room went black.

I woke up tied to a chair and a duct-taped mouth. My head was spinning and it was hard for me to focus. Once my vision started to become focused I noticed that we were in a room alone.

"How does her pussy taste?" he asked me inches from my face. I blinked back tears, because I didn't know what he was going to do to me. I was tied up and lightheaded. He hit me with gun again across my face.

Wham!

I moaned in pain but he was unrelenting. He hit me again. The room started to spin again. It was spinning so bad that I thought I "saw a putty cat." I was just that dizzy.

"I can't believe she was playing me with you." He spit out a glob of spit onto my face. I felt it run down my cheek and hit me on my thigh.

Nobody knows I'm here and this crazy nut is about to take my head off. I don't know where his wife was. I was hoping that he had not killed her in a fit of rage. It wasn't looking good as he kept on going back and forth to the window. It was like he was expecting someone else to come.

"So all you do is straight pussy?" he asked me. I nodded yes.

"So you never tasted a real dick before?" I nodded no.

"Well, today is your lucky day." He laughed. I started to cry harder now because I didn't want to be raped. I watched as he unbuckled his pants and pulled out his penis.

I moaned in fear while shaking my head side to side. He had a big dick for the size of a guy he was.

"You like that?" He slapped me in the face a couple of times with it. I could tell it was getting harder with every slap on the face.

"You like it?" he yelled at me and slapped me harder with his penis. I nodded yes to appease him. "Well, you about to taste it."

He ripped the tape off of my mouth with force that caused me to cry out.

"Bitch, shut up!" he put the gun to my temple. I hushed instantly.

"Open your mouth." I hesitated. He hit me with the gun again. "Bitch, I said open it." I obliged this time and opened my mouth. Salty, sweatiness is what I tasted as he pumped my face slowly. I was fighting for oxygen, because the girth of this dick filled my mouth. Even though I didn't do dick per se, I wondered why his wife would be dipping out on all of this. An average woman didn't just pass up on a dick like this. But, then *it* happened. He came. He was a one-minute brotha. Now I knew why she stepped out on him. At least that was part of it.

"Ahhhhhhh . . . mmmmm." He began to shake violently and pulled out until the tip of his penis was on my lips. Then I felt the warmness of his seed hit the roof of my mouth causing me to gag and try to spit it up.

"Bitch, you betta swallow that shit." He held my mouth closed to ensure that I did. I swallowed to assure him that the deed was done.

"Taste good?" he asked with his face inches from mine. I silently nodded yes. He didn't know I had stored his seed underneath my tongue. I was not swallowing shit. Before he could blink I had spit his own seed right back at him in his face.

"You swallow that shit!" I boldly said. I knew I was going to die, so why not go out with a bang.

"You bitch!" He slowly wiped his face with his shirt. "You gonna die for that shit." He stood up, aimed the gun at my head.

Chapter 32

Alex
Being Schooled
May 23rd 10:15 A.M.

I was sitting in my room thinking of my girl, trying to study for finals, mulling over all the drama going on in my life right now. I got a call from Wallace asking me if I knew how to get a VHS player or something that could help him transfer one to Blu-ray disc. I just happened to have a VHS/DVD/CD/Blu-ray converter that I got from Wal-Mart when I first moved here. I was a gadget geek too. Technology was another one of my obsessions.

One late night when Ashley was asleep I went to her car and secretly attached a tracking device. Her car was a 2000 model that came without LoJack or any other kind of tracking. A couple of years ago the government mandated all cars come with one. But I know Ashley; she wanted to floss in an outdated convertible. She sure was spoiled. I can't blame her for wanting what she wants, but I was just worried about the way she was getting it. I didn't know, but did I know she didn't have a job, a legit one anyway.

"Man . . . all of this is just madness." I shook my head and got up from behind my computer desk and walked over to my closet to pull out some stuff to wear today. I picked out some mesh basketball shorts and a white

T. It was as simple as I could get it. When it came to
clothes I didn't care. I just wanted to be comfortable.

My cell phone beeped letting me know I had a text. I
picked up to see that it was from my girl.

LOVE YOU, BABY! . . . Your baby girl.

I spoke into my phone to text her back.

LOVE YOU MORE! . . . Your big daddy!

Since we have been together all we do sexually is phone
sex. I was still hesitant. I didn't want to go all the way until
I was sure she was the one. I still had self- esteem problems when it came to sex. Some things had changed and I
wasn't sure she could handle it. I was still learning how to
deal with it myself.

The ringing of my phone broke me out of my daze. It
was Wallace.

"Hey, are you outside?"

"No, but I'm about a couple minutes away. I just wanted
to let you know." Dude was something else. I just didn't get
him. He just didn't seem like the average gay guy. He made
me a little uncomfortable, but I rode with it anyway. As
long as he didn't try anything it was all right.

I quickly grabbed the equipment I needed for Wallace, two bottles of water out of the refrigerator, scribbled a note letting Ashley know where I was and exited
my apartment to wait for Wallace out front.

He pulled up and I hopped in.

"There's been a change of plans, I need you to go
with me somewhere else real quick."

"Okay." I was a still a little reluctant to just go off
with him without asking any questions. "Where are we
headed to?"

"I think I have found a lady that may have the answers to why my lover was killed."

"Really?" It crossed my mind to let him know that I was looking for the same info, but I kept it quiet, because I didn't know how homeboy was going to come at me when I told him that James/Jerry Parks was my biological father. "Man, I think that is awesome. I feel privileged for you to let me come along."

"I told you that I trust you, so it was the only logical choice I could make once again. Besides, I need somebody with me if shit doesn't go right." He laughed. I slightly chuckled, because I didn't want to die from nosiness.

He pulled off and I just stared out of the window the whole ride, making sure I kept my eye out for things and places I could place if I had to get away or come back for some reason.

A half hour later we pulled up to a detached brick house with a two-car garage attached to it. It was your basic two-story house.

We both got out of the car and headed toward the house we parked in front of. On the walk to the house I pulled out my cell phone and found my recorder so that I could tape everything that was said and replay it when I got home. I did the same thing when we visited my grandfather's house. Wallace was oblivious to it all.

When we got to the door he knocked. A few seconds later the door opened and a pretty old woman stood at the door. She looked to be around fifty or so because I saw a few gray strands of hair on her head. Nevertheless, she was very beautiful.

"Can I help you?" she asked.

"Yes, I'm looking for Michelle Jenkins. Does she live here?"

"I'm Michelle, what can I do for you?" She was so polite and mild-mannered.

"Well, I had to ask you some questions about Tyrone Jenkins. He was my cousin."

"Well, I really don't want to discuss him. He's dead and I want to leave it that way." She tensed up a little, while folding her arms against her chest.

"Mrs. Jenkins . . ." He paused. "I just wanted to get some closure on a situation and I was hoping that you could help me out. Please!"

"Well . . ." She looked like she was about to give in.

"All I want is to ask you a few questions. It will only take a couple minutes of your time. I promise."

"Okay, come on in." She backed up and let us in. "But only for a few minutes . . . I was just about to leave out to take care of some errands."

She closed the door behind us and then showed us to her living room.

"Okay." She sat down on her love seat while Wallace and I sat on the sofa across from her. "What do you want to know?" She cut to the chase.

"Do you know a James/Jerry Parks?" Wallace asked.

"Not directly, but I do know him and my husband had some type of affair while we were married. I thought you were going to be asking me questions about Tyrone?" My mind was going all a mile a minute. I couldn't believe that my biological father was a home wrecker.

"I'm sorry, Mrs. Jenkins, but I didn't know how you would react if I just came out and asked you information about James/Jerry."

"So you are saying that Tyrone was having an affair with James while you were married? And James knew he was married?" He paused and shook his head like he was confused. "No . . . no . . . no . . . I don't know if I can believe that. James just didn't seem like that kind of person."

"Well, it's true, he did and it was with my husband. I have evidence to prove it too. I'll be right back." She got up and went up some stairs, leaving me and Wallace in the living room.

"Wow, man. That is some crazy stuff," I said out loud.

"You telling me." He breathed out and put his head in his hands for a few seconds. "It's not what I was expecting. She's telling me that my baby was wrecking homes on purpose. That just can't be true. It can't." A few second later Michelle comes back downstairs with a red brick and a large manila envelope.

"Hear you go." She handed the brick and envelope to Wallace. I was curious to see what was in the envelope, but I let him finish what he came here for.

"What's this?"

"Well, inside the envelope are pictures and a DVD of my husband and the James guy in all types of sexual positions. The brick is what it was tied to when he threw it through the window. I don't know why I kept if for this long, but now since you're here I can get it out of my house. I should have gotten rid of it a long time ago, but I didn't. It's yours now. Along with all the painful memories and heartache I carried with me over the years." I saw a tear slide out of her eye and down her cheek.

"Mrs. Jenkins, I'm not sure I understand everything. Are you sure James intentionally tried to destroy your home?"

"I'm sorry about that." She wiped a tear away. "The fact of the matter is that James wasn't the first man my husband was messing around with. My husband was in and out of work so much, I really didn't know what was going on while I wasn't home. I had two boys to take care of and I was trying to maintain my marriage.

James just happened to be the one that did something about my mischievous husband. I knew my husband was up to no good, but I still tried to make it work for our kids. It was a huge mistake. I'm saying all of that to say, this James guy was probably duped into an affair with my husband. My husband was a good liar and he died believing some of them. I went to my husband's funeral here and I actually went to James's funeral that his mom had here too. I had to apologize for my husband's treatment toward him. It was only the right thing to do. I'm sorry for your loss, both Tyrone and James. It just shows you that everybody isn't who you think they are. Maybe they're just what you wanted them to be at that time in your life."

"Wooooow!" I spoke out in awe. I was floored. That was some very tight information she just gave us.

"Right . . . right," Wallace nodded his head in agreement. "That still doesn't explain why Tyrone murdered him. Do you know?"

"Well, I put Tyrone out after that incident. I didn't want him around my kids any longer. He didn't take it very well. He would stalk me and my children and call all times of the night. He'd sit in his car in front of my job and all manner of things. It had gotten to the point where he was making threats on my life and his children's lives. When he called my house one time he said that if he couldn't have his family then he would burn us all up in our sleep. That is when I got a court ordered restraining order. He called again and I told him if he called or came by again that he would be arrested. He didn't believe me and sure enough he came back by and was immediately arrested on the spot."

She wiped away some more tears and continued. "I breathed a sigh of relief when that happened, because that was the last time I heard from him. For a long time after that I prayed that he was doing well and living well, but with the news of him murdering another chick and James, I knew my husband let his lies and deceit drive him to murder two others and to kill himself. Maybe your ex-lover was a good guy in the beginning, but from the reaction I got from him all that time ago, he may have took the wrong path that ultimately lead to his demise. I can't tell you that for sure, but I been around for a long time and you as well. Some people just don't let stuff go and it consumes them and ultimately kills them or gets them killed." She stopped talking. "Well, I need to be going. I hope what I've said has helped you with your questions."

"Yes, you did and I'm sorry to disturb you." He got up and so did she. I looked at Wallace and he had a few tears in threatening to fall from his eyes. They embraced and held for a long time. I had to admit that the moment had me a little emotional too.

We exited the house and the drive back to his house was a completely quiet one.

Chapter 33

Wallace
Candid Camera
May 23rd 3:32 P.M.

"Unnnnnnhh." I pushed my manhood all the way inside him as I bent him over the chair. He was so warm on the inside. I paused so I could feel him as he breathed in and out as his ass muscles expanded with every breath he took. I then began to slowly pump his tight bottom until I was working in and out with ease.

"Yeahhhhh!" He threw back himself onto my manhood like I liked it. I was holding his hips as he clawed at my thighs to pump faster.

"You like that?" I asked Lex as I leaned over to nibble on his ear and lick his neck. My heart was beating on his chest like a drum. I grinded and grinded my manhood in him so he could feel what I was feeling: passion.

I took my manhood out and started to grind it between cheeks to tease him. He was reaching and grabbing trying to put it back in.

"You want some more?" He turned around and mouth kissed me. It was sloppy and wet, causing me to grind on him harder. I could feel the latex condom heating up both of our skin from the friction.

"Yes. . . . yes. . . . yesss . . ." he hissed as I eased it back in. His head flung back like I had hit a nerve or something. That alone caused me to almost erupt inside of him. It had been so long since I had some. I was surely going bust a big load. I needed to badly. He must have sensed the urgency of my nut so he started to throw his ass back even faster once again.

"Wallace! . . . Wallace! . . . Wallace! . . ."

"Huh . . . huh . . . huh?" I jumped up off of the sofa in fright. I looked around the room confused for a second. "What's wrong?" I asked Alex who had a puzzled look on his face.

"I'm almost finished setting up the equipment so we can look at these tapes you got."

"Okay . . . okay." I must have fallen asleep waiting for him to set up the equipment. I was exhausted after hearing the news about James and my cousin Tyrone. It was almost too much. I didn't know if I could take anything else. I looked down at my pants and noticed a wet spot on them. Then I remembered the dream I just had.

"Alex, I'll be right back." I rushed out of the living room into my bedroom for a change of clothes and then into the bathroom to do a quick washup.

I showered real quick and got out and looked at myself in the mirror.

"Wallace what's going on with you man?" I shook my head as tears ran down my face. I had no right dreaming about Alex in that manner. It was totally uncalled for. "James is dead," I had to remind myself. I closed the toilet seat lid and sat down and began to cry. I wasn't ready to believe that my baby was a tyrant. "I miss you, James." I got up and splashed my face with some water to wash away the evidence of my crying.

"Is everything ready?" I asked as I walked back into the living room ready to go.

"Yep, it's ready to go." He sounded chipper. I was still embarrassed by what happened almost a half hour ago. I was a sick old man, preying on a young boy, because he looked like my dead lover. I was losing my damn mind.

"Well, you ready?" he asked me as he popped a VHS tape in the outdated VCR that was attached to something else that was then connected to my television. We both sat back on the sofa and he pressed a few buttons on his remote and the plasma screen in front of us came alive.

After a few seconds of the fuzzy, snowy screen an office scene popped onto the screen. I looked at amazement as I watched a little boy sitting on a long black leather sofa with his book bag fumbling with it. It was my brother David. I smiled because I remembered some of the good times we had as kids when we were really young. Those were the days. When we used to play together . . . you know, hide-and-seek in the house, camping out in our rooms, and so much more. It amazed me how things drastically changed between us. It was as if we were strangers. In fact, we were strangers. I knew nothing about either of my brothers or any of my family for that matter.

"Who's that?" Alex asked. I almost forgot he was in here with me.

"Professor Andrews," I spoke as we continued to watch.

"Wow, he was a little guy," he laughed.

"Yeah, he was."

A few seconds later another guy enters the room and stands in the middle of the floor with his hands in his pockets. I leaned in a little to try to get a good picture of who it was, but couldn't. Another few seconds later and my father popped back on to the screen. What happens next opens my mouth all the way.

My father and the other man began to kiss and fondle each other.

"Oh shit!" Alex belts out. "What the hell is this some sort of gay porn?" I unintentionally ignore him because my brother bolts to the door of the office. I could see him yelling something but I didn't know what, since the tape was without sound. My father walks over to my brother to say something to him while the unknown guy strips down and bends over the couch with his butt in the air.

I turn my head to look at Alex real quick. His mouth is open as wide as mine, neither one of us is moving away from in front the screen like a normal person would do.

Then something even more fouler happens. My father walks over to the guy and sticks his face in between his buttocks and tosses his salad.

"Whoa . . . whoa . . . whoa." I see Alex turn his head, but I continued to watch.

I then watch my father and this guy get up. My father pulls David, who is still at the door, back in front of the naked man. He says something to the David and then kneels in front of him.

"No. . . . no . . . no," I shake my head side to side. I watched the man suck my brother off. The man leans his head back and that is when I recognize who the strange guy is.

"John . . . fuckin' . . . Parks!" I yell out in fury. I look around to see Alex at the front door himself shaking his head side to side. He has tears in his eyes. Before I could say anything to him I felt my stomach churning and I grabbed my mouth as I sprinted to my bathroom to relieve myself. What I just saw was too much for me. That shit was too much for anyone to see. My brother/sister was right. I knew nothing. I did get the easy way out. I began to feel really guilty that they were abused and I wasn't. I was even more confused now. *Why wasn't I abused? Or was I,* I wondered.

After about five minutes in the bathroom I slowly made my way back into the living room. Alex was on the living room sofa. The television was off. You could tell he was crying, because his face was still wet from tears.

"You okay, man?" I asked with a still shaky voice.

"Nah, ma." I breathed in hard and put his face in his hands for a few seconds. I lean back on the sofa and just look up at the ceiling in a daze.

"James is my father," I heard Alex say.

"What?" I snapped back up. Fully alert.

"James Parks is my biological father."

"What? . . . how? . . . what? . . . Huh?" I stammered in confusion.

"My mother and James had an affair and James Parks is my father," he said it as plain as if he was saying 'I'm going to the store.'

The ringing of the phone put the conversation that we were having on pause.

"Hello," I answered.

"Baby, they have to take your father to the hospital, he don't look too good. I think you should come now," my mother spoke in between tears.

"Okay, " I spoke drily. I had no emotion for a man I never really liked or knew. I asked her the hospital and I told her that I would be there as soon as I could. I told Alex what was going on and he opted to go to the hospital with me. Truth was he looked a little worn-out, but I did have some more questions for him about the bomb he just dropped on me seconds ago. I had some questions for my mother. I needed to know if she knew about all of this molestation mess. I was boiling mad as well on the inside, but I didn't let it show. I was also worried about how I was going to handle seeing my father at the hospital. I just might have to kill him if he pulls through.

I pulled up to the hospital, but I wasn't in a rush. After what I just saw just a couple of hours ago, his ass could shrivel up as far as I am concerned.

"Wallace, I'm sorry about all of this, man." Alex stated. "I wasn't trying to use you. I just wasn't sure how you would respond to that kind of news."

"You know what Alex, right now I'm still trying to digest all of this molestation stuff. I can't fault you for keeping that secret. The truth is I probably would have done the same thing. I have so many questions right now that my head is swirling."

"Man, I would too, if that type of stuff was going on in my family. But, since we are connected in some way by all of this, I'm here for you." He had a real sincere look on his face. It was the same face that James had when we got married and he said "I do."

"While we being honest here, I have something I want to confess. I was attracted to you sexually. I grieved so much for James that your similar facial features lead me to believe you were him in some way. I just thought that you have an uncanny resemblance to him. Now that I know he was your father, I have to apologize for feeling that way without your knowledge."

"It's okay, man, and for the record, I'm not gay. Not that I have anything against that, that's just not my scene."

"Right . . . right . . . I understand totally." I nodded my head in agreement. It felt so much better to get that off my chest.

"So whatever happens in the hospital today, I got you." We gave each other a pound and exited the car for the hospital. We went through the normal security scanner and made our way to the floor where my family was. I looked over at Alex on the elevator ride up and he was in deep thought. I shook my head the whole time in awe of the fact that he was James's son.

When we got to the floor, David and a lady, who I assumed was his wife, were standing outside the room. We walked up to them and Alex greeted them both and went to take a seat in the waiting room across the hall. A few minutes later David's wife did the same. She was a little on edge I could feel, but I paid it no mind. I was here for my family.

David and I both walked into the room to see my mom and Rebecca sitting next to my father, who was hooked up to a lot of tubes. He was so frail it was hard to look at him.

"Hey Ma, What's going on?" I really, really wanted to know about if she knew about the whole molestation thing, but I let it slide for the moment. Looking at my father in the hospital bed almost made me compassionate for him, but then I looked at my transsexual brother and DL brother and compassion became lost on me again.

"Well, his body is starting to shut down. He is loosely coherent, but it is touch-and-go. The doctors said he could go at any moment. I just don't know what to do. I—I . . . don't want to lose him," she cried and buried herself in my chest. I rubbed her back trying to console her. It confirmed for the fact that she could have not known about what was going on.

"I'm sorry, Ma. But maybe it's his time to go." I tried to reassure her. "We all have a time to go, his is coming."

"How . . . how could you say that?" She pulled away from me and looked at me angrily. She was hurt by the truth I could tell. The bearer of bad news was never looked upon favorably.

I looked over at Rebecca and David, who were looking back at me in fear. They must have known I was going to blow the lid off of the situation. I couldn't hold it in me any longer.

"He wasn't the man you thought he was." I looked her square in the eyes.

"Wallace, what are you talking about?" She looked confused. It was now or never. I could see my brothers in the background shaking their heads no, but I had to do it.

"You husband is the reason your children are the way they are. He started this mess. He let some man take their innocence." I pointed toward my brothers whose eyes had tears threatening to fall.

"What are you talking about?" She stepped even further back.

"Your husband and our father let a man molest your children."

"He did what?" Her face was twisted. "What? . . . How? . . . That's not true. It can't be true." She shook her head in disbelief.

"Believe it!" Rebecca popped up out of her chair and seconded what I was saying. "He wasn't what you thought he was. I am twisted because of his sick ways." She scowled and turned her head toward my father's bed and then at David like he was supposed to be next to confess.

"He touched you?" She walked over to Rebecca and gently rubbed her face. "Why didn't you say anything?"

"I couldn't Mama, I couldn't . . . He warned us not to; me and David."

"David, baby is that true?" She walked over to where David was sitting. Tears were streaming from his face like a running faucet. He nodded his head yes and he stood up like a baby and hugged our mother. He was the one who cried the hardest. I was crying now too.

We all crowded around my mother and cried for a few minutes. That's all we did.

We heard someone clear their throat in the room. We broke apart to see John Parks standing in the room with us.

"What the fuck are you doing here?" I cursed. I was hot and boiling mad. He had the audacity to walk up in like he belonged.

"It's a family reunion ain't it?" He laughed really hard.

"Who is this?" my mother inquired.

"Your husband's mistress." I smirked John's way. He didn't like it one bit.

"His what?" She shrieked in shock.

"This is the muthafucka that turned me into the woman I am today," Rebecca hissed.

"Uhhhhh . . . mmmm," We all turned to see my father began to moan and his face begin to twist up. John rushed over to his side.

"Baby, you okay?" he asked. My father was nonresponsive. My mother, on the other hand, looked like she was about to pass out.

"Maaaaa!" I yelled out as I came to her rescue. She had blacked out and was about to hit the hospital floor. I grabbed her just in the knick of time. While I had her, both my brothers saw it fit to take their frustration out on John Parks. They commenced an ass-whooping that I could feel with every blow.

Pretty soon the room was filled with nurses trying to get my brothers off of John. It was too late, because

John was now unconscious. They carried him out and they made my brothers leave the room while I tended to my mother.

Chapter 34

Alex
All Fall Down
May 23rd 6:03 P.M.

"Baby, what are you doing here?" I asked as I watched her walk in the hospital waiting room. She and Professor David looked like they had just got into a fight or something. She looked surprised. She then looked around the room like she was confused.

"Ohh . . . uhhh . . . visiting my father." She sat on the other side of the room like she was afraid to sit next to me.

"Oh, he's sick?" I asked, concerned.

"Yeah, our father is dying." Professor Andrews spoke up. I had almost forgotten he was in the room. I looked at his wife and she had a nervous look in her eyes.

"Our?" I looked at Professor Andrews.

"Yes, our."

"Y'all brother and sister?" I asked Rebecca.

"Well . . . sorta." She was shaking like a leaf on a tree branch in a windstorm. I started to look at her funny.

"Sorta?"

"You mean you don't know?" Professor Andrews asked me with a perplexed look on his face.

"Know what?" I asked confused, looking back and forth between the professor and Rebecca.

"Please. . . . Please. . . . just stop!" Rebecca yelled out.

"What's wrong, baby?" I went over to her to try and comfort her, but she got up and stood by the door. "What's going on?"

"She's not a she." Professor Andrews spoke up letting the cat out of the bag. "She's a he."

"What the fuck!" I shot up out of my chair. "Nah . . . nah . . . nah. . . . You lying. *You lying!* She doesn't look like a man . . . She couldn't be . . . could she?" I shook my head from side to side in confusion. "I'm going to ask you one time and one time only. Are . . . you . . . a man?"

She shook her head yes. Then I lost it. Like lightning I picked up the ceramic vase that was on one of the end tables and threw it at his head. Professor quickly got up and restrained me because I was going for blood

"You muthafuckin' faggot . . . how could you? You . . . you tricked me. When the fuck was you going to tell me? When?"

"I—I—I—was going to before we got intimate." The she-male was crying hard.

"I'm so muthafuckin' glad I didn't fuck you. . . . oh my god. . . . I was about to fuck you. Oh my god! Oh my god! . . . I'ma kill you." Oddly enough no nurses or security came to see what the commotion was about yet. I sat down for a second to catch my breath and get my thoughts together.

"A fuckin' man," I mumbled to myself.

I looked over at Professor Andrews and his wife, she had tears in her eyes and she was shaking her head from side to side. Like she couldn't believe it herself.

"What are you shaking your head for bitch?" I looked at Rebecca in confusion. She had her eyes locked with Professor Andrews's wife.

"Your ass is doing the same damn thing to him," she hissed. My mouth hit the floor.

"What?" Professor Andrews jumped up. "What are you talking about?" He looked at Rebecca.

"You married to a man." She smirked. "Sorry dear brother, but you been shacking up with Thomas Jones. A man."

"Oh shit!" I belted out.

"You . . . you can't be." He shook his head from side to side. She eased out of her seat and edged toward the door right next to Rebecca.

"Thirty years . . . thirty years . . . thirty years," he kept on repeating. "How could you do this to me?"

"I'm so, sorry . . . I'm sorry, baby . . . I'm sorry, baby. . . ." she pleaded. He just looked at her. And stared and stared and stared. I was kind of scared of what he might do. It was only a few seconds but it was crazy quiet in the room. Then he charged her and started to punch her, and then I realized again that it was a man, and then I realized that that same thing happened to me minutes ago and I said fuck it and charged after Rebecca who was still in the corner of the room by the door. We were all fighting and throwing shit around. Security and nurses broke us up and the police came and arrested us for hitting women. They didn't know that the two ladies were actually men. Both of us men were ashamed that we were in that type of situation

Wallace and his mother stood by as he watched the police escorted me and Professor Andrews off to jail. I shock my head in shame. I didn't want anything on my record. And I didn't want to disappoint my dad, but it was what it was right now. I was headed to jail.

Chapter 35

Shawn
All At One
May 23rd 8:31 A.M.

"Baby, you okay?" I heard Mona ask me as we sat in BWI Airport waiting for our flight to California. We had all the kids with us. I had found James's mother and we were going to get some closure for her and us.

"Yes, Mona, I'm fine, but I will be better when we get this situation under control." I have been calling Alex and Ashley's phone and getting no response. They both went straight to voice mail as soon as I hit the button to call them. I didn't let Mona know all that was going on, because I didn't want to worry her. I just told her that I wanted James's mom to meet her grandkids since she never met them. I don't even know if she even knew about them. I couldn't keep them from their other family any longer. I had to get used to the fact that they had three families instead of the two I let them see. I was selfish and God was dealing with me about it now. I just hope nothing happened to them for me not tying up these loose ends.

"Damn, Shawn!" I mumbled to myself.

I got up out of my chair and walked over to the large window to get a moment to myself. I was emotional and I wanted to be alone. I just hope my kids forgive me for being so selfish and secretive.

"Daddy, what's wrong?" my daughter Diana came over and asked me. She was fifteen now and very beautiful. A spitting image of her mother.

"Nothing baby girl, just looking at the planes take off."

"Okay, can I stand here too?" she asked. She wasn't my daughter biologically either. She knew it and she didn't treat me any different.

"Sure, why not." I put my arm around her shoulder and pulled her in tight. She laid her head on my shoulder. Moments like these made being a father worthwhile. If I lost anyone of them I don't know what I would do.

"I like how the planes take off and land, Dad. It's really cool. When you said we were taking a trip to California to see Alex and Ashley I asked a couple of my Facebook friends about their first plane ride experiences. Most people say the plane taking off is the scariest part. Some people said that being in the air and going through turbulence is the hardest. But even more people say that the landing part is the best, because it brings a release of calmness over you."

"Oh, really?" I said as I stared out of the window looking at the planes land and take off. Truth be told, this is my first plane ride and I don't know what to expect. What I had to do on the other side of this plane ride was bothering me the most.

"Yep, but you know what I figured out, Daddy?"

"What is that, baby girl?" I looked at her inquisitively.

"I figured that just like life, this plane ride is about the whole experience. In life you go up and you go down and your going through may be rough. There is always a beginning and an end, but you must go through something to appreciate both the beginning and the end."

"Where'd you get that from, Diana?" I asked, shocked. She had no idea what I was going through but yet she answered my fears with a perfect analogy.

"Bible study." She smiled.

"Good girl. . . . Good girl." I kissed her on her forehead. "You don't know it but you just made Daddy's day." She smiled with her braces on her teeth like I just gave her a hundred bucks. The information she just gave me was priceless. I had to do what I had to do now and that was save my family. God is something else.

". . . out of the mouths of babes," I mumbled to myself as we walked back over to where Mona and the other two children were.

"4665 flight to California is now boarding. Please make a single-file line at the departures gate at this time." A polite female's voice filled the air above us, letting us know our flight was ready to go. Within minutes we were on the plane and taking off. Several hours later we were on the landing in California. And just like Diana said, it was an experience that I had to go through to get through to the other side.

We picked up our luggage and made our way to rent a minivan for our stay here. Alex and Ashley didn't know we were here and I hoping that they were doing what they were supposed to do, but I knew that was asking too much. Alex was nosy and Ashley had control and selfish issues; all a recipe for trouble. I called their phones and I watched as Mona did the same. She asked me what was going on, I just assured her that this was almost finals time and they probably shut their phones off for that reason. It was a lie, but I hoped that it was a reality.

Chapter 36

Ashley
Hurt People, Hurt People
May 23rd 2:33 P.M.

Just before he pulled the trigger to the gun, he walked away. I was thanking Jesus in every way imaginable at this time. I wanted to scream for help, but the gun he had suggested that I keep it shut. Jesus was the only one that could save me from myself and this lunatic. Seconds later I see him bring out Ebony. She was beat up pretty bad. I shook my head in shock. She had a busted lip, a black eye and a lump on her head. I was in and out of consciousness, so he could have been beating her when I was unconscious or something like that in the other room. She looked bad nonetheless. He still had the gun in his hand and my hands were still tied behind me. His ass must have been a master at kidnapping or something because he had my hands tied pretty securely. I tried and tried but to no avail. I was stuck. My cell phone was on the table in front of me and it looked like it was off. So no one could even reach me if they tried. Times like this I prayed that I told Alex what I was up to, but I had to be a bitch and now I was reaping what I sowed. Again, it was a little too late to be feeling regretful.

"You like tonguing down my bitch?" he growled almost. He didn't know that it was quite the opposite. I was the one being tongued down by her. I didn't say anything I just stared at him. He was manhandling her some kind of rough too. "I'm going to show you how it is really done." He proceeded to pull down her pants, push her over the arm of the sofa. Her eyes were dead-set on mines. It was like she was saying "I told you so." It made me feel even worse than before. I had not only put my life in jeopardy but I also put hers in jeopardy as well. *Lord, please help us! I'm sorry for all that I've done. Please hear me, now.* He pulled out his manhood and started to stroke it to an erection. For some odd reason I was getting turned on as he stroked himself. I watched him as he pushed himself into her. He exhaled like it was taking away his stress just by entering her. I never got to experience that feeling from a man. Didn't know if I ever wanted to.

He slowly started to pump her and with each pump tears flowed from her eyes. I didn't know if she was enjoying it or what. Then all of a sudden he switched gears and started slamming into her womb like he was power driver trying to break ground. She just lay there silently and took it like it was an everyday occurrence. I kind of felt sorry for her. He didn't show her any kind of care or anything. Wham, bam, thank you ma'am! And roll over and go to sleep. A typical man. He wasn't taking care to take care of her as well as himself. But then I thought about our sexual sessions and I did the same thing. I wasn't treating her with care either.

Hurt people, hurt people, popped into my head. It was something my grandmother used to say to me. I was just getting it now. I was just realizing that I was hurting and I needed help. I was angry at God for letting me be this way and not changing me when I asked him to. How could He let me endure such an unnatural thing? But I wanted a release from something that I wasn't too sure I wanted to give up. Then again, sitting here tied up was a real persuasive tool to get me to think about my lifestyle. It's funny how God does things in unconventional ways to get us to see it His way. I can't have it both ways. *I see now, God. I see. Not my way but yours. I relent. I surrender. I give up.* My head slumped down on to my chest and I cried like a baby. Everything that was going on around me was a blur as I sobbed uncontrollably and openly.

"Bitch, what are you crying for?" Ebony's husband walked up to me and barked at me. I ignored him and continued my long cry. He slammed me in the head with the gun again.

He walked away from me and over to Ebony. He pulled her up off the chair with force.

"Me or her?" He looked at Ebony. I was confused by his question. She was too. He handed her the gun. I understood then, but he verbalized it. "I need you to choose between me and her right now. You know what I mean?"

She nodded. "I . . . I choose you, baby!" She trembled in fear.

"Now that I know who your choice is, you got to shoot the bitch for trying to tear our home apart." He was behind her and he lifted the gun up with his arms around hers. She had a look of remorse on her face. He had a sick smile on his face. It was like he was going to enjoy watching me die.

"Ebony, don't do this. You don't have to do this. I'm sorry for all that I've done to you. I'm sorry!" I begged and pleaded softly.

Ebony was now standing with the gun with a silencer pointed toward me all by herself.

"Do it for us, baby. Do it for us." He was standing beside her, coaching her like he was her drill sergeant in the army or something. I saw her squeeze the trigger and smile, like she was getting payback.

Pop!

Chapter 37

Wallace
It's Over Now
May 23rd 6:40 P.M.

"What the hell happened in here?" The police had just carried Alex and my brother off to jail. My mother sat on the side of me while I questioned my brother and sister/brother-in law.

"Well, we—" Rebecca looked at my mother and then at Grace. Both had tears in their eyes. "We did some bad things."

"What do you mean bad things?"

"We weren't quite honest with our men." She shook her head in shame. "They didn't know that they were dating/married to transsexuals. We didn't mean to hurt them. It's just that we—we—"

"We wanted someone to love us for us and not what we used to be," Grace chimed in. "We went about it the wrong way and now it's all over. We are back at square one."

"How could you?" my mother asked with her hand over her chest. "You can't play with people's feelings like that. It's just plain wrong. Wrong I tell you." She had a really disappointed look on her face.

"Ma, I know. I'm sorry for it now. I really am."

"I can't blame them for acting out the way they did when they found out," Grace said solemnly to my mother. "I am sorry for hurting your son. I did love him though."

"Sweetie, you couldn't have. You don't love you, so how could you know about loving someone else? I think you two got just what you deserved. I don't know about how you got the way you did, but I *now* know about my son's plight. It doesn't excuse the actions though." She looked at them with a pitiful face.

I shook my head in unbelief.

Then Grace spoke up, "Ma'am, I was molested as a child and it severely damaged my sense of who I was or supposed to be. I wanted to be a man, but being so young and being molested, I thought I was supposed to be. I was always a pretty boy and my molester always said I was as pretty as a girl, so I thought that God or somebody had made a mistake and this is what I was supposed to be. He messed me up bad. That is how Rebecca and I met; at the reconstructive surgery office. We've been best friends ever since. We lost touch all this time, but we still are good friends."

"Okay." My mother spoke as she nodded her head.

"Sorry for letting the cat out of the bag earlier." Rebecca grabbed Grace's hand and squeezed it. "I was caught up in the moment. I didn't mean to hurt you."

"It's all right. It would have eventually come out anyway. Thank God he didn't kill me, though. Even though I've been feeling half dead for most of my life anyway." She was crying really hard now. I personally couldn't imagine going through any of that. The surgery and all. I liked men, but getting my manhood cut off was out of the question. Sad thing is manhood has nothing to do with what you got between your legs. That is a small part of it. It was about total being. These two had their manhood stripped from them at a young age.

"It's such a shame. All of this mess." My mother shook her head with tears in her eyes.

I wrapped my arm around her shoulder and pulled her toward me.

"My babies are messed up because of me not paying attention to what was going on in my house."

"Well, Ma. That is partially true. You couldn't be everywhere and with us at every turn. And these two should have said something to someone no matter what," I stated as I looked on to the two deceivers.

"It's not that easy, when you have someone like Daddy doing stuff to you." Rebecca sniffed back some tears.

"Lawd, I don't know what to do. Truth be told, your daddy and I did separate for a small period of time. We were having problems and we decided to take a break. I didn't know he was doing that guy in there. You guys actually were too young to remember. I didn't know he was that way. I would have never left him around you boys. I just thought that I was too nagging and putting a lot of stress on him. His practice was just starting and we were struggling and he just snapped one day. He said he needed a break and he left. It hurt me to my heart. You boys and the Lord were the only things that keep me sane. I just can't believe I missed all of this. I—I—don't know what to do. A mother is supposed to know when something is wrong with her family. I was too wrapped up in saving my marriage and my husband's happiness, that I neglected you boys. I wasn't paying attention to the signs. For all of this to come out now. I—I'm so brokenhearted. I failed you boys. I failed. "

"No, Ma. You did a wonderful job on all of us. Don't blame yourself for Dad's actions. He made those decisions and that is the truth. Him and . . ." My voice trailed off. I immediately went to the videotape that I saw earlier today and tears filled my eyes. This was a real, real bad situation for my family. Anyone's family for that matter. I wouldn't have believed it if I didn't see it with my own eyes.

"John Parks is his name." I finally spoke up. I shook my head in shame and confusion.

"How do you know who molested me?" Grace interrupted us.

"Excuse me?" I asked. "He molested you too?"

"Yes, he did. And I think he molested my cousin Jerry too. His own son. The sorry son of a bitch." Her face twisted up in anger.

"What? You're Jerry's cousin?"

"Yes, why do you ask?"

"He was my lover." I lowered my head.

"Oh, I'm sorry. I didn't know." Grace spoke with compassion.

"No need to be sorry. I'm doing fine with his loss now."

"Good . . . good," she spoke back.

"Look let me go down to this jail and see if I can get these two released." I stood up and stretched. "Ma, stay here I'll let you know what's going on and you do the same."

"Okay, baby." She kissed me on the cheek. "I sure will." I didn't know my mother well, so I didn't know how she could still be so quiet when she knew the man who was her husband let someone else molest them. I don't know if I would be so nice and stay by his bedside in the hospital.

"We'll go too," Rebecca and Grace spoke up together.

"No, I don't think that is a good idea right now. We need to let them cool off. I just need you two to be honest and let the authorities know when the time comes. Okay?"

"Okay," I hugged them both, because I know they too would be having a difficult time to adjusting to what is going on now that their partners know about them.

***

I walked out of the hospital totally exhausted. I was in over my head for sure. I slowly walked across the parking lot toward my car.

I've never experienced so much drama in all my life. I lived drama-free almost all my life and up until I met James, my life was pretty calm. Even with me selling drugs and all of that. I loved him, but, man; if I would have known that it would have led to all of this then I would have never hopped in his car. But, on the other hand, if I had not met him I wouldn't have found out about all of this mess in my family and I wouldn't have gone looking for answers to questions I didn't have. As of right now, I wasn't sure how this was going to end, but I hoped that it all ended well.

I finally got to my car and heard footsteps behind me. I quickly turned to see John Parks behind me. He had a couple of bruises on his face and a swollen lip.

"Wallace, can I talk to you for a minute?"

"Man, I don't think that's a good idea."

"I know, but there is just something that I needed to tell you. It's about your father." I looked at him and wondered what he could possibly tell me about my father that I wanted to hear or cared about hearing. I should have been breaking him off another ass-whooping just for my mother's sake, but I knew she wouldn't approve of it. Even though she did let my brothers whip on him first. I also had an unbelievable tolerance for forgiving and letting go of people wronging me. I didn't like it as a kid and even now, but it was a part of me, so it naturally happened. Now I'm not saying I'm God with the forgiveness piece, but I do let stuff go easily.

"Man, make it quick." I leaned back on the trunk of my car, folded my arms and waited for him to start. His old ass was good-looking though, I had to admit. James probably would have looked like him at this age too. If he were alive.

"Look, your father and I had a relationship that wasn't like everybody played it out to be. I wasn't a home wrecker. We just had a natural bond. At first we were client-patient and then we became friend-lover, it was wrong. I know that now. I was seeing him for my issues and against policy he started to tell me about his past and then we just clicked. One thing led to another and we started getting sexually involved and then he suggested that we involve your brothers. At first I was against it, but the more he talked about it the more I gave in. He said he could never do his sons himself, but he wouldn't mind watching someone else doing it. Twisted and hellish it is. And I accept my fate or eternal damnation for it. I let my demons run me and my love for attention from your father consumed me and I was forever lost. You know he always talked about you. You were his favorite."

I thought back on how my father treated me as a child and the things he said to me. I just couldn't see how I was his favorite son and the fact that he could treat me the way he treated me.

"That can't be true. He hated me and then he put me out of his house."

"I know, I know." He nodded. "That was a front for your mother, he didn't want to let on that he and you had the same affliction. You were a mirror to him. He wanted to beat it out of you verbally, seeing himself in you tore him apart. He would cry and cry in my sessions with him. He didn't want you to be like him, but since you were, he thought it only fair that your brothers suffer the same fate. He didn't want you to be alone in the house with the affliction he shared with you. You know what they say one bad apple spoils the bunch. That's what he did. He thought he was making it even, but he only made it worse."

"Nah, man you telling me some real sort of crazy shit right now. He had to be mentally challenged to think like that. I mean real crazy. That kind of crazy you can't hide. I mean he was a freaking psychologist. How he gonna be one and need one too? I'm not wrapping my mind around this man. This ain't no normal shit here you telling me."

"True, but it is the truth. You ever hear of a functioning drug addict, well, your father was a functioning crazy. Loosely put." He chuckled a little bit, but I didn't find anything funny. My father had literally screwed up his family intentionally.

"Look, man, I got to go. I can't . . . I can't . . . I just got to go." I got up off the trunk of my car and walked around to get in the driver's side.

"Wait . . . wait, I need to ask you something," he said with pleading eyes.

"What now man?" I said a little pissed off and disgusted. "I don't want to know any more about my father. You said enough."

"No, I want to know about my son. What was he like?"

"He wasn't like you." I looked at him sternly. "Nothing like you."

"I never meant to hurt him, but I was so young when we had him and I was confused about my sexuality and I took it out on him. I know it's too late to be apologizing, but I am. I loved my son. Well, I tried to love him. I—I—I know now that I did the worst thing a person could do to a child and I will never be able to forgive myself for it. So, I'll ask you again. What was he like?"

"Your son was the most loving, attentive man I knew. He loved with all that was in him. I'm learning now that he wasn't a saint, but he was a victim of circumstance and malicious treatment. All he wanted was genuine love and attention. We had that in the short time that we were together. But his past caught up with him and it didn't end well for him. It was no one's fault but his, but I am pretty sure that if you would have tied up the loose ends in your mental health, demons and such and got the help that you needed, he just may have ended up on a different path, but that's too late now. What's done is done."

Tears glistened in the corner of his eyes and fell one by one down his cheek. His tears were fifty some odd years too late. He should have gotten the help he needed then and he wouldn't be here asking about a son he could have gotten to know if it had not been for his foolishness.

"You know the sad thing about all of this? Your son has children that may or may not have to deal with the same things he did. You see he left this earth with loose ends too, but hopefully before it's all over they won't have to go through any of the pain and hurt that you pushed him into."

"He has children?"

"Yes, and you met one and didn't even know it."

"When?"

"The young guy that was with me when I met you first, that was your grandson. But don't worry about seeing him or the others, because he has witnessed you and all of your foolishness firsthand. I'm positive that he will be having nothing to do with you now that he knows all about what you did to his father. So go back under the rock you crawled from up under and chew on the fact that you never enjoy the privilege of being a grandfather. I hope you and my father meet in hell . . . Favorite son. . . . Huh. Y'all are some fucking lunatics."

I opened my door to my car and pulled off, satisfied that I got one in for James.

Driving down the road I couldn't help but thank God that I was not molested. That is just something that I don't think I could deal with. I'm not an expert on the subject, but I'm pretty sure that being molested does a whole lot of damage to one's psyche. It just destroys a person from the inside out. I am sure that James would have had some kind of normal life if he had not been molested. I just wasn't sure if he was gay before or after he was molested. I am sure that the molestation didn't help. I feel the same way about my brothers. Both were molested, but turned out completely different. It just goes to show you that tampering with someone's sexually can have all kind of adverse affects: gender identity, violence, DL syndrome, and all kinds of mess. This world has some messed-up people, with messed-up minds. You just don't know who it is. It could be someone close, even in your own family. Even a parent.

"Man, I thank God!" I hollered out to no one in particular. It could have be a lot worse for me. A lot worse.

I pulled into my driveway and made my way into my house. It was a quiet night in my neighborhood, but my mind was still on overload. I walked into my living room and past the television that held my family's painful secrets. I shook my head in shame. I walked into my kitchen, grabbed me some lunch meat and bread to feed my empty stomach. I wolfed it down along with a Valium to ease my mood. I jumped into the shower with hopes of being able to jump into bed and get a good nap in. When I exited the shower I noticed a messaged on my phone. I dialed my voice mail. My mom's voice came on.

Wallace, baby, your daddy is gone. He just died. Call me when you get this message.

Her voice was just as calm and serene. I listened to it a couple of more times, not know if I wanted to be true or not. I was pretty sure I knew everything that I need to know about him. So I decided to call my mom back in the morning. He was still going to be dead anyway. I know it sounds selfish but I need a small break away from everybody and everything, before I had to go and see if I could get David and Alex out of jail. I set my alarm, crawled into bed, grabbed the picture of James off of the nightstand and cried myself asleep. I woke up a couple of hours later still cloudy, but relaxed.

Chapter 38

David
Player Got Played
May 23rd 9:43 P.M.

"All this time I was on the DL, I was being scammed in my own damn house," I mumbled to myself. It was ironic how I was sleeping with a man my whole marriage and didn't even know it. I was creeping with a man on a man. I felt so dumb, so used. But I knew that this is what my hand called for. It was the one I was dealt and now I have to deal with it.

I looked over at Alex who sitting on the other side of the cell, with a worried look on his face. I couldn't help but feel sorry for him. He didn't even see it coming. That really has to have him messed up in the head. Dating a woman that is really a man. I would have hated to see him if they had done anything sexually. I really think somebody would have been writing two obituaries right now: his and my brother's.

Then I started to think about how I was secretly trying to pursue him. Man, I felt like a rat. Here he is trying to date a woman and me pursuing unknowingly just to find out you dating a transsexual. Against my better judgment, I decided to go over and talk to him about my intentions. I needed to get this off my chest. We were in the cell alone, so I knew I didn't have to worry about someone listening to our business.

"Alex, can I talk to you about something?" I walked over to where he was and sat a couple feet away from him on the same bench he was on.

"Sure, what about?" He was lying on his back and he got up to focus on me and what I was about to talk about.

"Well, I haven't been completely honest about my intentions with you."

"Okay." He spoke with a plain face.

"I have been secretly trying to see if I could sleep with you. I didn't know if you were gay or not and I thought that you were attractive and I wanted you."

He got up off of the bench. I flinched a little and leaned back. I didn't know what he was going to do. He looked at me for a few seconds and then he proceeded to walk up to me. He reached out arms as if he wanted something.

"What?" I asked confused by his gesture.

"Give me a hug." he said.

"A hug?" I asked, dumbfounded.

"Yeah, man."

"Did you just hear what I said?" I looked at him real hard. "I said I wanted to fuck you."

"I know that, but I also know what happened to you." He had a sincere look on his face.

"What do you know?" I asked, not sure if he really knew about me and my past.

"I know that you were molested. I know that you were pushed into who you are right now. But I also know that you need help with all that you are going through. So give me a hug and stop holding all of it in. You can lean on me and cry on my shoulder if you want to. "

I slowly got up and embraced him and he did the same. I leaned my head on his shoulder and cried like

I was a baby. I cried so hard that I started to wail, but he didn't let go, even when the guard came to check on us. He still held me like a baby. After a few minutes I pulled away and sat back down on the bench to get myself together.

"Now there are some things I want to tell you." He sat back down himself.

"Okay," I sniffed back a few more tears.

"Well, the man who molested you is my grandfather. He was one of the people I was trying to locate. I didn't know that he was who he was. What I do know is that he is not a well man. I apologize on the behalf of him. I don't know if it will help but, I'm sorry for all of the pain he put you through and your family. That is why I forgave Rebecca. Sitting over here at first I was angry at her, for withholding such a thing from me, but I know now that she was holding on to something far greater than her identity. She was also holding on to a lot of hurt, pain and shame. I can't hold that over her head. Don't get me wrong, I'm still a little mad, but I will get over that. I just hope you guys get the help that you all need."

"We will . . . we will." I nodded my head in agreement.

"That's cool." He smiled.

A few hours later, Wallace showed up to get us out. After Grace and Rebecca called down and explained the situation to the arresting officers, we were released.

Wallace dropped me off at the hospital where my car was and proceeded to take Alex back home.

I pulled up to my house and struggled to get my head together. I entered my house and looked around. It was a different feeling in the house now.

"This was all a lie." I moaned in pain. "A lie that you contributed to . . . fully." My conscience spoke back to me like "I told you so."

"Well, it couldn't last forever." I walked up to my mantle in the living room and looked at the pictures of me and my "wife."

"I'm a liar, you a liar, don't you wanna be a liar too." I sung the lyrics to a song we sung in elementary school. I didn't know that shit would come back to bite me in the ass now.

The only good news I received today was the fact that my father was now deceased. Wallace told me as soon as he saw me in the jailhouse. I can't even say I was happy about it. I just heard it and said okay. How do you respond to finding out that the man who was supposed to love and care for you, but did the complete opposite, has died? I knew for sure that I was going to need years of counseling and help. That was a present to myself. I was going to make it. I had no choice but to. I had family that I pushed away for so many years to help me. My mom and my brothers. I just need to make this one call to get some much-needed answers.

Chapter 39

Grace
Breathing for the First Time
May 23rd 11:30 P.M.

I was sitting over my aunt's house in one of her spare bedrooms, crying my eyes out. When I called and asked her if I could come over for a couple of days, she didn't even ask any questions. She just said "sure, baby." I was a little dumbfounded and confused that she didn't question me or any of that. Truth be told, all I want to do was kill myself. It was official. I was all alone. I couldn't even go back to my home or my job. I had nothing left. I had a bottle of sleeping pill that I had stopped to get at the pharmacy before I got here. I figured dying in my aunt's house was best. Since she was the only family I had left.

My cell phone rang and I sluggishly got up off the bed to go see who it was. I was hoping it was Ashley so I could tell her where to go and how to get there. In a way, I was so glad the lies and secrets were out of the bag. I wanted to tell that freak of a girl to get on away from me and be done with her for good. Who is saw on the caller ID caused me to stall for a few seconds before answering.

"Hello." My voice was barely above a whisper.

"Hey," I heard my husband speak into the phone in the same tone. There was a few seconds of silence before he spoke again. "Can I talk to you for a few?"

"Yes." Tears ran down my cheek like a waterfall. I was shocked that he would even want to talk to me about anything after all that went down. I know I wouldn't have had anything else to do with me after all I lied to him about really being a man.

"Did John Parks molest you?"

"Yes . . . yes he did." My bottom lip trembled in emotion. All that I endured as a child flooded my mind once again.

"Well, he did the same thing to me." He spoke and his voice was a little throaty, it was as if he was holding back tears.

"Really?" I spoke in awe. "He molested you too?"

"Yes, he did and my brother too."

"Really?" I was shocked again. All of the time that Rebecca and I were friends we both knew we were both molested, but by the same man is what threw me. It was almost unbelievable. But then I thought about it and it made sense. He was a serial molester; we just didn't know that we were all molested by him. I became furious all over again. I wanted his head on a stick. I wanted to kill him, like I was about to do myself. But that would be too easy for a slimy bastard like him.

"Yes, we all have him in common. But I'm not finished. I was lying just as much as you were in our relationship. I was still seeing John on the regular."

"Seeing him?" I asked, confused.

"Fucking him," he said making it clear for me. "For the last past thirty years I was still fucking him on the regular. Whenever I said I was staying late at work I was going over to his place and doing him."

"Wow." I had my mouth wide open. "I'm sorry, I'm not judging you. I'm just shocked that we both got away with what we got away with for so long. But, then again, when we got married we never really asked any of those questions normal people asked. I could hide behind you and you hid behind me. The perfect front for all those years. Not knowing we had more in common then we talked about."

"So true," he agreed. "So that is why I am calling you. To let you know that I forgive you. I can't hold that against you when I was doing what I was doing."

"Thank you." I spoke with a smile. It was nice to have all of the secrets out in the open. It was like I was breathing for the first time in all my life. "Well, I forgive you too."

"Thank you too." I could almost feel him smiling on the other side of the phone.

"Can ask you something else?" he asked

"Sure."

"Were those really birth control pills you were taking?"

"No, they were hormone pills. They keep me feminine. No facial hair and the like."

"So that is why the pharmacist looked at me all funny whenever I picked up your prescription. If I would have opened the bag I would have found out the truth."

"But I knew you were a man and most men don't even want to look at that stuff," I informed him.

"What about the feminine pads and all of that?"

"Just a show," I informed him.

"The condoms you made me wear?"

"Just a precaution too. I had to make me not wanting to get pregnant believable. The fact of the matter was I couldn't get pregnant. Doctors can make a man a woman, but he can't give men a womb. Only God can do that."

"Wow," was all he said.

"Yeah, I feel the same way you do."

"Instead of teachers, maybe we both could have been lawyers, because we both have mastered lying to others and ourselves." I let out a slight chuckle and so did he.

"So where do we go from here?" he asked.

"I don't know," I answered. "I really didn't think you would call me after all that we have been through. I wouldn't have blamed you anyway."

"I feel you." He spoke softly.

"Well, tell you what. Let's keep all of this to ourselves and the few people that know about it. The school doesn't need to know about it. It will be our little secret."

"Okay," I agreed. "But are we still gonna live together as husband and wife?"

"No, I don't think that is a good idea."

"You can come back home for a little while, but I think since you have your mother's house that it would be best for us to slowly start to live apart. We can still be married on paper for the sake of our jobs and all. But realistically, I don't think we can be together and successfully get the help we need."

"Okay." I had to admit I was not completely happy with being alone on my own, but he was right. It was the best thing for both of us.

"So, I'll see you in a couple of days." My voice cracked up a little bit. "Give us both some time to get used to moving on separately."

"See you in a couple of days." He hung up the phone.

I laid back on the bed for a little while longer before I went downstairs to talk to my aunt to fill her in on all that went down. Not once did she judge me or say "I told you so." She just sat there and listened as I told her every detail of what was going on in my life in the last few months. I left out the business about Ashley, because I had to get some info from Ashley before I said anything to her about it. After my aunt and I talked she fixed me dinner and I went back upstairs to my room. I called Ashley's phone but it went straight to voice mail. I didn't leave her message, because I wanted to discuss what I had to ask her face-to-face.

Chapter 40

Alex
The Truth Is...
May 23rd 9:35 P.M.

"Hey, you want to come in and rest for a minute?"
I asked Wallace as we pulled up to me and Ashley's
apartment. I had driven us back to East Los Angeles,
since he had gotten very little sleep. All I had to do
was put in my address and the car spoke the directions
through the speakers every step of the way. I was tired
too. All I wanted to do was go to sleep and start fresh
tomorrow.

"Sure, let me get a small nap in before I go home."
Wallace looked exhausted.

He parked the car and I noticed that there was a car
that I didn't recognize in the spot where Ashley usually
parks. And Ashley's car was nowhere to be found. I
had not seen Ashley the whole weekend. And here it is
Monday and she still not home.

I put my thumb onto the fingerprint reader on the
front door panel and the door buzzed to let us into
the building. I did the same thing when I went to go
into my apartment. I got the surprise of my life when I
opened the door and walked in.

"Hi Ma, hi Dad." My mother came over and hugged
me first; then my dad came over.

"Hey, Shawn." Wallace smiled and then shook his hand. "Long time no see."

"Yes, it has been a long time. How is everything going?"

Wallace looked at me and then at my parents. "Well, we had quite an adventurous last couple of days."

"Yeah, it's been really eventful." I smiled awkwardly.

"Is that the reason why both you and Ashley's phone been off?" my father asked curiously.

"Well, I left my charger here at home. That is the reason why my phone is not on right now. Ashley's phone, now that is a different story. I have no clue about that. She has been tripping lately."

"So when was the last time you saw her?" He had a concerned look on his face.

"A day or two ago," I answered.

"Do you have a clue as to where she may be?"

"Shawn, what's going on?" my mom asked him with the same amount of concern.

"I think Ashley's is acting like her father. James, I mean." Shawn looked at Wallace like he expected Wallace to zap or something. Wallace just shook his head. I think that if I hadn't told him and he had just found out about it now, that he would probably went off. I would have.

"Oh, no!" My mom put her hand on her chest and then sat down on the sofa.

"What's wrong, Ma?" I sat down beside her. My father paced a little bit before he sat down as well.

"Well, um, Alex baby, James Parks, you biological father, was a very disturbed man. He had a very bad temper problem and he had a tendency to lash out on people when he didn't get his way."

"That's not true," Wallace interjected. "That wasn't the only side to him." He looked angry.

"Excuse me, who are you anyway?" My mother looked confused and pissed off at the same time.

"I'm James's husband. His widower," Wallace proclaimed, almost sticking his chest out proudly.

"His what?" My mother looked shocked.

"Ma, James and Wallace were married back in Baltimore. They were in love."

"In love?" My mother looked surprised. "James was only in love with himself and money. Oh, and making me and my husband miserable."

"I don't know what he did outside of my presence, but I know he wasn't a completely uncaring person. He was just misguided and misunderstood."

"I'm sorry," my mother apologized. "You know, you are right. James wasn't completely uncaring; he did leave some money for his three kids for college in his will."

"Three?" Wallace looked at me, surprised.

"Yes, I have another sister that is by James too," I explained to Wallace.

"Wallace, I'm sorry I didn't tell you this before. I just didn't know if I could trust you or how you would handle it," my father spoke as he looked at Wallace with sincerity.

"You know what, I can't even fault you for holding out on me. Truth is I didn't know who James was when we hooked up. I should have taken my time and gotten to know him before I jumped into something with him. Now I see, I had some issues too. I wanted someone I could love and trust and be with. I thought James was that one. I still do. I'm just getting to know him now, after his death. I should have done that before we got heavy into it. But it all happened so fast and I didn't get him the right way anyway, so I guess I got what my hand called for."

"I'm sorry, Wallace. I'm sorry for your loss," my father spoke solemnly.

"Well, it was good while it lasted." He smiled. "Anything else y'all want me to know, so I can move on with my life?"

"Well, there is one more thing." My father looked at my mother, me, and then at Wallace.

"Wallace, Alex, I wasn't completely about my relationship with James. Before he met you, Wallace, James and I had a short sexual relationship."

"But, you said—" I spoke up.

"I lied to you, Alex. I lied." My father hung his head down low and looked at the floor. A few seconds later he picked his head up and looked at all of us again. "I couldn't handle you knowing the truth, I'm sorry."

"It's okay, Dad." A tear slid out of my eye. I could see that this was a great pain for my father. "I've told you so many times that I love you no matter what. Nothing will change that. You my pops."

He smiled proudly.

"Thanks, son, but I'm not finished." He looked at Wallace and then at my mom. "Mona, I need you to know that I was attracted to Wallace and when I introduced him as a client to you I lied."

"Did anything ever happen?" My mother looked at Wallace and then my father. I was a little curious myself.

"Nah, Mrs. Black. Your husband never once tried anything with me. Truth is, I wanted to, but he never let on that he was attracted to men and I kept my distance. It was partially the reason why I moved back to California. Your husband helped me get through a rough time in my life. And I am extremely grateful. So please don't be mad at him."

"Shawn, baby I had faith that God would keep you, so I'm not even mad at you. I'm glad you told me though. I need you to remember, that your family loves you and that is unconditional."

"I know now, baby." They embraced for a few seconds and then pulled away.

"So how we gonna find Ashley?"

"Don't worry Dad, I got that covered. I put a tracking device on her car without her knowledge." I smiled.

"Alex!" My mother looked at me disappointed. "That's not right. That is an invasion of her privacy."

"Sorry, Ma. I was just looking out for my sister."

"Honey, holler at him later. We need to find Ashley. There's no telling what she has gotten herself into."

"Okay, Dad. I got the tracking software installed on my phone. We can find her with no problem."

"Good, let's go." My father hopped out of his chair and headed for the door. We all trailed behind him as we made our way toward his car. I hopped in the front seat and plugged my phone up to the car charger and we pulled off.

Chapter 41

Shawn
Who's Ya Daddy?
May 23rd 10:25 P.M.

It was dark outside when we pulled up to the complex that Ashley's car was parked in and parked right beside the car that Alex said was hers. I was extremely curious as to how she got a car and how she paid for it, but I was more worried about where she was and why her phone was off.

"What we gonna do?" Mona asked me with fear on her face.

"I tried her phone again, it is still off." Alex chimed in from the front of the car.

"So how do we find her if her phone is off?" My mother asked another fear-filled question. "We definitely can't go door to door looking for her. Can we?"

"Well Ma, even though her cell phone is off, the phone she has still emitted a signal letting us know her location no matter what. It's for emergencies. Most cell phones have them now. I can pick up her signal in a few short seconds." He hit a couple of buttons and was ready to go. "Got it. She is right in there or at least her phone is in there. Apartment three B." He pointed to a building that was about thirty feet away from where we were parked.

"Okay, so what are we waiting on?" Mona moved toward her car door and hopped out.

I hopped out of the car on my side and walked around the car to where Mona was standing. "Mona, baby. I think it is best for you to stay in the car. Let us men go up there and get her. We don't know what is going to happen. I need you to stay here just in case something does and we need your help or the police."

"That's my baby too," She looked at me with tears in her eyes.

"I know baby, but it may not be safe." I pulled her in my arms. "I don't want anything to happen to any of us, especially you baby." I walked to the side of the car where Alex was and said, "Alex, I need you to stay here with your mother. Wallace, do you mind coming with me?"

"Sure, let me grab this real quick." He reached under his seat and pulled out a gun. I looked to see where Mona was. She was snooping inside of Ashley's car, so I was glad she didn't see the gun he pulled out. She would have definitely freaked out. Even I was a little scared. I wasn't a gun man by a long shot.

"Okay, you ready?" Wallace asked me as I got out of the car. Alex gave us the exact apartment and we made our way over to the building

"Yeah, man. Let's get this done." I had to admit I was a little scared, because the last time I was in a situation like this was when I found out that James was dead in Sherry's apartment. I don't know if I could bear the thought of finding my child dead or hurt really bad.

We got to the entrance of the building and tried the door: it was locked. It didn't have a fingerprint reader on the door like the apartment that I had for Ashley and Alex, because this was sort of a lower-income apartment complex. It was just one of those regular key entry doors, where every occupant had to have a key to get in.

"It's locked Wallace. What we gonna do?" I looked at him confused. I just wanted Ashley alive and well.

"Hold on." He reached in his pocket and added on a silencer to the gun. He then aimed it at the lock and fired. There was a small pop and he tried the door to see if was opened. Sure enough, it was. I breathed a sigh of relief as we were one step closer to getting to Ashley. My mind was racing with all kinds of thoughts and almost wanted to cry out of anger for not coming clean about all of this earlier. But that was too late. We crept up the carpeted stairs toward the apartment number Alex gave us.

"What are we going to do know? We can't just knock on the door and ask for her. If somebody is trying to harm her then it might push them into doing it."

"Right . . . right." He nodded. "Let me think."

A few seconds passed by and we heard the door to another apartment open across the hall. We both tried our best to act like we belong, because the neighborhood we were in wasn't a bad one but it wasn't a good one either.

"Hello, young men," an old lady spoke to us as she pulled out her laundry bag and detergent in front of her door. She had on a night coat and a scarf, so I assumed that there was a laundry room in the building, like most apartment complexes.

"How are you doing, ma'am."

"I'm good, baby." She smiled, but she still looked at us with suspicion.

"Y'all fellas okay?" she asked.

"Yes, ma'am. We are just fine." I smiled and looked at Wallace who was smiling too. He must have just got the same idea in his head that I did.

"Ma'am, we do have a problem though." My smile turned into a frown. I spoke with a hushed tone, because you could hear your voice bouncing off of the stone walls that surrounded us.

"I think my daughter is in this apartment right here and I think someone might have her here against her will. We don't want to let them know that we are here for her. So I really need your help." My eyes were pleading with her so hard.

"Well. . . . I don't know about that, young fella. I don't know what you fellas are up to. I don't want to get involved with any foolishness. I minds my business in here. I don't want any trouble." She spoke in the same hushed tone.

"I'm sorry, ma'am. I'm really desperate right now. You're my only help." I pleaded. "God knows I'm not lying. I wouldn't play around with my daughter's life like that. So I'm begging you please. . . . Please." A tear snuck its way out of my eye and down my cheek.

"Well okay," she hesitated. "But what do I ask for?"

"Ask for some laundry detergent." Wallace spoke as he handed me the lady's detergent she had by her bag.

"Okay." She walked up to the door. Wallace and I stood on the side of the door. When she knocked, and a person answered. It was a man. While she was asking for the detergent, me and Wallace rushed passed the old lady and bombarded the apartment before he could even think.

The guy had a gun but Wallace punched him before he could get a shot off.

Chapter 42

Ashley
The Rescue
May 23rd 10:37 P.M.

I was sitting in the chair, still tied up. They thought I was dead. Shit, I thought I was too. When Ebony pulled the trigger she closed her eyes, like most timid women do when they have a gun in their hands. The contact of the bullet threw my head back and then I slumped forward like I was dead. The truth is the bullet just grazed my head. I knew this because I felt the blood running down the side of my head and drip on my lap. They thought I was dead. Thank God neither one of them bothered to check to see if I was really dead. I could hear them in their kitchen rummaging through cabinets and drawers. I assumed they were looking for something to get rid of me in. I dared not lift my head in fear of getting caught alive. In those few seconds that my head was down, I prayed to God that he would send someone, anyone, to get me out of this mess. Then there was a knock at the door. I silently mouthed *Thank you, Jesus*!

I heard what sounded like an old lady asking for something and then a loud commotion that sounded like someone being punched.

"Ashley! . . . Ashley!" I heard what sounded like my father calling my name. It was too good to be true.

"I'm in here . . . in here." My voice was faint, but I used all I could to speak up at that moment. The look on my face when my father ran into the room and began to untie me made me feel instant relief.

"I'm sorry, Daddy. . . . I'm so sorry," I sobbed really hard.

"It's all right, baby. . . . Daddy's here now." After he successfully untied me, he scooped me up in his arms like I was a baby and carried me out of the apartment. It was like it was a dream as he carried me out. I thanked God profusely as my mother and brother ran up to me and tried their best to console me. I was placed in the backseat in between my father and my mother as an unknown man hopped into the car a pulled off. I laid my head on father's shoulder as we drove off. Before long I was fast asleep as if I was a toddler on a long car ride.

I awoke in a hospital bed after what seemed like days in the bed. I felt my head and face; I had a couple of Band-Aids on my head. My mother was sitting in the chair next to the bed.

"Hey, baby." She rubbed my hair back like she used to do when I had a fever. "How are you feeling?" I looked at her with tears in my eyes again. I escaped with my life and I was grateful to God for coming through once again.

"I feel alive." I spoke with sincerity. "I'm sorry, Ma. I didn't mean for any of this to happen. I—I—"

"Ashley, baby . . . Stop, I'm just grateful you're still alive, baby. I thank God that he spared your life. He's got it all in control. So baby, just lay back and rest. Rest, baby." And that I did.

The next day the doctor released me. I had a mild concussion from being hit in the head with a gun, and was told that I would have a permanent scar from where the bullet grazed my head, but that was the extent of my physical damage. On a trip or two to the bathroom in the hospital, I would look at myself in the mirror and pull my hair up to look at the scar on my head. It wasn't healed yet, but I knew that this was a constant reminder of almost losing my life. I kneeled down right there in the bathroom and I prayed.

Heavenly Father, I played around and almost lost my life. Thank you, Jesus, for not letting me die by my own hands. Thank you, God for keeping me. Thank you, God for my nosy brother Alex. Thank you God for my parents. Thank you, God for all of this. After all of this I know that you are with me. I know that you won't ever leave me. I know that you will always be right here. God I didn't trust you. I didn't trust you with me or with my issues. I apologize God. I apologize. Forgive me, God! Father forgive me. In the name of Jesus, I cry out for forgiveness. I cry out for peace. I cry out for your love. I cry out for your touch. Oh, God forgive me! Change me, God; make me what I'm supposed to be. What you created me to be. Wash away my desire for unnatural things. Take it away, God. Please take it away. In Jesus' name I say amen.

I stayed on my knees and sobbed and cried for a few more minutes until I got up and got myself together to leave.

Emotionally, I was still touch-and-go. I would bust out crying at the drop of a dime. And I was scared to even leave the house for the first couple of days that I was home. I had finals for my classes I had to take, and thankfully I was doing my homework and studying in between my madness.

***

About two weeks after narrowly escaping with my life, my father said he had a surprise for all of us. So him, my mother, me, Alex, Diana, Li'l Shawn, my baby sister, Brittany and the guy named Wallace piled into a van headed to a destination known only by my father. I found out from Alex that Wallace was our biological father's husband. They were legally married.

My father said he had someone he wanted us to meet. I was curious as to who it was. We pulled up to a house in the Hawthorne area. It was real nice one level ranch-style house.

We got out the van and we all walked up to the door of the house and my father knocked. When it opened, my mouth hit the floor. Sister Bella Jones stood before us.

"Hello Ashley dear." I looked at my father and mother, confused.

"Ashley, Alex, Diana. . . . Meet your grandmother. This is James's mother."

"Really baby?" My mother looked at her and then my father.

"Come in everybody . . . come in." She stepped back.

When we walked in the house, she invited us to sit down in her living room. There were pictures of my biological father spread out around the room. Everybody took their turn walking around the room, looking at the pictures and various items. A couple of minutes later Grace walks in the room. I was in shock. I was not ready to see her. She looked surprised to see me too. Neither one of us said a thing to either. I was wondering how she was related to my newfound grandmother.

After about a half hour, everybody was ushered out to the backyard, where there were decorations and things like that. Along the back of the large yard big sign read *Happy 70th Birthday*. After about another hour, the backyard was filled with about twenty more people who I learned were more of our newly discovered family. I was smiling, because I was really happy to meet them all. We were taking so many pictures that I had lost count. Everybody was commenting on how all of James's children looked just like him. My father didn't frown one time and neither did my mother. On a trip to the bathroom, I ran into Grace and she pulled me into a room and closed the door.

"I'm sorry for treating you the way I did. I was wrong for using you the way I did." I immediately apologized.

"No need to apologize. I got what I deserved." She began to break down everything that went down over the past two weeks in my absence. It was one big mess. I shook my head in awe.

"So everybody knows that you are a man now?" I asked.

"Yes, they do," Grace spoke somberly.

"Wow."

"It's not that bad." She wiped a tear from her eye. "It's all out in the open now. The only ones that won't know is the school. Could you please keep it that way?"

"No problem, just as long as you keep the secret that we were intimate."

"Sure." She smiled. "I got one question though."

"Okay, let's here it."

"How did you find out about my secret?"

"Well, nobody knows that my brother had plastic surgery on his penis, but me. I know that is kind of close for a brother and sister, but it's true. Anyway, in the room that they placed us in so we can review some sample of the doctors' work, there were two books and my brother was looking at one and I was looking at the other out of curiosity. When I flipped through the pages, I came to yours and almost peed myself. I took a quick couple of pictures with my phone real quick and presto, black-mail."

"Wow, I never thought the money I saved by letting the doctor use my pictures in a sample book would come back to haunt me. That is just scary."

"I know," I cosigned.

"All right, another question."

"Okay."

"Why would you knowingly have an intimate relationship with me and you knew I was a man?"

"Well, in God's eyes it was a man and woman relationship."

"That is so true. I never really looked at it that way." Grace nodded.

"Truth be told, whoever the doctor was that hooked you up down there, he was a master. Your shit worked just as well as mine and I'm the real deal." She smiled a little and looked away.

"Well, he did earn his money, but he wasn't God. Because there will be no babies coming out of here no matter what he fixed down there."

I agreed with Grace, "True, true." Then, "You ever feel like you made a mistake?"

"Yes, sometimes. But it's too late for all of that now, right?" She frowned.

"I would say so." I nodded. I looked out the window and then at the door. I was ready to go. The air was a little too thick for me at the moment.

"Again, I want to say I'm sorry. I really am. I didn't know how deep your secrets hurt you. I know I wouldn't want the same thing to happen to me. "

After a few more seconds of silence, we both hugged and exited the house to go back to the party.

"So how do you know Professor David's wife?" Alex asked as I sat down at the table with him.

"Oh, we're just good friends." I smiled. He didn't need to know everything. I mean really. Got to keep something between us girls.

Chapter 43

Alex
The Showdown
June 13th 3:30 P.M.

"Ohhhh . . . okay." I said to Ashley as I got up from the table and went to fix myself a plate of food. I brought Ashley back a plate as well. We both sat and watched our two families mingle and get to know each other. It was nice to have a family and no more secrets. Well, almost no more secrets. I saw Professor Andrews walk in the celebration and go over to talk to his wife. He looked happy, but that could have been a front. After all that went down I was still a little shook myself. Shit, everybody I dated from henceforth was a suspect until proven a woman. And that shit was hard nowadays. Transsexual and transgendered men were passing like they were born the way they were remanufactured to be now. But, men weren't God and they couldn't change everything. No matter what they did, they couldn't make men get pregnant and have babies. Doctors and science can clone cells and all of that, but they can't create a womb inside of a man. God gave men the gift of creativity, but creation is in his hands. Men will try, but will never come close to it.

"Fuck all y'all muthafuckas!" Everybody turned around to see my crazy grandfather standing at the back gate of the yard. He had a gun in hand and he staggered a little, so I knew he was drunk. People at the celebration started to huddle together. I always wondered why people did that in movies and things. Now I knew why. You don't want to be singled out by a madman with a gun. So right now I was stand next to my grandmother and Professor David. The music was still going, but I could only hear the beat of my heart as it raced. I can't help but think that everyone else was having the same experience too. "I didn't get an invite to this so-called party."

Everybody was on freeze.

"Man, why don't you just leave and let us be. You've done enough to this family and others." Wallace spoke up.

"You don't know anything about what I've done. All of them probably deserved it. " As people say a drunk man speaks a sober man's heart. He was doing it for sure. The gun was being waved like it was a bouquet of flowers. His arms would flail and people would duck. I looked at my mom and dad; my father had her and my sister and brother behind him. "Y'all was just waiting on me to give it to ya." he laughed and his head roared back.

Pop! Then there was a shot in the air, but it wasn't from my grandfather's gun. Professor Andrews had a gun in his hand too. There was a couple of screams. The crowd then broke away from both of them and the two aiming the gun at each other like it was a showdown.

"David, baby, don't do it," his wife/husband hollered out in fear.

"Yeah, don't do it with your punk ass," my grandfather spoke with disdain. "You were always a faggot-ass punk anyway. I don't know why I let you fuck me for all these years." There were a couple of gasps from the crowd.

"Why are you here?" My grandmother stepped from the crowd and next to Professor Andrews. "You don't belong here. You left a long time ago. We were happy when you left. Leave now and don't come back." She spoke with authority and firmness, but he still didn't budge.

"You don't know nothing, you old bitch." You could see the spit flying from his mouth. He was definitely wasted.

"I know you better get out of here. I know that." She spoke again. She was very serious. "God don't like ugly. Look at these people. They will never be the same and it is your entire fault. But I forgave you a long time ago. I prayed for you to get peace and to come to God, but I see now that you had your own plans. God have mercy on you. I think that it is best that you leave here now. I can't stop this young man right here from pulling that trigger and taking your life. You might even take his in the process, but something tells me that he feels like he doesn't have anything to lose." She looked at David and put her hand on his shoulder. It was like she was telling him to let it go. In her eyes was forgiveness. David looked at her and then at him again. Tears flowed from his eyes. I started to cry too. All that he went through on those tapes flooded my mind and I was balling too.

"Bitch, hush up. I got the gun. I'm doing all the demanding up in this here party." He was waving the gun again with every word he spoke.

"Go ahead and leave, John." Professor Andrews still had his gun pointed at John. He was shaking and I was afraid that his anger would cause him to let off a shot. "Just get out of here. Leave us be." The two guns had everybody's attention.

"All right, all y'all want me dead." He held the gun to his mouth and pulled the trigger. Women were screaming terror-filled screams. We watched as my grandfather's body slowly fell and hit the ground. It was unreal. I had never seen anything like it in my life. It took awhile for the women and some of the men to stop crying. My father and mother were both consoling each other, my sister was hugging my grandmother and the professor and his wife/husband were embraced. The ambulance and the police showed up. They questioned everyone as to what happened to my grandfather. Everyone had the same story. He committed suicide. They took our names and numbers and told us that they would be contacting us if need be. I am not happy that it ended this way. I hoped things would have worked out better. He could have gotten help or something. But, then again, maybe that was his fate. That was the way he was supposed to go. It is all unfortunate. After all the commotion died down and most of the family went home, we made our way into my grandmother's house again. I, for one, needed to sit down or maybe even a drink. Well, not a drink. I didn't want start something new. I just need to hear something good or positive. My parents and I had a little bit of blood on us. My grandmother gave us some spare clothes she had in the house. She just happened to be collecting for a church clothing drive. They weren't stylish, but they worked. My parents, Wallace, Me, Ashley, Li'l Shawn, Diana and my baby sister, Brittany, sat around the living room quiet. No one knew what to say it was such a strange and crazy experience; to see someone take their life. I know my little sister would have some questions for my parents. I am pretty sure they knew what to say. They were very experienced parents, indeed.

We were all sitting in the living room when my grandmother came in the room with a photo album.

"This here is all the pictures and memories of Jerry or James, as you know him." She was all smiles. I was too, in fact, everyone was as we sat back and listened to my grandmother told us stories about each picture that she pulled out of the album.

"Let me tell y'all some things about my baby." She looked at all of us as we sat in a small circle around her plush living room. "I knew my baby was special from the day he was born." Her smile beamed brightly, almost lighting up the room.

"Most people don't know my baby was a miracle. Yes, he was." Some tears flowed down her sagging cheeks. "I was not supposed to be able to have any children. But God blessed me with him. Jerry Emmanuel Parks. Emmanuel means *God with us*. And I knew that God was with me and him. He was my little miracle. Hmph! . . . The moment I laid eyes on him I knew I had the best thing in the world." She paused, took a deep breath and continued.

"But I lost my baby trying to keep his father and the roof over our head. You see, I ignored my mother and father's teaching—that a man was supposed to love and support his wife and the wife was supposed to stay at home and tend to the children. I took the first man that paid me some attention and gave him everything. Not knowing the cost. The cost that would not only I would have to pay, but my son with his life, and even to his children." She looked at us with remorse in her eyes. I wanted to run over and hug her and squeeze her and tell her that it would be all right. But, I sat still as she continued.

"You see I was in a vicious cycle and didn't even know it. My parents sheltered me in life so much so that when it was time for me to experience things I went at it head-first. I too did the same thing to Jerry. I thought that if I could keep him in the house at all times, with very little contact with the outside world that he would be safe. Little did I know that the enemy was in my home the whole time. My ex-husband was evil. He took my child's innocence. I didn't pay attention to the red flags that were being waved in my face. Y'all, I was *so* blind. I would come home and my baby would be all over me but I would be too tired to do anything for him or with him outside of dinner and homework. My baby boy was a happy-go-lucky boy anyway. He really didn't need anyone to entertain him. He knew how to do that by himself. My baby didn't have any friends. It wasn't because he couldn't make them it was because I thought that I could be his only friend. I was wrong. Oh, so wrong.

"Look, I'm rambling on. I'm sorry about that. I just want all of you to know that my son's life was changed by some of my choices, some of his father's choices, but most of all, his choices. You see I have learned over the years that my choices just doesn't affect me, but they effect everyone around me. I sit here and look at all of you and I see some of my choices in you. The good and the bad. My son had an effect on all of you. Good or bad, he did. I ask that you forgive him. He was carrying some of my loose ends and didn't even know it. So I too apologize."

"I say to you all that we all make wrong choices and we have to live with those consequences. Though it is not always an easy feat. It can be done. I'm a living testimony to it. Forgive yourself and forgive others. It is the only way to truly live life freely. When I die I want to know that I don't have anything holding me down. I want to fly away free. I sit here today with my loose ends tied up, right here and right now. I feel good. I feel blessed. I feel old." She reared back with hearty laughter and so did the rest of us. We sat for hours and listened to Mama Bella as she told us more stories about Jerry and his life. I was truly full of joy when we left her house late that night.

All and all I was satisfied with how things in our family turned out. Especially, the still being together part. God has been good to us and we definitely have a testimony to give.

Alex's Epilogue

Starting Fresh

"Good-bye, Cali." I sat back in my seat on a plane, waiting for the plane to take off. Ashley and I were headed back to Baltimore. Life pretty much went back to normal after all of that went down out here almost two years ago. Or as normal as it could get. Both Ashley and I graduated with our degrees in college and in life. Outside of my degree, I learned a lot about myself and life. I learned that when you go searching for things you really never know what you are going to get into. The people that I have met over the last few years have changed me in profound ways. I thought I was looking for a lost father, but I found out that what I was looking for I already had in me, as my newfound grandmother said:

"You are your father. You carry pieces of him with you and you didn't even know it. I'm talking about the way you walk, the way you talk. You nosy as can be. Your father was quick-minded and so are you." I smiled and looked on in amazement. I loved this lady and haven't even known her that long.

She continued, "I know you told me that you were looking for his family for medical reasons, but I can tell you that you will get what you will get medically. God knows you can handle it and he got you whatever may come. I'm a witness, baby. God is good. He'll be good to you. Keep on living and you will see."

I was so glad for each and every thing that happened here. The good, the bad and the downright ugly. I can say that I have seen some things and made it through it. When think about my biological grandfather, I wish that things didn't turn out the way they did. But there is a season and a reason for everything. It may not seem right at the time, but one day it will. He seemed crazy, but I knew that there was a hurt man in there screaming for help, but too prideful to get help. Having secrets will do that to a person. Thinking we can fix everything, we hold it in until it festers and then we pass it on to our offspring unknowing. Loose ends are a mutha. You never know who you are affecting when you keeping quiet about your secrets. But we made it. The Black family made it. My sister was a prime example of what can happen with loose ends, but she too made it, with God's help.

I watched as Ashley progressed into a new woman. Over the last two years Ashley and I became closer than ever. She had totally stopped having sex with women and had been on a few dates with some men. At first, it was hard to swallow, but I knew that if anybody could change a person, God could and Ashley was a proven witness of God's ability.

But before we left California we both had long private conversations with my grandmother and we were told not to discuss it with each other and that is a vow we both keep to this day. It was a stretch for my inquisitive self, but I did. Sadly, my grandmother passed away at the ripe age of seventy-two. We had only known her for two years but we would visit her often and she would tell us all about our father and how we were some much like him. She would cook us dinner and would watch some home movies she had of James. There were only a few and they were short in length, but I got a glimpse of James/Jerry, his father and mother, when he was very, very young. They looked like a happy family, but that was only in the few minutes we got to see it. No one knew the secrets lurking in the shadows, but we would all experience the backlash from them. We all would reach back and look at it and say, *But God. But God. But God.*

"But God, but God, but God." I mumbled and smiled to myself as I looked out of the window next to me. Life has its ups and down, but I knew that all and all it would be all right. I would be all right. When I get off of the plane in Baltimore, I don't know exactly what is going to happen or what I am going to do but I am sure going to make the best of it.

Wallace's Epilogue

Alive and Well

I sat in my car and cried tears; tears of joy, tears of sorrow and tears of gladness. Today was the day that the sign for my restaurant was being put up. I was finally the owner of my own business. It wasn't a dream anymore. It was now a reality. I sat in awe and watched as the workers put up each individual letter. It was an experience to remember.

"Park's Place." I smiled real hard. That was the name I named my restaurant. "This for you baby." I looked up toward heaven and smiled even harder. I knew my baby was smiling down on me.

I found out from a personal conversation with Mama Jones all I wanted to know about James. The conversation we had over the phone a couple of days after we left her seventieth birthday celebration gave me some very good insight into James's past: his early years.

"Good morning, Ms. Jones." I spoke in a mild tone. I was sitting in my room in a corner with a picture of James in one hand and the phone in another. "Do you have a couple of minutes to talk?" It was a Saturday morning and I was off from work. I still had on my boxers and socks. I hadn't even cooked anything to eat. I had a dream about James last night. It was like he was telling me to call his mother and get the truth from her.

I knew what other people had told me about him, but as the saying goes, "Mama knows best." I am sure she knew him better than anybody.

"Yes, baby. I have some time to talk." Her tone was just as pleasant as it was when I first met her. "You want to know about James I figure?"

"Yes . . . yes, ma'am."

"What is it that you want to know about Jerry?" She livened up a little.

"Well, Ms. Jones." All types of questions were flooding my brain. The one that would be first wasn't an easy pick.

"Call me Mama."

Mama? That threw me a little. I wasn't expecting that. I knew that she was a Christian woman and most Christians didn't condone homosexuality or the marriage of two men. She never judged me though. So I'm assuming that it was for the love of God and her son that she treating me with such love.

"Okay . . . Mama. Did James have anger problems as a child or a destructive nature?"

"Wallace, Jerry evolved over time. Like I told everyone else, and I'll tell you the same. Jerry was a mild-mannered child as a kid. He was giving, loving and playful. He was very affectionate as well. But, I noticed early on that he was passive-aggressive, something I am myself. He had his bouts of anger, but you had to push him to it. It was never something he just did. Most of the time he would get teased in school because he was so quiet. We would talk about it, when I got the chance, but Jerry would always be the bigger person and try to befriend people in spite of the negativity they pushed his way. Now he was no angel, let me say that. He had a smart mouth on him and that didn't help. But he was honest and considerate. Son, what I am trying to say is that you knew Jerry as you knew Jerry. Yes, he hid some things from us all. But, one thing is sure. He loved and lived. He didn't have a picture- perfect ending. That doesn't mean that he didn't touch lives. He touched yours. It's not one's beginning, middle, or end that defines the life of a person. But if you can say that you loved with everything in you and fell, but got back up to love again, than you are blessed. Wallace, don't mourn for my son any longer. His life is an example. Take from it what you will. But you can't discount the love. He chose to let God love on him through another individual. Enjoy your memories of him. Never let anyone dilute them. You understand?"

"Yes, ma'am. I understand."

"Good, son. Now get yourself in church and live your life. Let God's love reign in your heart still. It's the only thing that is worth anything. Love is the blood of your soul and spirit. It keeps you warm when this world gets oh so cold."

"Yes, ma'am. I agree."

"Good, now Mama got to get off this phone and head on out. Keep in touch, son."

"Good day, Mama." I hung up that phone so refreshed and enlightened. I finally can move on with my life and live.

Tap . . . tap . . . tap.

I was broken out of my daze by the Mexican guy that was installing my signage.

"All done." He smiled at me. I smiled back as I got out my car and looked up at the bright red letters. I pulled out my phone and took a few pictures to send out to family and friends.

I walked up to the door and used my thumb on the finger reader to open the door and I flicked on the lights and the place lit up like stars shining at night. It wasn't huge, but it was mine. All mines. You see, after my father passed away and was buried, we found out in his will he left us all some money. I used my inheritance to do what I want to do all my life: Open my own restaurant. It was really ironic that he tried to make me do what he wanted me to do, but him dying brought it to fruition anyhow. It just taught me that dreams of a true believer can be deferred a little, but if they hold on long enough it will come to pass.

After I secured the doors to my new establishment, I made my way over to the graveyard to have a talk with my father. It was a talk that we should have had when he was alive, but he pushed me away thinking it was for my good.

It was breezy day and the wind pushed me around a little as I made my way through the cemetery toward his plot.

"Wassup, Pop." I played it cool, like I wanted to do when he was alive. I always wanted a good relationship with my father. A father-and-son bond is what all boys dream of. I didn't get it, but I decided against being bitter about it toward him now, standing in front of his burial plot.

"How's it going?" I knew there wouldn't be an answer back, but I did it anyway.

My mom had put a real picture of him on his headstone. It was a picture of our family. We looked happy. I thought we were.

"Dad, I'm opening up my restaurant soon. I know it's not what you wanted for me, or maybe it was. From what I was told you were trying to save me from being like you, but I guess I will never understand that. I forgive you. I really do. You did the best you could with what you had. I see that now."

I breathed out and looked around at all the leaves and loose debris the wind was blowing around. It was nice to be alive. It was nice to have a family again, minus my father. I missed James, but that too will pass. They say it is better to have loved and lost, than to have never loved at all. That was so true. In this case, I didn't lose. I actually got my family back looking for what I lost.

I walked slowly back to my car, whistling the whole way. I was a happy man indeed. I felt so free . . . so alive.

Ashley's Epilogue

The Promise

As the plane taxied down the runway and lifted off of the ground into the air, I thought about the last couple of years. It was a mess. I was a mess and I barely made it out with my life. I looked over at Alex who had this huge smile on his face. He was still goofy, but I loved his butt. He was my right-hand man. I treated him some kind of terrible. I was a real piece of work. But that was then, this is now. I am changed. It wasn't an overnight process I tell you. It took lots of prayer, from my three grand-mothers, me and, I know, my parents as well. I was done with women. Yeah, most people don't think it's possible to change up, but I am a living witness to it. God can do anything, as long as you are willling to give it over to him. He not gonna take something you want to hold on to. You got to want to let it go. And sure enough, I did. It wasn't the lifestyle for me. It wasn't a lifestyle period. It was hell. One bad situation to the next. Being with a man ain't easy, but put two women in a relationship together and it is mass chaos.

Almost losing my life wasn't the only factor that changed my attitude and mindset. It was the conversa-tion by grandmother had with me days before she died that persuaded me to get my act together and fly right, permanently.

"Baby girl, you got to promise me you not end up like your father. Bitter toward people for the wrong they did to ya. You got to let it go. You got to take the chance that God has given you and make something of it. Make me proud. Make Jerry proud. Make your parents proud. But most of all . . . make you proud. Hold your head up, baby. You special and don't let nobody tell ya different. God chastises those that he loves. Baby, that little scar on your head is God's love on ya. It's not a reminder of the gunshot wound. It's a reminder of His love. Just for you. You understand?"

"Yes, ma'am." I smiled as she reached over and rubbed my head right where the scar was located. Her touch was so gentle. "I understand."

"Now baby, I'm not no judge or no jury, but you know you need to leave that foolish lifestyle behind ya. God got some blessings with your name on it. That wonderful voice you got there is gonna be an instrument for Him. I have seen what it did to the people in the church. God don't make no junk or mistakes. You got to use it honey. God don't take stuff back, so you have no choice but to use it. Don't let the devil lie to you and tell you different. You healed of your sins. You got the blessings in your belly. Use them, baby. Use them. Your voice is your weapon. I am so glad God brought me you two. I thought I lost my only son, just to find out that God had triple the blessings in store for me. I wish it wasn't so late in my life, but God is God.

"Ashley, baby." She paused and softly wiped her thumb across my cheek. She gazed deep in my eyes and I in hers. I felt a connection so deep. It was pure love. It was God's love. I knew it. It radiated like none other. It pierced my heart and tears flooded my eyes. "Repent and turn away. Never look back. Never."

"I won't, Grandma. I won't." She pulled me into her arms. "I promise."

I laid there in her arms for at least an hour. It was a promise that I was going to keep. *No looking back.*

I really didn't have a clue as to what I was going to do career-wise when I got off of this plane, but I knew one thing. I was going to keep my promise to her, but not just for her but for the people counting on me and my testimony.

"I promise!" I whispered to myself as I placed the headphones on that the airline gives you. I put my head back and smiled, because I knew I was blessed to have made it this far. The sky is the limit for me and with God, I will supersede that as well.

Grace's Epilogue

I'm Doing Me

I sat on the deck of my mother's house, but it was mines now. I thought that I would be an absolute crazy person right now. Who would have thought that I was still hanging in there? I have been here in this house for a year now and I am loving it. I have been through counseling and I am working on me. I am so happy about it too. I am still at the same school as David, but now I am a dean. My life is moving in the right direction and I can't stop smiling. Yes, sometimes I get a glimpse of my past when I dwell on the past, but I am getting over that as well. David calls and checks up on me and I am glad that we are still friends even after all of this mess. I even helped him adopt a sweet little girl. He is such a good father. You can tell that he was made to be one too. He so in love with her and she is enamored with him. At times I want to get jealous because I still feel a little cheated out of a regular life. A normal family, but it is what it is. God still loves me and I know that. I have no doubt in my mind.

I still have my bestfriend, Rebecca and we are closer than ever. In fact, she decided to move in with me so that we can be close to one another. We do everything together. Rebecca and I learning to be up-front about identities, with ourselves and others. She had a new man now and he knew all about her and loved her for her. I was just hoping to find the same one day. But for now I was happy with me doing just me. Nobody else's extra baggage. I had tons of my own that I was still unloading. I will know when it is time to start another relationship, but until then, I'm doing me.

David's Epilogue

We are Family

"There you go, Amiyah." My adopted daughter and I were in my backyard playing with the Hula Hoops that we brought from Wal-Mart today. She was five years old and she consumed most of my time. But it was worth it. It was what I dreamed of all my life. A family of my own. And even though I didn't have a wife to share it with I was content with just me and her.

"I got it Daddy! . . . I got it!" She twirled and twirled. She was growing up so fast. I was so excited to have her here in my life.

"I see . . . I see." A smile plastered my face. I can't say I don't have any depressing days but I do notice some good changes in me. I am more honest with myself and I am more honest with people.

Two years have passed and Grace and I are officially separated. I can't say that I don't miss her. We did share a house and a life for over thirty years together and one just doesn't get over being with someone for so long just because they split apart or broke up. I have been doing the counseling thing for the last past two years as well and I am getting a fresh start. I know what you are saying, why bring a child into my life when I still have some issues. The truth is, she's helping me and she doesn't even know it. She my anchor. She keeps me focused. Children keep parents focused, most of the time.

Parents know they have a responsibility to that child or children and they have to push to make a home for them all. That is what I plan on doing; making a home for the both of us.

Grace and I talk periodically about what is going on in our life and what we are learning in our sessions. It's a part of the healing process for us both. And our agreement still stands at work; we are still married, but just on paper. I know what you are thinking, it's still lying. But you have to understand that people just wouldn't understand or tolerate it for all that matters. People are still prejudiced against gays and even though they may not show it, it is still present, just like any other prejudice.

My mom, my brothers, and I have bond as a family as well. We have dinner together several times a month. We are stronger than ever. My mom loves being a grandmother. She can't get enough of Amiyah.

A couple of years ago, I didn't think it would end up like this. You know, happy. But with God and family, anything is possible. Anything. The love I have for myself and my family transcends all of my prior and present issues.

Shawn's Epilogue

Home Again

I sat in my seat at the gate where Ashley and Alex's plane would be landing. BWI airport was bustling so waiting for Ashley and Alex's flight to arrive was a breeze. Mona decided to stay home with the kids, while I picked them up. I was kind of glad to come alone. I can say I was an extremely proud father. I had successfully raised two brilliant children. They both made me really proud. I am learning that raising children isn't a science. There is no one book that can tell you how to handle certain situations when it comes to raising them. I learned understanding, love, and patience is the key. I also learned that they are going to have to go through some things no matter what I do to shield them from it.

Mistakes and mess-ups were a part of life and everybody gets their turn. Ashley and Alex sure did get theirs, but they both were better for it now. They didn't share their entire experience away from home with me and some things I know need not be said. It was lessons for them and their lives. I just hoped that they learned from them. I'm glad that I still get to be Dad to them.

I sat in my chair with my iPod on listening to some gospel music. I was in good spirits and I loved being that way. My own practice, a loving wife, two graduates, and two more teens and a little one. I had a full life.

A half hour later, I noticed Ashley and Alex coming off of the plane. I have to admit I got a little misty- eyed seeing my two babies coming toward me. If Mona was standing next to me, I knew she would have run up to them and squeezed them with all of her might. I was a real man now and that is what I did I ran up to my children and squeezed them with all that I could. I was a blubbering mess. I cried so hard it was hard to see. They were successful, even with all of me and their mother's slipups and all of the drama. I cried so hard I trembled.

"I love you guys so much." I kissed both of them on the cheek right there in the middle of everything that was going on. You would have thought that they had just come home from war. It in fact was war they had come home from. It was one they had on the inside. I've learned that we all have personal wars going on inside of us. And that we need to have each others' backs in these personal wars. "I am so proud of you two. So proud."

"We know, Dad." As usual they looked around a little embarrassed at this display of emotion that was going on in front of the world. But little did they know that they too would have even more tests and drama in their life that would teach them to be them regardless of where they are. This was the beginning of their lives. I prayed that they learned from the drama they survived back in California, but I know that life is about the expected and unexpected. I raised them the best I could and I know that God is with them and cares for them far more than I ever could. I was just temporary.

We made our way toward the baggage claim, picked up their bags and jumped on the shuttle to get to our car.

I let Ashley drive home.

"So what are you guys going to do tomorrow?" I asked curiously.

"Sleep in." They both chimed in together and laughed. I totally understood. Everyone needed a break after finishing college, even if it was only for a few days.

"Well, you guys know that you will have to share rooms. And you guys might not like what your brother and sister have done in your absence." I laughed as we drove.

When we pulled up to the house it was a little dark, but I could see the lights on in the living room. As soon as I opened the door, Ashley and Alex were bombarded with kisses and hugs from Mona, my mom, her mom and their brothers and sisters.

"My babies are home," Mona exclaimed with tears in her eyes. My baby still looks good. I was definitely hitting that tonight. We were closer than ever and we couldn't get enough of each other.

Everybody gathered together in the dining room, where there was a huge spread of delicious food that Mona, my mother, and her mother took time to cook.

I prayed over the food and we ate 'til we were all stuffed. It was a great time indeed. We talked and danced and sang karaoke. None of us knew what tomorrow would hold. But I am sure we can handle it. We've been through much and yet we are still here, by the grace of God.

A Closing Letter to the Reader

Well, you made it through book three. Take a breath, sit back and relax. Thank the Lord God that you didn't have to experience anything in these three books and if you did, you survived. There was so much going on in these books that it made my head spin and probably yours as well. There were some scenes that were over the top and just downright nasty. But they served a purpose not to just entertain, but to enlighten and educate at the same time. I dared myself to do certain things and I did it. For most, the response from readers was shocking and sometimes appalled, but the point was made. I personally thank you, the reader and friend, for picking up these three books and giving it a chance. Simply because I took a chance. Fail or win. Some say my faith or Christianity was questionable because I wrote it the way I did. The books did not define me and I am proud of my salvation and didn't need to defend something that was freely given in spite of me. I am not saying that it was right. I'm just stating the facts. At many times during the writing process I wanted to stop and walk away. Thank God I had friends and loyal readers like yourself that pushed me to keep it moving and finish what I started. I can't name them all so I'll just say it. . . . Thank you, everyone! Everyone with encouraging words, criticism and simply . . . love. It was appreciated and noted in my heart.

A Closing Letter to the Reader

Both Sides of the Fence, the series was an experience for me. An unplanned one too. When I sit back and think about all of it, I am so grateful that these three books happened. It pushed me to finish what I started. And helped me to set goals and get it done. I can't tell you how many people have confessed to being molested to me, men and women, and experiment on that other side of the fence and I was able to tell them that they can get help and where to find it. It also saddens me to realize that so many people's story won't get told because of shame or grief. I myself, never being molested, really could never put it into words how to deal with the act or violation therein. I commend people that do get help and do confess these deeds. I pray for the victims and the ones that were the predators as well. They need just as much help as the one they victimized, but that gets overlooked by severity of the crime. Chances are the molester was molested and the cycle can be continued if not dealt with appropriately. I'm not speaking as an advocate for either, but as a call to give help and compassion to both parties. It's just right.

When I think of the Black family in my book and the black family in America, I think that we can do better. Most of our problems stem from lack of communication and listening to that communication. We keep secrets and we even take some to the grave, supposedly, but unbeknownst to those who did so, they left those loose ends for the living to tie up and/or deal with after they are gone. Drugs, violence, are discussed on a regular, but molestation and homosexuality in men and women go untalked about. There may be someone in your family that has been molested or tampered with but fear of judgment or shame causes them to keep it all in, which in turn comes out in adverse ways:

A Closing Letter to the Reader

promiscuity, drugs, homosexuality, and violence are some the ways people that may have been molested act out, but are not limited to just those attributes alone. It varies greatly.

Take a real good look at your family. Are you talking about your problems or are you just pushing them under a rug? Pretty soon that rug is going to develop lumps and then hills, and then mountains. Please don't wait until it's too late to discuss it or we are burying a loved one because of a secret that we let take them out. Your children are waiting for you to talk to them and it is time for *you* to start talking to your children or any family member that you see in need of help. The time is now for the black family to get it together and stop letting the enemy in us and in the world take what God has promised us:Life and life more abundantly. So let's start talking so we can truly start living.

Peace and Blessing, M.T. Pope

PLEASE. . . . PASS THE WORD, NOT THE BOOK

Look for me on:

www.facebook.com/mtpope
www.myspace.com/mtpope
www.wix.com/mtpope/bothsidesofthefence
www.urbanbooks.net
www.twitter.com/mtpope

Purchase my books on:

Please leave a brief review, if possible. Thanks
www.amazon.com
www.barnesandnoble.com
www.borders.com
www.half.com
www.EBay.com
www.tower.com

E-mail me at:

chosen_97@yahoo.com
chosen_97@hotmail.com